HOLMES AND HOUDINI

AIRSHIP 27 PRODUCTIONS

AN AIRSHIP 27 PRODUCTION

Holmes and Houdini
© 2016 I.A. Watson

Published by Airship 27 Productions
www.airship27.com
www.airship27hangar.com

Interior illustrations © 2016 Rob Davis
Cover illustration © 2016 Chad Hardin

Editor: Ron Fortier
Associate Editor: Charles Saunders
Marketing and Promotions Manager: Michael Vance
Production and design by Rob Davis.

ISBN-10: 0-9977868-0-9
ISBN-13: 978-0-9977868-0-4

Printed in the United States of America

10 9 8 7 6 5 4 3 2 1

BY I.A. WATSON

One likes to think that there is some fantastic limbo for the children of imagination, some strange, impossible place where the beaux of Fielding may still make love to the belles of Richardson, where Scott's heroes still may strut, Dickens's delightful Cockneys still raise a laugh, and Thackeray's worldlings continue to carry on their reprehensible careers. Perhaps in some humble corner of such a Valhalla, Sherlock and his Watson may for a time find a place, while some more astute sleuth with some even less astute comrade may fill the stage which they have vacated.

—Sir Arthur Conan Doyle, introduction to *The Case-Book of Sherlock Holmes*

1. MORIARTY'S DEATH MASK

From the account of John Watson MD:

As Sherlock Holmes and I met at the breakfast table on that fateful 4th May 1902, not even the detective genius of my life's friend could warn that it marked the final period of our long partnership and an end to my days at 221b Baker Street forever. Whilst I recalled the macabre significance of that date on the calendar, Holmes remained absorbed in the Sunday edition of the *Times*—a policeman had been murdered in St Pancras.[1]

I helped myself to Mrs Hudson's excellent kedgeree and waited for some sign of my companion's mood. He refolded the newspaper, set it aside for his clippings books later, and reached for the butter dish.

"I apprehend that you wish to discuss something, Watson," Holmes noted as he carefully buttered another round of toast. "You have twice made that characteristic cuff-tugging gesture which indicates your intention to broach some difficult subject. You have sugared your tea, which you only do these days on occasions wherein you are perturbed. And you continue to glance at the brown-paper package which arrived yesterday from George Newnes Limited of Southampton Street, Strand,

---

1 This murder was also referenced in "The Adventure of Shoscombe Old Place".

that you charmingly fancy to have concealed from me beneath your Aberdeen coat beside the elephant's foot walking-stick stand."

I put down my fork and chuckled. "I should know better after all these years, Holmes, than to try and surprise you," I confessed. "May I enquire if you have also discerned the topic I have been trying to broach?"

Holmes completed his meticulous buttering. He broke off a corner of the toast and flicked it to the floor for the dog to devour, took a bite himself, then demonstrated again those keen powers of reasoning which readers of my annals have marvelled at no less than I.

"You have newsprint on your fingers, which means you have already consulted the Times broad-sheet; yet the paper remained folded and had never been opened when I took it up. You therefore consulted the front page only, most likely the masthead to confirm the date as one to which I might still be sensitive. You brought in the parcel while I was shaving, believing as you often do that the apparent clutter of our chambers would prevent me from noticing its presence. And you have new boots, which habitually you only purchase after you have received some financial windfall. From this I conclude that you wish to present me with the new edition of one of your accounts of our cases from the box of complimentary volumes forwarded by your publisher, but are unsure of how I might receive the gift if I am in a black mood."

Holmes was, as usual, correct. Over the winter of 1901 and through to Easter 1902 I had returned to chronicling my remarkable friend's exploits for the readers of the *Strand Magazine*.[2] However, I knew that my literary endeavours did not always commend the wholehearted recommendation of their principal subject.

I shifted my coat and brought the heavy parcel to the breakfast table. "My recent serial has proved popular," I admitted. "Mr Conan Doyle has arranged for a collected edition to be released to satisfy public demand."

"And the public must be satiated at all costs?"

"The truth must be served. On how many occasions has your work gone ignored whilst the men you have assisted have been swathed in glory for their triumphs? How much has a broader dissemination of your methods shaped modern forensic investigations of criminal activity? I trust that as your friend I have some delicacy about how I present your activities to the world."

I was cautious because Holmes did not entirely approve of the

2 The account in Strand Magazine from August 1901 to April 1902, the first published for eight years since the reports of Holmes' apparent death in "The Final Problem", occasioned massive public interest. Hundreds queued to purchase each magazine on its publication day.

publication of his memoirs. Although he did not forbid it, and indeed assiduously reviewed the results of my labours and even on two occasions added accounts of his own,[3] he was often troubled by the compromises of the literary style required to tell a compelling narrative. Holmes' own monographs generally required a more academic and therefore less dramatic tone.

My breakfast companion relented. "Come, Watson. Show me your book and be done with it. I doubt that your description of our old adventure in Devon will contain any worse inaccuracies or obfuscations than your publications of former years."

I took the letter-knife and sliced away the parcel string. The lid came off, revealing six red-spined author's copies of my new work. I lifted one out and passed it to my friend. "Here you are, then. My account of the mystery of the Hound of the Baskervilles."

Holmes turned the cloth-bound volume over in his long thin hands, admiring the weight and texture. "Your publisher has spared no expense in preparing his first edition, Watson. This and the advance which has new-shod you so lavishly suggest that he expects a ready market for your writing."

"I am gratified that my chronicles of your work find so ready an audience," I admitted. "I have been careful to select for release a case which dates back to 1889, before…"

"Before the Fourth of May 1891 and my 'fatal' tumble at the Reichenbach Falls," Holmes supplied. "The grim anniversary, which we have both assiduously avoided mentioning as usual. Yet it was that occasion which prompted you to release a flurry of your accounts of cases we had undertaken together. You believed me dead and therefore no longer requiring the anonymity that might otherwise assist a detective in the pursuit of his occupation."

"Assist a normal enquiry agent, yes," I responded, picking up the old argument. "But not a consulting detective who specialises in those cases where others have become baffled. That unique occupation you have created for yourself requires a level of publicity sufficient that the difficult puzzles you so value might come to our door."

Holmes laid the volume beside the marmalade and returned to the toast-rack. He had long since reviewed my notes about Sir Charles Baskerville

---

3 "The Adventure of the Blanched Soldier" and "The Adventure of the Lion's Mane" are the only canon stories narrated by Holmes rather than Watson. "The Adventure of the Mazarin Stone" is told in the third person.

and the deceptive and dangerous Stapleton, and had undoubtedly included the periodical *Strand Magazine* episodes in his voracious pile of reading.

He had kindly not mentioned the most personal change I had made to the account; in 1891 I was not, as the published annal suggested, resident at Baker Street. Holmes understood why I wished to avoid explanations of my domestic arrangements and descriptions of my marriage to Mary.[4] It was now eight years since her passing; I was ready to lay her to rest.

Since my friend seemed in an approachable mood I determined to push my luck. "There is a launch for this volume this afternoon," I mentioned. "A literary gathering in Bloomsbury. I don't suppose you would be interested to attend?"

Holmes declined. "I can think of few greater wastes of my time, Watson. Nor do I wish to endure the questions of your ebullient literary agent Doyle, who exhibits an endless fascination with the minutiae of my work. Please accept my apologies and appear without me."

We were interrupted by a short knock and Mrs Hudson's entry to our sitting room. She hefted a brown-paper parcel somewhat smaller than the

---

4 Holmesian historians find Dr Watson's marital history a source of much lively speculation and debate. The internal evidence of the "canon" of Conan Doyle-published accounts offers incomplete and occasionally contradictory evidence. It is certain that in 1889 Watson married soldier's daughter Miss Mary Morstan (c.f. "The Boscome Valley Mystery" and "The Stockbroker's Clerk"), whom he had met the year previously during *The Sign of Four*. Watson's "own sad bereavement" is referenced on the occasion of Holmes' return after Reichenbach Falls in "The Adventure of the Empty House", suggesting Mary's death during the interim of Holmes' three 'lost' years, 1891-4. After that time Watson returns to Baker Street for a prolonged stay.

W.S. Baring-Gould's definitive biography of Sherlock Holmes argues that Miss Morstan was actually Watson's second wife. Watson leaves no Canon record of his adventures with Homes between April 1883 and October 1886. Baring-Gould speculates that Watson spent the period from January 1884 to August 1886 overseas tending to his alcoholic brother, supporting himself with a medical practice in San Francisco and meeting Miss Constance Adams, who likely became Watson's first wife. He asserts that Watson and Miss Adams married in England on 1st November 1886 but the lady died a little over a year later in December 1887. This theory explains an anomaly of Watson describing his married state in "A Scandal in Bohemia" and other early stories that significantly precede his 1889 matrimony. This does not explain a continuity gaffe in which Watson's wife visits her mother in "the Five Orange Pips", which references and is therefore set after *The Sign of Four* wherein Mary Morstan's mother is stated to be dead. Watson records "The Five Orange Pips" as occurring in 1887 while he recounts *The Sign of Four* as happening in 1888. This perhaps illustrates how Watson sometimes obfuscated dates, names, and places to protect clients' identities.

The earlier Mrs Watson, whomever she might be, certainly assists in simplifying what are otherwise significant continuity problems in the published material.

Of course, none of this helps with Watson's reference to a current wife in "The Adventure of the Blanched Soldier", set in 1903!

Some Holmes enthusiasts have gone so far as to deduce six wives for the energetic doctor, but those theories are undoubtedly beyond the scope of our present footnote.

box my books had come in, wider than it was high, tied with twine. "This has just arrived, sirs, by private messenger," she informed us.

Holmes regarded the package with considerably more interest than the prospect of a buffet with Arthur Doyle. A Sunday delivery was unusual and promised novelty. He gestured for our housekeeper landlady to lay the item on the breakfast table and ruthlessly cleared dishes and post to make space for it. He was quite excited.

I looked to see what might have commanded his attention. The parcel seemed ordinary at first glance. Then I apprehended some of the features which had engaged Holmes' detective enthusiasm.

"This paper is old," I observed. "The ink of the address has faded with age also."

"And the string," Holmes added. "Note the coarser weft and the discolouration from the bleaches used a decade ago. But the stamps are modern, post-marked yesterday afternoon at Charing Cross. Curious that the package was sent to a delivery agent who would forward it to us on the Sabbath when the general postal service sleeps, when the parcel might have been deposited direct on our doorstep with Saturday's last post." He picked up his lens and examined the brown paper. "This has been stored for a long time in a dry dusty place out of the light. See where it has been brushed down with a soft cloth before mailing?"

He produced a pocket-knife and carefully sawed through the string. I looked at the neat copperplate writing in blue ink that read 'Forward to Mr Sherlock Holmes, 221b Baker Street, London,' but could find nothing unusual about the inscription. There was no return address. Abrasions on the packet indicated a pasted label directing the parcel to an intermediate delivery agent had been removed.

Unwrapped, the cardboard box proved to be of a common kind, without any identifying script. It was sealed with paper tape that had become brittle and dry with the passage of time. When the lid was opened it revealed yellowed newspaper packing.

I seized upon the date on the papers. "18th March 1891." The ancient pages were reminders of that time. "The Great Blizzard was passing.[5] The SS Utopia collided with HMS Anson in Gibraltar harbour with 564 lives lost. And the London-Paris telephone system was officially opened."

Holmes ignored my elementary deduction and unwrapped the object that the crumpled papers protected. It was a black ceramic mask of the

---

5 The "Great Blizzard of 1891" covered south and west England with extensive snowdrifts from 9th March. Channel storms sank 14 ships. The weather caused around 220 deaths. Holmes avoided the snows by being out of the country at the time, on "the matter of supreme importance to the French government" mentioned in "The Final Problem."

kind sometimes used in funerary rites, cast from a mould taken of a corpse's face.

I recognised that countenance, the prominent forehead, the sharp nose, the thin calculating lips. Though I had never met the owner of that visage I knew it well from Holmes' papers. My breakfast churned in my stomach. The sculpture was in the image of Professor James Moriarty!

The events of eleven years earlier welled back. It was then that Holmes had appeared at my medical practise in great haste, hunted by the deadly Colonel Sebastian Moran at the behest of Moran's deadlier master. Years of painstaking work to track down the consulting criminal at the heart of Europe's underworld had finally exposed the disgraced scholarly Professor as the secret co-ordinator of much that was nefarious across Britain and the Continent. Holmes was within mere days of closing the net upon him. Moriarty had ordained the detective killed before the noose could be tightened and had pitted all his vast ingenuity and terrible resources to achieving that end.

Holmes and I took refuge across the Channel. Moriarty and Moran followed us. Yet the final confrontation between the foremost minds of our age came without either the Professor's lethal gunman or myself present. Holmes met Moriarty alone, and both men tumbled together into the lethal 820 foot chain of waterfalls at Reichenbach, Switzerland. Moriarty was gracious enough to allow Holmes to leave me an explanatory note before their ultimate clash.

When I finally arrived at the falls and found my friend's cigarette case set aside to hold the farewell he had written, I had really thought it the end. The fierce cataracts of that dramatic descent in Bernese Oberland are terrible and formidable. Survival is considered impossible.

I alerted the authorities, of course, starting by rousing the police at nearby Meiringen and then the municipal force at larger Interlaken. A through search was made along the Reichenbach stream and the Aar River into which if flows. No bodies were ever recovered.

I looked at the pottery countenance of Holmes' most competent adversary. Moriarty's face seemed to sneer back at me, confident, cunning, intelligent, ruthless. I found my voice. "Holmes, you survived that confrontation. Could he…?"

"If any man had the resource then it was James Moriarty," my friend considered, "but I do not believe it to be so. The Professor was my match in many things, perhaps my superior in some, but he spent his days as a spider lurking at the centre of his web while I spend mine as a hunting hound chasing prey. My knowledge of *baritsu*[6] saved me in that last desperate struggle so that I never suffered that full lethal tumble into the teeming waterfall. I saw my enemy fall."

"Moriarty still had allies, though. Could one have retrieved the body? Revived him? As a medical man I an aware of many odd incidences where subjects of drowning..."

Holmes assuaged my fears. "You will recall that on the occasion of my supposed death, a death I indeed believed awaited me when the Professor and I plunged from that path, I was also being stalked by the deadly Colonel Moran. He in turn was only the first of several dangerous associates who had avoided the net that closed on Moriarty's organisation on three continents. I spent the following two years secretly assisting in those men's downfall before I could reveal my survival to the world, or to you."

"I well recall it. Sebastian Moran was the last of them to be taken. I was there."[7]

"Then be assured that Moriarty was not still alive during that mutual hunt, or my task would have been far harder. It was the loss of their head that made those lieutenants of crime vulnerable. Those who were not swept up by Gregson, Lestrade, and Hopkins in England, by Wilson Hargreave in New York, by Lebrun and LeVillard in Paris, scattered like frightened jackals, vicious but uncoordinated. Had their head survived they would have caused far more harm than they did before each one fell."

Holmes tapped the death mask. "Besides, this image betrays none of the signs of a body crushed by a high drop or submerged in water. This cast was taken while its model was alive. See the twin holes left at the nostrils to allow the subject to breathe." He turned the morbid object over in his hands, half-delighted, half-appalled that his 'Napoleon of Crime' still had new ways to baffle him.

---

6 There is no martial art called baritsu. A plausible case has been made for baritsu being a typographical error, authorial mishearing, or even a copyright protection change from bartitsu, an eclectic fighting style founded by Doyle's fellow contributor to *Pearson's Magazine*, E.W. Barton-Wright. However, Barton-Wright did not found his art until 1899, more than a decade after Holmes' possible use of it to fend off Professor Moriarty. The actual technique by which the great detective escaped his greatest enemy therefore remains unknown.

The "Baritsu Chapter" of the New York Sherlock Holmes Club was founded in 1948, and in 1977 it spawned the Japanese Sherlock Holmes Club, which has around a thousand members today.

7 Watson's account of Holmes return and the capture of "the second most deadly man in London" appears in "The Adventure of the Empty House" in *The Return of Sherlock Holmes*, 1903.

"What then must we make of this?" I puzzled. "Why send such a grotesque *momento mori* on the anniversary of his passing to the man who occasioned that end? What does it mean?"

Holmes ruthlessly pushed more breakfast china aside to make room for his investigations. "Glazed plaster," he began, tapping the mask with his fingernail. "The mix of powder will be telling but must wait for later. The image is well made, doubtless based upon a template made from life. It is the work of an artist."

I had never seen James Moriarty in life but was well aware of him from the photo-plate on his book jacket, from Holmes' copious files, and from the images the periodicals had printed of him after his death. The mask's caster had somehow captured that serpentine expression, the glint of genius tethered to utter malice that characterised the man.

Holmes examined the reverse of the mask and made a noise of interest. "See here, Watson. An inscription!"

On the transverse of the forehead were a string of strange symbols. My first impression was of hieroglyphs, but they were not. Nor were they the marks that chemists used to use to indicate pharmaceutical formulae.

"A code?" I suggested. "Like the Dancing Men?"[8]

Holmes examined the symbols more carefully and made a copy for further study:

"I confess to having no idea where to begin with those," I told him.

Holmes frowned too. "They are figuratively in the mind of Professor Moriarty, Watson. We cannot expect to fathom them easily."

He spread out a fresh stack of paper, took up a pen, and began to scribble. He occasionally stopped to measure some element of the mask or its engraving with a ruler or magnifying lens. He sometimes hopped up to heave a reference tome from a shelf then discarded it on the floor.

"I take it you will certainly not be accompanying me to my literary reception, then?" I asked uselessly.

---

8 Holmes had addressed the problem brought by Mr Hilton Cubitt of Riding Thorpe Manor, Derbyshire, which featured an obscure string of stick-figures in various poses, four years previously in 1898. Watson presents the account in "The Adventure of the Dancing Men" in *The Return of Sherlock Holmes*.

Holmes did not even hear the question.

⸺⸝⸜⸺

It may not surprise the reader to know that I attended the Bloomsbury event without Mr Sherlock Holmes; indeed, I am not entirely sure if he noticed my departure from Baker Street. I arrived at the reception venue a little before four and was escorted immediately to a back room where I was to be briefed by my agent on what was to follow. I had been warned that I might have to say a few words but hoped to avoid it. Public speaking makes me uncomfortable.

"Ah, Dr Watson," Doyle's harried assistant greeted me as I entered the gallery foyer. "Um, yes…"

Galpin looked even more flustered than usual. Perhaps the strain of ushering caretaker and stewards to place chairs for the reading and to set out buffet tables, the worry of preparing for the elite literati of the publishing world and for the popular press had got to him. "Good afternoon. Where is Doyle?"

"Mr Conan Doyle[9] is in the back room, sir," the nervous little secretary revealed, "but…"

"He asked to have a word with me before this circus starts. I hope he doesn't think he'll inveigle me into reading some extract from the book. Bad enough that I have to say a few words. He promised an actor or professional reader."

"Yes, yes he's engaged someone…"

"This way, is he?"

"Er, he is, only…"

I grew impatient with the dithering Galpin—it is only in comparison to Holmes that I seem tolerant of blitherers, and I own to being somewhat nervous myself on that occasion. I dodged round the assistant, past the red cord that separated off the rear chambers, and passed into the back of the gallery in search of my literary agent.

---

9 Scholars remain at odds over the famous author's surname. His baptismal registration at St Mary's Cathedral, Edinburgh lists his Christian names as Arthur Ignatius Conan while his father's name was Charles Altamont Doyle. Michael Conan was his godfather. In young adulthood, Doyle began to use the compound Conan Doyle as his name and signature, but when he received his 1902 knighthood, a mere six months after the time of our present story, he was gazetted as Doyle alone. The British Library and the Library of Congress both list his works under 'Doyle' On the other hand his second wife took the name Jean Conan Doyle.

I followed the sound of raised voices.

I was surprised to discover Doyle engaged in a difficult argument with a furious young woman. She clutched in her fist a crumpled pamphlet which she waved in the author's face for emphasis.

"This…!" she scolded, lips curled back to show her teeth, "this scurrilous piece of apologia! How dare you traduce the integrity of witnesses who have seen first-hand what you dismiss as prejudiced fallacy?"

Arthur Conan Doyle was not one to back down from an argument, but neither was he so ungentlemanly as to raise his voice to a lady. "Madam," he replied with what dignity he could muster, "the document to which you have taken offence contains nothing but truth. I served as a volunteer doctor at Langman Field Hospital at Bloemfontein between March and June of the year 1900. I am quite familiar with the Boer and the Kaffir, with the terrain, health conditions, and conflict of the region."

"You left for the comfort of England before the worst consequences of British policy occurred," the passionate woman accused. "I was there too, more recently than you, mere months since, as secretary and amanuensis of Mrs Fawcett on her government commission. Or do you wish to call me a liar also?"

Doyle warmed to his defence. "Consequences? What of the consequences of a different policy, madam? That appears to be the point no critic of our methods will answer! When Boer rebels will not face us like men but hide out in the veldt to commit atrocities and massacres by stealth, and leave us with no choice but to remove from them the means of foraging, what shall we do with those non-combatants who are necessarily left homeless and without means of support? Send them to the Afrikaner lines? There were none. The rebel force had split into a hundred factions. Leave them to starve? No, we took them in, gave them security in guarded laagers from the Kaffirs who might prey on them…"

"Kept them confined in close quarters and did not allow them to leave," the young woman interrupted. "Sent their men overseas and left women and children on short rations, without access to clean water, soap, decent food, to die of starvation and disease in your concentration camps!"

"We gave what comfort we could to an enemy population, while our own women and children suffered similar deprivations of war—with no such consideration from the enemy!"

"So I read in this grubby little document of yours, Mr Doyle," the lady sneered. She waved again *The War in Africa, Its Cause and Conduct* by Arthur Conan Doyle. "Yet it fails to make adequate apology for the one quarter of that interned population who have died in those camps. One quarter, sir, of over ninety thousand Boers and who knows how many blacks? And most of those deaths of children!"

I felt the need to intervene. I dislike seeing any woman so upset and any man so besieged. "Excuse me," I interrupted. "This seems to be a difficult moment but I was asked to come back here for a briefing?"

Doyle and his Nemesis both turned abruptly. Neither had recognised my presence until then. Doyle seemed abashed to have been discovered in such an altercation. The impassioned woman turned her gimlet gaze on me. "Dr John Watson!"

"Ma'am." I raised my hat. "You have me at a disadvantage."

"Yes." She turned back to point at Doyle. "Your esteemed literary agent libels the good work and good name of Emily Hobhouse and is lauded for it by a complacent government because he is associated with you and Mr Sherlock Holmes. And thus you collaborate with him to cover up mass murder!"

"Miss Hobhouse is the lady who first visited the Bloemfontein camp and reported concerns about the conditions there," I recalled.

Doyle snorted. "Miss Hobhouse spoke no Dutch, had no experience of the Boer character, and knew nothing about the regular conditions of South African life. Furthermore, she is a known radical, related to the M.P. Charles Hobhouse whose political leanings are well known. She was only present in the colony at the invitation of the Liberal firebrand Leonard Courtney to stir up trouble for our government. Of *course* she found things of which to complain."

"It does not require advanced language skills to recognise a starving child," the lady responded. "Nor to see meat and flour rancid with maggots, nor to count thirteen latrines for 3,500 people…"

"Meanwhile, I was seeing fifty or sixty loyal British soldiers a day die in our single overstretched military hospital," Doyle responded. "For every man killed in combat two more died of disease and poor rations."

The door from the main hall opened and a man I did not know slipped in. He paused, uncertain, as he encountered the conflict raging in the backroom. The fellow was a stout round-faced fellow with small spectacles, dressed in a rumpled suit of American cut. He blinked in surprise and told Doyle, "Um, Galpin wished me to mention that they're waiting for you."

"Oh yes, Mr Doyle, *don't* keep your illustrious literary friends waiting," the lady hissed. "Go and let them applaud you while Boer children die in brutal British camps that you will defend to the death!"

The newcomer heard this with alarm. "That's probably not the message you want to concentrate on," he advised my agent. His accent was curious, some mix of American and Eastern-European. Holmes later defined it as Slovakian.

"Madam, volume and rhetoric do not make your arguments any more valid, only less palatable," Doyle responded to the Fury that assailed him. "Now I must withdraw from this unsolicited harangue and attend to business. Mr Beck informs me that our event is about to begin. Please have the courtesy to leave us to our affairs."

"Neither do evasions, slurs, and propaganda make crimes any less immoral," his opponent shot back. She had a spirited line in repartee and was not yet ready to concede the floor.

"It's clear that there are points to be made on both sides," I interjected, attempting diplomacy. "The issue is an emotive one, provoking strong opinions from all quarters. I wonder, however, whether this is the best time to debate them? Or what could be achieved by such a discussion under these circumstances?"

The angry woman glared at me, nostrils flaring splendidly. With some effort she regained control of her temper. "You are correct, Dr Watson. It is a waste of time to argue with a fool whose mind is set." She swivelled away from my agent and stalked away to the main hall, where she was finally intercepted by two attendants and escorted from the premises.

The man Doyle had named as Beck watched her go. "If only the people who get mad at me looked like that," he sighed.

"By Jove, Doyle," I breathed, "I thought for a moment she was going to tear your heart out and eat it whole."

"She and her whole suffragette contingent are like that," Doyle warned. "They choose the facts they want to argue about and ignore the context around it."

"She said she had been to the camps. With Mrs Fawcett?" The papers had made much of the 'Ladies Commission' sent to test whether unofficial reports from the concentration laagers were true. Scholarly academic Mrs Fawcett, considered 'a safe pair of hands' by the government despite her feminist leanings, had instead delivered a damning appraisal of how badly wrong Lord Kitchener's well-meant internment policy had gone.

"I'm not saying there was no mistake, Watson. Only that the alternatives were worse. You've seen war. You know that often there are no good choices. Sniping at the decisions made in a desperate hour has always been the sport of the armchair analyst." He picked up the crumpled leaflet the departing lady had thrown at his feet. "That is why I wrote this, in defence of the British. We are so slow to speak on our own behalf, as if it were bad manners to correct malicious criticism."

"This probably isn't the time to reflect on it, gents," Beck advised. "You have a whole bunch of self-important bigwigs out there waiting to meet the good doctor." He held out his hand to shake. "Martin Beck of the Orpheum Circuit, the American theatres group."

"Delighted. John Watson."

"I'd figured that. You're the guy we've all come to see." He glanced back down the corridor where the lady had vanished. "Didn't expect a side-show as well."

"Who was that remarkable critic?" I ventured to Doyle.

"Mrs Kent, relic of the late Liberal pamphleteer Giles Kent. A woman of considerable temper."

"So I noted. Was she invited to your gathering?"

"Certainly not. A gate-crasher. We can only be grateful that she did not shackle herself to something—or someone." Doyle snorted and regained his good humour. "I'm sorry, Watson. This is only a distraction. It is more important that we introduce the world to the good Mr Sherlock Holmes once again."

"I agree," chimed in Beck. "Your return to publishing his chronicles has caused quite a stir."

It was some time since I had released accounts of my friend's cases to the general public. As Holmes had noted, my first forays into print had occurred when I thought him dead. Upon his return I had quietly withdrawn from issuing more material. It was only lately, as a growing sense came upon me that I was changing, and the world with me, that I had obtained my comrade's permission to recommence publicising a selection of my chronicles.

"It seemed a good idea when I picked up pen to make sense of my notes," I admitted. "I had not expected such interest after so long a break."

"Nine years only whets the public's appetite," Beck assured me.

Doyle nodded agreement. "Now come. We'll make our grand entrance. There's a hundred or more people out there who want to meet the great detective's companion—a good many of them buyers or reviewers who I would like you to charm."

"I'm not exactly the chap you need for that, Doyle."

"You are exactly the chap, Watson. Be yourself—forthright, decent, perceptive, and trustworthy. Leave it to me to do the rest. Oh, and you'll need to make a few remarks."

There was no escape.

I returned to Baker Street quite late but the mantles were still lit and Holmes was still poring over books on his desk.

"You should have come along after all," I told him. "Met a very interesting fellow by the name of Beck. He's the managing agent for that chap whose exploits you've been following—Harry Houdini. They're back in London for a short season before heading to the Continent again. We're invited to their big launch."

Holmes looked up from his studies. "And who was the lady that so engaged your attention, Watson?"

I stopped short, frozen in the act of hooking my walking-stick into the rail around our hatstand. After all this time Holmes' acuity can sometimes take me by surprise.

He chuckled. "Come, Watson, credit me some familiarity with your habits. As you hung your hat just now I could not help but notice you had taken the trouble to straighten the brim. Likewise you have smoothed your moustaches, a gesture you perform unconsciously in the presence of or when contemplating some member of the fairer sex who has captured your interest. My conclusions are hardly the stuff of novels."

"There was a brief encounter with a very irate lady," I confessed, "but I was not the principal cause of her chagrin. Poor Doyle received the full broadside however."

"Yet you wished it had been you who was the focus of her attention."

"The lady was… she had other urgent interests." I noticed that Holmes had propped up Moriarty's mask on his music stand to better study the sigils engraved on the image's transverse. "Have you made progress in deciphering the code or learning the purpose of your macabre gift?" I wondered, to change the subject.

Holmes allowed the deflection. "How like the Professor to baffle me even after fourteen years in the grave—or wherever his corpse ended up. And how characteristic of him to discern where lie the weaknesses in my learning and the gaps in my fund of data and exploit them so thoroughly."

I moved over to examine the mask again. "What do you mean, Holmes?"

"Why Watson, on your very first venture into the world of literature you mentioned composing a list of my special areas of expertise and of deficiencies that seemed remarkable to you. You noted my understanding of politics was variable and that my knowledge of literature, philosophy, and astronomy was nonexistent."[10]

"I know you better now," I admitted. "Were I compiling such a judgement

---

10 This assessment appears in Part 1 Chapter II of *A Study in Scarlet*.

today I would accede that you have a comprehensive knowledge of those plays in which you performed during your stage days with Sasanoff's players. Indeed, you often quote the Bard to illustrate your point. Your familiarity with politics has also improved as several of your cases have involved political motives and you have educated yourself on the relevant matters."

"But my familiarity with astronomy remains feeble. Of what value is the motion of the planets to the career I have chosen? You know my ignorance—and so did Professor Moriarty!"

I frowned. "Whereas Moriarty was a noted astronomer and caused uproar in the scientific community with a book on that subject."

Holmes tapped an open volume of the thin self-published *Dynamics Of An Asteroid*. "Moriarty knew well how to baffle me. That is why he chose the one field of scientific endeavour where he knew most and I knew least."

"What has astronomy to do with someone sending you a clay image of our old enemy?"

"Everything, Watson!" Holmes jumped up and took three long paces to the blackboard where he had chalked up the symbols discovered on the reverse of the death mask. "You wondered what these vaguely hieroglyphic images portrayed? Perhaps you might recognise these other sigils instead?"

He quickly sketched out another series of symbols:

"I presume you know these, Watson?"

"What doctor would not? Several of them are used in pharmaceutical notation for the prescription of medication, a hold-over I believe from the alchemists of the middle ages associating elements with celestial bodies and ancient deities.[11] The marks you have drawn are the astronomical symbols for the objects in our solar system, beginning with the sun and

---

11 Of Holmes' list, the first symbol, the sun, also represented gold. The second, Mercury, represented the liquid metal also known as quicksilver, as well as the planet. Mars, fourth on Holmes' chart, also meant iron. Saturn, third from the right, represented lead. A crescent signifying the moon meant silver. Venus' symbol, third from left in Holmes' list, was later associated with copper. Other alchemical and scientific sigils were not tied to planetary bodies. Their use went back at least to Basilius Valentius' alchemy table in his Last Will and Testament circa 1670 and was well established by the time they were codified in a key in Kenelm Digby's *A Choice Collection of Rare Secrets*, 1682.

then listing each planetary body outwards from Mercury to Neptune."[12]

"Indeed. And these I am familiar with because of my professional interest in poisons and diagnostic chemistry. What Moriarty knew might baffle me for a short time at least are these other astronomical symbols."

I looked at the obscure chalked characters with renewed interest. "You have discerned what they are?"

"I have. They are the correct astronomical marks for the asteroids, written in the order by which they were discovered. Ceres, observed in 1801, was given the first of the symbols in the list, derived from a stylised corn-cutting sickle. As for the others..."

Holmes passed me a list he had scribbled showing the meaning of the signs:

Ceres - a sickle - 1801
Pallas (Athena) - a spear – 1801
Juno - a sceptre – 1804
Vesta - a sacred hearth – 1807
Astraea - a scale of justice – 1845
Hebe - a cup – 1847
Iris - rainbow and star – 1847
Flora - a flower, specifically an English rose – 1847
Metis - eye of wisdom and star - 1848

"There have been other discoveries since," my friend reported. He had clearly been catching up on a field of study that Moriarty had known to be a weak spot. "Hygeia in '49, Parthenope, Victoria and Egeria in '50, Irene and Eunomia in '51 and so on. Psyche, Thetis, Melponeme, and Fortuna, all spotted in '52 were the last asteroids to be regularly awarded their own icon. Thereafter a convention of a circle and the order number of the body's observation sufficed. Exceptions were Proserpina, the twenty-sixth discovery, which was awarded the pomegranate as a symbol, Bellona and Amphitrite, the twenty-eighth and ninth respectively, and Leukothea and Fides in '55."

12 Pluto, formerly recognised as our solar system's ninth planetary body, was not discovered and named until 1930 and was therefore unknown to Watson. Pluto has recently and controversially been demoted by the International Astronomical Union to a minor planet designated 134340 Pluto. It is now ranked with Ceres, Pallas, Juno, Vesta, newly-discovered Eris and many other not-quite-large-enough space objects that have not "cleared the neighbourhood" of other masses around their orbit to become gravitationally dominant. However, Pluto's demotion has not gone unchallenged; the states of New Mexico and Illinois have both passed motions retaining Pluto's planetary status and several senior astronomers have questioned the IAU's findings or its constituency to reclassify the body.

"You have had a busier Sunday afternoon than I!" I admired. Whatever the origin of Moriarty's effigy, it had galvanised Sherlock Holmes as I had not seen him for some time. Gone was the disinterested logician who had casually solved the affair of the Counterfeit Coiner only a month before with a mild contempt for criminal and detectives alike.[13] Now Holmes' gimlet eyes were sharply focused, his prominent brow furrowed with concentration. "Have you any idea yet why such symbols might be engraved upon the back of an image of Moriarty, or what that image being sent to you might signify?"

"I have given it much attention, my friend. At first I considered whether the years of discovery might be relevant to some kind of numerical difference code. I am now reviewing the possibility of some algorithm regarding the names of the astronomical bodies. I confess that James Moriarty was my superior at advanced mathematics. If he chose to challenge me on that battlefield he would most certainly prevail."

"You speak as if Moriarty himself set you a test."

"Who else? It is too calculated at my areas of ignorance to have been devised by any other. The mask to provoke my interest, prepared in advance and presumably bestowed on some trusted lieutenant with instructions for its use. The unfamiliar symbols encoded in the clay. Its calculated arrival by special delivery on the exact anniversary of our fatal encounter. No, Watson, this challenge is directly at me—for revenge or some other purpose I am yet to discover."

I looked at that pottery countenance. Even the mere clay image of that criminal spider who had once squatted at the centre of Europe's most terrible criminal organisation seemed evil and threatening. Moriarty glared at us from beyond the grave.

"What then is the message that you were meant to take from this artefact?" I asked, more nervously than I might have liked.

"It is too soon, Watson, too soon to say! But I will know. I must know. And I shall!"

I was woken by the tread of Holmes' boots on the stairs up to my bedroom before ever his urgent rapping sounded on my door. I was already reaching for my dressing gown before his "Quickly, Watson!" prompted me to haste.

---

13 This case is mentioned in passing in "The Adventure of Shoscombe Old Place".

Readers of my accounts will realise that this was not an unprecedented interruption of my reposes. A glance at the clock told it was as 7:21 a.m. "What's the matter, Holmes?"

My flat-mate furrowed his brows. "We have had an intruder."

I turned back to the dresser and found my service revolver.

"Too late for the Beaumont Adams, Watson. Our interloper has been and gone, taking with him what he came to get."

I hastened after Holmes, down the stairs to our sitting room. "And what did he want?" I enquired.

Holmes gestured to the empty music stand where Moriarty's death mask had been displayed.

Mrs Hudson was present, clutching her pinafore and looking round as if she might still spot the thief lurking behind a piece of furniture. "I don't know how he could have got in, Dr Watson," she protested. "I'm always most particular about seeing the downstairs doors and windows locked and bolted."

A thundering up the stairs from the hall below announced the return of our page from his inspection of the perimeter. "Nothing as I can see without touching anything that Mr 'Olmes might want to examine," he reported. "None of the bolts is open. He couldn't 'ave gone out and pulled the shots across after 'im."

Holmes held up his hand for calm and quiet. "There are already several lines of investigation which suggest themselves," he told us. "An obvious question is how the thief knew that the object he sought was here. In tracing the delivery from the company who brought us the package yesterday he may have left some trail himself. A visit to the agency was already on today's agendum. However, I must first consider what physical circumstances can tell us about our uninvited caller."

"Then I'd best be seeing about breakfast," Mrs Hudson insisted. It took more than a larcenous intruder to disrupt our housekeeper's diligent schedule. "Will you be needing the boy?"

Holmes looked over at our eager page. "You might ask the street lads if they noticed anything last night," he told the youth. "Also if anyone was asking about the house yesterday."

"Yessir!" our house-boy agreed, haring out of the room and downstairs even as Mrs Hudson's chiding about decorum echoed after him.

I picked up a *Times* from the pile of newspapers that Holmes had delivered daily. "Investigate my armchair for clues first would you, old man?" I asked the great detective. When he pronounced himself satisfied I took a comfortable seat and browsed the front page while he crawled over our home with a magnifying lens.

My eyes were drawn to another article about the House of Commons debate over the situation in South Africa. As hopes of a negotiated settlement of peace grew there was still fierce opposition from the right for any kind of deal with the Boers. The Liberals continued to demand the government be held to account for the administrative blunders that had caused so much misery and suffering in the concentration camps.

I confess that my mind wandered to the redoubtable Mrs Kent assailing poor Doyle like a vengeful Valkyrie. Miss Hobhouse was the radical reformer who had been expelled from the colony for her troublemaking and who had first revealed the abuses and horrors of the internment system. Mrs Garrett Fawcett had led the Ladies' Commission that had confirmed much of what had been reported, whose report had belatedly spurred the government towards reform. But surely those troubled Boer widows and orphans had no more passionate nor so beautiful an advocate as Mrs Kent?

"Here is where our intruder entered," Holmes announced from the window that looks out over the rear yard, the one directly opposite the big bay onto Baker Street. "There are unmistakable signs of a blade being slipped beneath the sash to press aside the restraining clasp. Not a pen-knife, I would judge. Larger. What the Americans term a Bowie knife, or perhaps a bayonet."

I snapped from my reverie and set aside my reading. "How did the thief get up to an upper story window?" I wondered. "A ladder?"

"I do not perceive any such marks from here, Watson, though I will of course make a ground inspection shortly. My first suspicion is that our robber simply climbed up the brickwork." He leaned dangerously out of the open casement. "Yes, it's easy to see from here. Mortar chiselled out between the stones to allow handholds. Interesting."

"An acrobatic burglar, then, and a good one."

"And a diminutive one, judging by the distance between grip-holes. Not as tall as five foot six, I'd judge, and light. A child, possibly, or rather a half-grown youth. Yet deft at turning catches. It is not every would-be thief who can trip open the fastenings on our windows at Baker Street."

"Deft and small, then," I summarised. "Does that suggest any particular rogue from your comprehensive index?"

"There are three dozen who might attempt this kind of entry with this level of competence," Holmes considered. "However, the wise career house-breaker would normally have better sense than to try and burgle from Sherlock Holmes. Such an action would draw my attention with judicial consequences."

"Here is where our intruder entered."

"Perhaps for a very significant reward?" I suggested. Then, my imagination darkening, I added, "Any one of them would have done such a thing at Moriarty's behest."

"And did," the detective conceded. "You will recall the occasion that these rooms were set on fire when the good Professor wished to send warning or distraction." He paused to reflect. "Some few of those men who were arrested during the great roll-up of Moriarty's organisation fourteen years ago might have served out sentences and be released onto the streets by now, but I doubt that any of the specialists who might attempt this would remain fit and limber enough to pull it off after a decade of rock-breaking. A newer generation would have less reason to follow the orders of a dead man who can now be only an underworld legend."

"Then we cannot draw too narrow a list of suspects by simply listing those capable of the intrusion."

"I fear not. Even if the professional house-breakers of London are too awed by my reputation to attempt such a thing there are many others who are not local talent that might manage the feat. Less who might have the initiative and intellect to recognise my notes on the code and to steal them also, though."

I realised for the first time that Holmes' desk had been disturbed and that the chalk had been wiped off the blackboard where the sigils had been copied.

"A futile attempt to halt me," my friend sniffed. "As if I had had not now memorised every salient point. It suggests, however, that our thief or his employer was keen to understand the meaning of the Moriarty code himself—which further raises the possibility that someone knows what the code is meant to tell."

"What is our course of action now, Holmes?"

"For me, a closer examination of our house and grounds and then some necessary work amongst the seedier denizens of our fair city. I note from your calendar that you have arranged a luncheon with your new showman acquaintance Mr Beck. I suggest that you keep your meeting and that we rendezvous at three at the Old Bailey."

"Newgate Prison?" Holmes intention seemed clear. "You intend to visit Moran."

The detective nodded and cradled his fingertips. "Who better to understand the mind of the master than his most faithful hound?"

I met with Beck at the Savoy Grill on the Strand,[14] which I had heard did excellent kippers. We ordered Yarmouth bloaters[15] in butter sauce and settled to our meal. The portly American was delighted to push across a pair of complimentary tickets to his client's first return performance at the Lyceum.

"Come if you can," he encouraged me. "It'll be a riot—although not the kind that occurred in our debut there last year."[16]

I knew of the strange events at the venerable Wellington Road theatre from Holmes' clippings book. "Your Houdini is an interesting character," I opined.

Beck snorted. "You have no idea! Well, perhaps you do, given your fellow-lodger. I first saw Harry Houdini in a little backwater called Woodstock, Illinois, peddling a mixed act of card tricks, conjuring, and escapology. Tracked him down at a Minnesota Beer Hall where he was calling himself the King of Cards. Encouraged him to concentrate on the locks and chains stuff—you can't throw a stone near a vaudeville stage in the States without hitting a dozen 'Is this your card?' merchants, but there's very few can do what that man's able to with a sealed box. Signed him exclusive to the Orpheum—that's my entertainment outfit. I've been trying to manage him ever since."

"Trying?"

"Oh, Harry has his own ideas about what he wants to do. The ideal client would turn up at his performances, sober and punctual, do his act, take a bow, talk to the press, and retire quietly till it's time to get on the train to the next venue. That's all we agents ask, really."

"Houdini is not sober and prompt?"

"Oh, that's not my problem, Dr Watson. I could handle an unprofessional drunk. I have done. But a guy who insists on chasing down frauds and hucksters, who'll never turn his back on a gal in distress or a puzzle that can't be solved? It makes for an exciting tour, you know?"

I couldn't restrain a sigh of sympathy. "There are some men who are fated for such extraordinary adventures, I'm afraid."

---

14 The luxurious 268-room Savoy Hotel was opened in 1890 by opera impresario Richard D'Oyly-Carte. Under its original manager César Ritz it became famous for the quality of its formal restaurant and its separate 'Bar and Grill', some of the finest dining in London.

15 These smoke-cured ungutted whole herring must not be confused with kippers, which are more-smoked lightly-salted split herring. Though rarely served now, bloaters and kippers were both immensely popular Victorian dishes. It is perhaps characteristic of Watson to order so English a dish in the restaurant of renowned French chef Auguste Escoffier.

16 Details of Houdini's memorable performance are available in Jim Beard's "Houdini Brings The Curtain Down" in *The Amazing Harry Houdini*, ISBN-13: 978-0692586563

"And some who have to put up with 'em," Beck replied. "Come to the opening if you can. Houdini's a big admirer of Sherlock Holmes. He'd like to meet him."

"Holmes is shy of publicity," I warned. "I doubt he'd wish to participate in Mr Houdini's show."

Beck shook his head. "Actually, your friend is about the *only* famous man in the world who I'd keep off a stage with Harry. Houdini's in the habit of getting Police Chiefs and Lord Mayors and what-have-you to search him before he gets locked up, to prove he's not made any preparations to cheat his captivity. I don't think it'd be smart to ask Sherlock Holmes to do that, do you?"

I chuckled at the thought. "Probably not."

"Just call in and enjoy the show if you can. We'll be debuting a new trap. I can't say what, yet, but it's good. And we'll be doing one of Houdini's big set piece challenges two days before, a stunt at Tower Bridge next Saturday. It'll be big."

"I can't make any promises. Holmes has a new case which is drawing all of our attention."

"And he doesn't want any distractions, right? Obsessive about getting every detail nailed down and shining a light into every shady corner? Yeah, I've been there. Still, if you do drag him out to the show make sure you call backstage before or afterwards. I know Houdini would be pleased as punch to meet you and your pal."

Our conversation progressed on, comparing and contrasting our unusual friends. Beck outlined some incidents that had distinguished Houdini's European tour so far. I described Holmes' recent adventures at the Priory School and the affair at Thor Bridge.[17] The American agent revealed some details of his principal's exploits in the Parisienne catacombs against the notorious Far Edge Club.[18] I sketched out some background on the Abergavenny murder and the case of the Six Napoleons.[19]

Eventually our talk turned to our mutual friend Arthur Conan Doyle,

---

17 Chronicled in "The Adventure of the Priory School" in *The Return of Sherlock Holmes* and "The Problem at Thor Bridge" in *The Case-Book of Sherlock Holmes* respectively.

18 Described by I.A. Watson in "Houdini and the Catacombs of Paris" in *The Amazing Harry Houdini.*

19 Watson also references the Abergavenny murder in "The Adventure of the Priory School". "The Adventure of the Six Napoleons" is told in *The Return of Sherlock Holmes.*

whom Beck had met under odd circumstances.[20] That in turn led me to casually enquire, "What of the young woman with whom he was engaged in such lively discussion?"

The theatrical agent smiled. "Ah, yes, I observed that you noticed her. Very notice-worthy, Mrs Morgaine Kent. Widowed for some years, you know. I asked Galpin about her afterwards."

"She seemed to be a lady of strong views. I fear I might have offended her."

"She sure got Doyle worked up, didn't she? You Brits have gotten yourselves in a proper tangle over this South Africa stuff. I don't know whether as former colonials who won free from your empire's tyranny we should be rooting for the Boer rebels, or as trans-Atlantic partners in democracy we should be cheering you as you stand up for helpless settlers against armed raiders."

"It's a complicated matter. Do you happen to know where I might find Mrs Kent to make amends for any offence?"

"Or to continue the argument?" Beck suggested. "She was part of Mrs Fawcett's Ladies' Commission, wasn't she? I guess you could apply at Mrs Fawcett's National Union of Women's Suffrage Societies[21]—if you dare."

Newgate Prison sat brutal and brooding in the last days of its seven hundred year reign of terror.[22] Since at least the twelfth century the gaol had served to intimidate, imprison, and destroy London's criminals. Twice rebuilt, after the Great Fire and eighteenth century riots, the huge looming slab of *architecture terrible* had been our capitol's greatest and

---

20 Outlined by James Palmer in "Houdini and the Spear of Destiny" in T*he Amazing Harry Houdini.*

21 Mrs Millicent Fawcett presided over the 1897 remerger of the National Central Society for Women's Suffrage and the Central Committee, National Society for Women's Suffrage to become the NUWSS, the Suffragists who campaigned for women to have a vote in elections and to have the right to hold property on their own behalf. A year after the time of our present narrative the Women's Social and Political Union split away to become the more radical and militant Suffragettes. Mrs Fawcett remained in her post as President of the NUWSS until 1919, the year after it succeeded in its objective of women's electoral enfranchisement in the United Kingdom.

22 Newgate Prison closed later in 1902 and was demolished in 1904. The site is now occupied by the Central Criminal Courts, commonly known as "the Old Bailey".

most unrelenting bastion of justice. Public executions had taken place outside its gates during my lifetime.[23]

Within the narrow cells of that old fortress had languished King Charles I's prosecutor John Cooke, condemned for regicide, Venetian libertine Giacomo Casanova, Protestant martyr John Frith, Quaker William Penn who founded Pennsylvania, Daniel Defoe, Ben Johnson, pirate Captain William Kidd, the U.S. Congress' first stenographer Thomas Lloyd, Sir Thomas Malory, *Times* founder John Walter Senior, and a veritable who's who of London criminals from Jack Sheppard to Dr Neill.[24] The man Holmes and I had come to see matched even the worst of them in infamy.

"Holmes and Watson," sneered former Colonel Sebastian Moran as he was led into the claustrophobic interview room. He rattled his gyves and sat on the metal-framed chair across from us.

I had been present eight years ago when Moriarty's right-hand man had finally been arrested. I had witnessed him being questioned by Sherlock Holmes and inspectors of Scotland Yard's Detective Branch. I had last seen him being dragged from the dock with a life sentence for the attempted murder of my best friend. Only his deceased master's cunning precautions had saved him from homicide charges that would have seen him dangling in a noose.[25]

---

23 W.S. Baring Gould asserts in his excellent biography *Sherlock Holmes* that John H. Watson was born on Saturday 7th August 1852. Executions were carried out in the street before Newgate from 1783 when the London gallows was moved there from Tyburn. The last public execution was on 26th May 1868, of Fenian bomber Michael Barrett for the murder of twelve people. Thereafter civil death sentences were carried out inside the prison courtyard away from public view. Newgate Prison was the principal training ground for public hangmen.

24 Thief and rogue Jack Sheppard became celebrated in 18th century London for escaping prison on four occasions and for making a fool of dreaded 'Thief-Taker General' Jonathan Wild. A supposed autobiography sold at his eventual execution is held to have been ghost-written by Daniel Defoe. The thief's posthumous popularity was such that for forty years licenses were refused for any stage production with the name 'Jack Sheppard' in the title for fear that his behaviour might be emulated. Macheath in *The Beggar's Opera* was based upon Sheppard.
Thomas Neill Cream was an early serial killer, a physician who blackmailed his patients and poisoned several prostitutes and other victims. Unverified reports claimed this his last words on the scaffold were, "I am Jack the...", which was taken by some as proof that the Ripper had finally met justice. However Cream, almost always referred to as Neill in the newspapers, was already in prison at the time of the last three Ripper murders.

25 In "The Adventure of the Empty House" Holmes advises Inspector Lestrade not to press charges for Moran's thwarted assassination of the detective but instead to bring an indictment for murder of the Honourable Ronald Adair. However, Moran was still alive and imprisoned at the time of "The Adventure of the Illustrious Client" in September 1902, suggesting that he had evaded that capital conviction and received a life sentence on some lesser offence.

"What's this then?" enquired the killer whom Holmes had once termed 'the second-most dangerous man in London'. His face was thinner than I remembered it and sapped of its outdoor tan, but his eyes still burned with the fury and hatred I recalled of old. "Do you think that a few years' stretch in this miserable dungeon will have weakened my resolve to say nothing that can assist you in your enquiries?"

"What useful information you possess has gone somewhat stale by now," Holmes informed him. "Even as you returned home to bungle your assassination attempt upon me I had already ended every other part of the late Professor's organisation. The London police had long-since taken Kirk, Fenner, Jenson, Gunnell, Partridge the financier, Wenlock from the Foreign Office and all the rest. Of them all you are the last survivor. In Europe I had rolled up the disparate cells of Moriarty's affairs, as well you know from your frustrated attempts to track me across the Continent whilst I carried out my own posthumous justice."

"The Norwegian named Sigerson," Moran growled, recalling the pseudonym under which my friend had travelled in those years when the world and I had considered him lost to the Reichenbach flood.

"And others. I did not 'return to life' until I was certain that you were the last active agent of Professor Moriarty's inner circle, and then it was time for our final act."

"I almost had you in Tibet."

"As an old tiger hunter such as yourself should know, near-misses do not count." Holmes pursed his lips. "We are not visiting you to trade reminiscences or to revisit old grievances, Moran. Nor do I expect or require you to divulge information about a criminal organisation that is a decade past destruction. Indeed, were you to walk free from Newgate today you would not recognise the underworld you once knew so well. A new generation of villain has grown into the places your ilk vacated; not so organised perhaps, but vicious and deadly in their own right and jealous of the territories they have carved. You would not survive your liberty long, I fear."

"Then why are you here? I was not invited to Dr Watson's book launch."

I stirred at being mentioned and mocked. "If it had been up to me you would have hanged for your crimes."

"You did enough," hissed the old soldier. "Stripped of my rank, disowned by my regiment. I owe you for that."

Holmes interrupted his bile. "There is perhaps one matter on which you and I might be in accord, Moran. You have always been loyal to your employer Moriarty."

The prisoner glared at Holmes. "The Professor was my friend, a great man. You destroyed him."

"And the world is safer for it. However, it is possible that someone may be meddling in one of his schemes, using your late friend's genius for his own ends."

Moran looked up sharply. Even though the man was wan from imprisonment and restrained by cuffs I braced myself to dive on him if he went for Holmes. "What do you mean?" he said.

"Yesterday, the anniversary of my final tussle with James Moriarty, I received an extraordinary and detailed clay cast of his face; a death mask. It was evidently modelled while the Professor was alive and had been packaged up before or around the time of his passing. Inscribed upon the image's reverse were several astronomical symbols which I suspect to be a coded message."

Moran froze, his narrowed eyes intent and dangerous.

Holmes continued. "Last night this item was stolen from our rooms by someone of significant skill. Enquiries amongst the usual sources have proved useless save to indicate that the theft was not commissioned from one of the regular professional housebreakers of London. Now whilst I own that Professor Moriarty might have been devious enough to foresee his own death, to prepare a puzzle on a memorial mask for me, to commission its sending on a particular anniversary of his demise, and to then arrange for the item to be pilfered again to promote the mystery, it seems more likely to me that at least one of these things has been done without your late employer's intent. What do you say, Moran?"

The expert rifleman thought for a moment. "It seems that someone is attempting to use the Professor's preparations for his own benefit," he concluded.

"You knew about the mask, then?" I asked him.

He nodded reluctantly. "In those last few days when Sherlock Holmes had grown from amusement to nuisance to significant threat, when his net was closing round us, Professor Moriarty spoke candidly with me. He foresaw a climactic confrontation. Never think your acuity greater than his, Holmes. 'Now events have progressed this far', he told me, 'our organisation turns on one death. If Holmes perishes within the next fourteen days then all is well. If he survives then everything is lost. I shall make my plans accordingly.'"

"And never has anyone come closer to ending my career," the detective admitted.

"Moriarty recognised the danger too. He made preparations, some known to me, others probably not. The mask was one of them, but I do not know his intention for it, or his motive."

"You think it was sent to us on his instruction?" I demanded.

"If so then I know nothing of it," insisted Moran. "As *your* master says, Watson, it seems unlikely that all the things that have happened were of the Professor's planning."

"Will you then co-operate with us in discerning what is going on?" Holmes asked the killer.

Moran's face twisted with a crooked smile. "No. Whatever plot is spawned is aimed at you as much as at my friend's memory. It can no longer harm him. It might yet harm you. I fervently hope so."

"Surely you wish to know who still has access to Moriarty's affairs?" I protested. "Or do you already suspect?"

"I believe our conversation is concluded, Dr Watson. I'm ready to return to my cell now. You've given me something to think about."

"And you have been most helpful," Holmes told him. "While attempting to obscure and baffle us you have been quite informative to the trained observer. From your reactions, posture, tone, hesitations, and eye motions, I deduce that you were aware of the mask's delivery before we mentioned it, but not of its theft from Baker Street. You know the message's purpose but not its content. You are baffled about who may have stolen the mask and frustrated that someone might intervene with a scheme with which you are familiar."

Moran launched himself across the table. Holmes deflected the hands aimed at his throat and pinned the prisoner until the surprised warden guards could wrestle him away. "You are the devil!" Moran spat at Sherlock Holmes. "The devil! I hope this is the case that puts you in your grave at last!"

I spoke to Moran as he was being manhandled away. "You know, after the hullabaloo of that book launch yesterday I had more-or-less decided not to publish any more of Holmes' cases, despite my agent's portuning. But you, sir, have inspired me to new literary endeavours. I think my next offering will be "The Adventure of the Empty House", detailing the surprise return of Mr Sherlock Holmes from apparent death and his capture of the notorious marksman and card cheat Colonel Moran!"[26]

---

26 This was the title and content of the first tale in the 1903 anthology *The Return of Sherlock Holmes*.

"*Kill* you!" Moran raged, struggling with his gaolers. "I shall kill you both!"

"Thank you for your time," replied the great detective.

—⟍⟋—

"What now?" I wondered as Holmes and I settled back into our rooms at Baker Street. Moran's violent response had disturbed me somewhat, but I knew it had excited my friend.

"Miss Sybella du Plessis, Watson," he replied. "As we signed the Newgate visitors book you perhaps did not apprehend that a lady had been to see Moran a scant week ago, his only visitor for many months. Alas, her signature did not resemble the script addressing the package to us nor the feminine hand on the newer label directing its delivery yesterday. Still, that is a lady who has much to tell."

"I noticed you talking to the gatehouse keeper."

"Yes. The men there were well able to remember a striking blonde-haired woman of considerable attractiveness who visited the deadly Colonel. She carried with her a letter of introduction and permission from an under-secretary in the Home Office whose name the warders did not note as assiduously as the beauty who proffered it."

"You sent off a telegram to your brother Mycroft," I noted.

"Who better to ferret out which officer granted such a pass?"

"Do you believe this lady was the sender of Moriarty's mask?"

"We have no evidence yet on which to formulate a firm hypothesis. There are other possibilities. We shall know more when the origin of the letter is uncovered—assuming it was not a forgery."

"You mentioned a visit to the delivery company," I recalled.

"Indeed. The parcel was delivered to them by general post, the Royal Mail service, along with instructions and payment for it to be forwarded to us unopened. The accompanying note has been disposed of, alas. Their office cleaner is conscientious in his duties. There is no other trail to follow there."

"Then we are stymied," I concluded.

Holmes helped himself to a shot of Scotch from the tantalus and poured another for me. "You forget the message itself, Watson. There lies the heart of the mystery, the secret recorded behind Moriarty's eyes." He gestured to his board where he had restored the hastily-erased symbols. Now a number was written beneath each glyph. 5, 3, 8, 2, 4, 2, 5, 5, and 7.

"You have cracked the code?"

"Perhaps. Let us set aside the astronomical significances for now, Watson, and consider the symbols purely as symbols. You will note that the various glyphs each have a number of terminators—that is dead ends where a pen would have to leave the page or retrace its route. The first symbol, Ceres, for example, has five such points. If we assign each symbol a numerological significance based upon its terminators then we have the sequence I have inscribed here."

"You believe the shape not the name to be relevant?"

"Remember that Moriarty's first love was binomial calculation. A glance at the thesis that won the Professor his chair will remind you that the innovative elements of his work with somewhat prosaic two-number calculus was his inversion of Pascal's triangle and the differencing of the elements."

"Holmes, for pity's sake," I pleaded. "It's a long time since prep school."

"One takes each pair of numbers and records beneath them the difference," Holmes explained. He took up the chalk and illustrated. "Thus five and three have a difference of two, and so on. So we end up with something like this."

$$5\ 3\ 8\ 2\ 4\ 2\ 5\ 5\ 7$$
$$2\ 5\ 6\ 2\ 2\ 3\ 2\ 4$$

"Now we use the same technique again to reduce another line, and so on until the inverted pyramid is complete."

$$5\ 3\ 8\ 2\ 4\ 2\ 5\ 5\ 7$$
$$2\ 5\ 6\ 2\ 2\ 3\ 2\ 4$$
$$3\ 1\ 4\ 0\ 1\ 3\ 8$$
$$2\ 3\ 4\ 1\ 2\ 1$$
$$1\ 1\ 3\ 1\ 1$$
$$0\ 2\ 2\ 0$$
$$2\ 0\ 2$$
$$2\ 2$$
$$0$$

He looked at me expectantly. "Er, yes," I answered vaguely.

"Reading down the edge of the triangle gets us two new sets of nine digit numbers," Holmes pointed out impatiently.

"So it does. Is that helpful?"

"Three simple processes, Watson. Three. Now remember what I mentioned about the asteroids discovered after the nine depicted with these symbols? The third to follow on, the twelfth in line of chronological discovery?"

"Holmes…"

"It was Victoria, Watson. Victoria!"

My friend seemed very excited by this discovery, but I still remained ignorant of the significance.

Holmes indicated his well-thumbed copy of *Whitbread's Map of London*, the definitive 1871 edition. "Take the two numbers down the sides as co-ordinates," he instructed. "Use the map Cartesians to discover a place."

I bent and traced out the location the figures might suggest—and gasped. "The entrance portico to Victoria Railway Station!"

"Victoria," Holmes agreed. "It might interest you to know that the Battersea Terminus there was refurbished in 1880 by the Ealing and Wandsworth Construction Co., one of the front companies used by Moriarty's accountant Partridge to legitimise the takings from his less salubrious operations."

A thought occurred to me. "Isn't the Battersea side being demolished and rebuilt now? The LB&SCR are planning a prestigious new station to stay ahead of the improvements made by the LD&CR and GWR."[27]

"Indeed it is, Watson! Might we dare imagine that Moriarty had his construction firm plant some further clue during their work on the site? A clue which is now in danger of being destroyed, provoking some forgotten accomplice to initiate his old leader's plan in haste?"

I glanced at the clock. It was not yet eight in the evening.

"Yes," Holmes agreed, interpreting my thoughts. "We should head south and inspect the station." He swept up his coat and made for the door. "Mrs Hudson! Cancel our supper!"

—✦—

---

27 Victoria Station grew piecemeal from the 1840s, and up to the First World War it was effectively two stations side-by-side. The London Chatham and Dover Railway (LC&DR) and the broad gauge Great Western Railway (GWR) operated the "Chatham Terminal". The larger "Battersea Terminal" was owned and administered by the London Brighton and South Coast Railway (LB&SCR), who also operated the integral 300-room Grosvenor Hotel (pronounced grow-venn-uh). Both stations were extensively rebuilt in the first decade of the 20th century, including erection of the red-brick Renaissance frontage which still characterises the second-busiest rail terminal in Britain today.

The Victoria Station now replaced by that grand renaissance redbrick was then a mere single-story length topped with wooden hoardings that read 'London, Chatham & Dover Railway' and beneath, 'Paris, Brussels, Cologne' and in smaller letters, 'Switzerland, Italy, India'. Behind the façade rose the barrel roof of steel and glass over the platforms. A line of hansoms queued up outside the entrance. A gust of steam welled from the interior.

"Another weakness you have observed in me," Holmes mentioned as we stared with field glasses at the old scaffolded frontage, "was my lack of reading in matters theological and mythological. I have had to quickly revise my knowledge of the Roman goddess Victoria. Adapted from the Sabine agricultural deity Vacuna and identified with the Greek Nike, she has given us the word *victory*, of which she was the personification. She was often depicted on Roman coins and buildings and had her own temple on the Palatine Hill, decorated with her symbols the star and victory laurel."

"I believe the station was named for adjacent Victoria Road," I mentioned, "which of course was named for our own late monarch.[28] Before that this was Grosvenor Terminus."

"The two characters have often been confused," Holmes lectured. "There was controversy when J.R. Hind first observed the asteroid on September 13th 1850 and used his discoverer's privilege to name it Victoria. B.A. Gould, editing the *Astronomical Journal*, insisted on the alternate name Clio, but W.C. Bond of Harvard College Observatory, then considered the foremost authority in the United States, adjudged that the naming condition of using a mythological female had been met and so upheld the designation. His was the opinion which eventually prevailed."

Holmes had clearly felt Moriarty's rebuke and had endeavoured to amend his ignorance.

"This is the spot that the code on the mask indicated, if the co-ordinates are not some bizarre coincidence," I observed. "You are presumably looking for some further clue in the architecture of the portico?"

"Oh, those are evident," Holmes told me absently. He handed the field-glasses across and pointed to a lintel on the apex of the roof. "The first is there, you see?"

I trained the binoculars where Holmes indicated, across the peeling

---

28 Queen Victoria's remarkable 54 year reign as Queen of the United Kingdom of Great Britain and Ireland and as monarch over the largest geographical empire in history ended with her death on 22nd January 1901. She was succeeded by her eldest son who became King Edward VII for the last nine years of his life and lent his name to the Edwardian period, the first decade of the 20th century.

frontage of the old station to the chimney stack over the waiting rooms. There was a mason's mark on one of the bricks.

"A star and laurel," Holmes supplied. "Astronomical symbol for the asteroid Victoria. But look then at the other crosspiece there."

I looked as requested and spotted another engraving. "Some kind of deer? Another asteroid mark? And the letter L?"

"No, Watson. Not any deer. You will recall the name of Victoria's discoverer?"

The image showed antlers. "A hind! J.R. Hind named the space-rock! And the L?"

"Not an L," the detective insisted. "It has no serif or swash. There is a plain vertical and horizontal leg and arm and nothing more. Clearly a mathematical rather than literary character, sometimes denoting a Pythagorean right-angle triangle. Assume the laurel and hind as two points in a diagram and the next location we seek is the third."

I looked around the concourse. With the gathering evening the upper levels of the construction were shadowed, making it hard to see any markings on lintels and pillars. The scaffolding around some of the stonework where demolition was due to begin further obscured our view.

"Moriarty loved his Pythagorean triples," Holmes reminded me. "Furthermore, he has kindly provided us with a key number, three, being the difference between his initial code of nine asteroids and the twelfth to which we have been directed. Three is the base of the most elementary of Pythagorean triangles, where $3^2 + 4^2 = 5^2$, as I'm sure your teachers would have beaten into you."

"Most painfully," I agreed. "So you propose to treat the two identified points as having an arbitrary distance of 3 and then extrapolate from there where the other point must lie."

"There are only two possible places, depending upon whether this is a right or left handed triangle. We shall examine both."

I can only imagine what the cabbies, porters, and travellers made of two grown men scrabbling round the iron support pillars on the platforms where passengers waited to alight onto their trains. Holmes ignored the spectators while I tried to appear nonchalant and felt obliged to lift my hat at the ladies.

My friend dropped to ground level and traced his fingers over the base of a pillar. "Yes, this is it," he cried. "See, Watson, the mark of Parthenope, the fish and star of the sirens!"[29] He indicated the almost invisible grooves that were barely discernable beneath thick black paint.

"The harp is also used to denote this asteroid," Holmes noted. "There are several variant sigils for these celestial bodies. I cannot believe that Moriarty selected the ones he did at random." He calculated the distance back to the roofbeam where the Victoria symbol had been engraved. "If we posit that the hart marker was the base, it being the one that is not an asteroid, then we might calculate another simple Pythagorean triangle using these other fixed points as the new base. Come!"

Holmes was thwarted in his theory, however. Our quest took us into the Ladies' cloakroom and to an altercation with a fierce and outraged attendant.

"The Professor had a vicious sense of humour," Holmes brooded as we were ejected onto the forecourt. "Let us try again."

"Holmes, I have no wish to be arrested for intruding upon a water closet," I argued.

"There is no need for that yet, Watson. We have enough observational information from our brief sojourn into the Ladies rooms to suggest that the same calculation will not avail us with our new co-ordinates. Suppose Moriarty selected another primitive Pythagorean triple? The next would be $5^2 + 12^2 = 13^2$. Let us return to Parthenope, ignore the siren-lure of the Ladies cloakroom, and pace that out instead."

I trailed after the eager detective. This measurement required rather more manoeuvring as the line took us past the Chatham line platforms

---

29 This ancient sign, reused as the symbol for the asteroid, has also been interpreted as originating from a representation of female genitalia.

into the adjacent Battersea Terminal. We purchased platform tickets, passed under the ornate wrought-iron gateway arch to platform 2, and discovered another engraved pillar.

"Hygeia," Holmes identified. "Parthenope was discovered just before Victoria. Hygeia immediately preceded Parthenope. It seems we have a countdown."

"And a confirmation," I added. Affixed to the metal support column was a small first-aid cupboard. "Hygeia was the daughter of the god of medicine Aesclepius, was she not? She has given us the word hygiene."

"Very good," approved Holmes. "Our next in sequence, the asteroid preceding Hygeia, would be Metis, the eye of wisdom beneath a star, last character in the mask inscription. Assuming we are to use ascending triples to calculate triangle bases then the next such formulae would be $8^2+15^2=17^2$—that is 64 plus 225 equalling 289, so we assign the distance between Hygeia and Parthenope as 64 units and trek 225 units at right-angles from the line, starting at Hygeia."

"What about $6^2 + 8^2 = 10^2$," I objected.

"Ah Watson, I see why you elected a military rather than an academic career! To be a true primitive triple the numbers cannot be divided down to a simpler formula. The equation you suggest is susceptible to universal division by two and puts us back with our initial calculation. No, we must travel this way, some three and a half times the distance between our previous two way-points."

There are times when I sometimes wish Holmes might err. However, we discovered the station clock fixed to the wall at the point he had calculated. A small maker's mark on its face displayed the predicted sigil.

"Next is Hebe, calculated by $7^2 + 24^2 = 25^2$," Holmes predicted. "That would put us somewhere by the parcel shed, I fancy."

We found the cup symbol on a drain cover beside the building. From there Holmes tracked Astraea's inverted anchor to a newsagent's stand and Vesta's altar to the lintel of the coal-house. Next was Juno's sceptre, calculated with the triple 9, 40, 41 to take us into the gentleman's cloakroom on the Brighton side—where the trail ran cold.

"Could you have miscalculated?" I ventured when Holmes had spent a futile thirty minutes scrutinising the walls, floors and fixtures of the facility to the bemusement of the ancient attendant.

"It should be here," my friend insisted. "Moriarty was devious but he did not cheat—not in mathematics at any rate. We are missing something."

"It's all clean, sirs," the worried one-armed veteran who kept the cloakroom assured us. "Are you from the company?"

"There is no need for concern—sergeant?" I ventured. There is a mark stamped upon such men that never entirely fades.

"Why yes sir!" The old fellow perked up at recognition. "Second Battalion King's Liverpool Regiment. Under Brigadier General Foord in Burma, sir. Until this." He indicated his stump. "Minhla."

He meant the costly British assault on Minhla during the Third Burmese War of '85. I slipped him a shilling. "Have you worked here ever since you shipped home?"

"Yessir. My captain was good enough to write me a recommendation. I've cared for these rooms since they was almost new."

Holmes looked up sharply. "Almost new?" He slapped himself on the forehead. "Of course! I'm a dolt. Moriarty has me so caught up in his maths and his mythology that I forgot about the Fenians!"

"Fenians? What have Irish insurgents to do with this?" I puzzled.

"It was them Fenians what bombed this cloakroom," the attendant supplied. "Back in '64 it was. A package exploded. Seven staff was injured."[30]

"Part of the Fenian Dynamite Campaign," Holmes lectured. "At the same time, bombs placed at Charing Cross, Paddington, and Ludgate Hill were discovered and defused. But this cloakroom was completely wrecked and was presumably rebuilt."

"Destroying the marker that Moriarty had left!" I recognised.

"Let us assume so. It makes plotting our next location somewhat more difficult, but since we know roughly where the Queen of Heaven should have been we can attempt to proceed. "Pallas' spear with the triple 28, 45, 53 if I'm not mistaken, Watson."

That took us back across the concourses and almost to the end of

---

30 Although some modern books such as Bernard Porter's *Origins of the Vigilant State: the London Metropolitan Police Special Branch Before the First World War* (Boydell & Brewer, 1991) indicate the station was empty at the time and no injury occurred, this is at odds with other accounts citing newspapers of the time, such as the story in *The Times*, 27th February 1884, page 10, "Dynamite Outrage at Victoria Station". It is perhaps beyond the scope of our present story to investigate the discrepancies.

platform eleven, outside the sheltering glass canopy and the interior lights. A late express hooted and began to drag its carriages out of the station. It pistoned away into the dusk, leaving only a spreading trail of steam and a line of glowing clinkers to show where it had passed.

"Did you bring a firearm?" Holmes asked me quietly as he inspected a grating at the walkway's end.

"No," I admitted. "Should I?"

"It might have been wise for both of us to arm ourselves. We are being watched."

I knew better by now than to peer around and seek our observers.

"Three men at least," Holmes went on. "One on the crossing bridge, another by the news-stand, and a fellow who imagines he is hiding beside the rails beneath the level of the platform. Might we assume that they have been set by whomever either sent or absconded with the death mask to watch us solve the puzzle?"

"You think that you are being used as a bloodhound to discover a secret that eluded others who might have tried to understand the code?"

"There are two significant possibilities. Remember that the mask had been sealed away for a long time, so no recent inspection would have been possible prior to our opening its package. Either the person who sent the item is checking on our progress or wishes at last to benefit from whatever secret it holds, or else the thief who now possesses the mask hopes we might offer the solution to its mystery. I do not insist upon either explanation, of course. Things may become clearer when our shadows make their move."

"What then shall we do, Holmes?"

"Well, here is an ingeniously disguised Pallas," Holmes pointed out. "The triangular top of the symbol is this triangular key-hole here on this grating. The plus sign embossed beneath makes up the sigil as it was on the mask. That leaves only Ceres and her scythe on our little treasure hunt, and the next highest triple sequence in order of ascending c^2 is 11, 60, 61. I do not think it is wise to lead our followers to that location. So…" He rose abruptly and pointed back to the entranceway. "There, Watson!" he proclaimed loudly. "Come, let us discover the final clue!"

I trotted after him as he strode with determined purpose towards the lost luggage counter. It was now after ten p.m. by the Metis clock and traffic had thinned inside the vast station. Holmes backtracked to the gentleman's cloakroom and had a brief exchange with the one-armed sergeant there.

"I am Sherlock Holmes. You have heard of me? Splendid. My good friend Dr Watson and I are on a case and we are being followed. When we have moved on would you be so good as to step out and alert the station manager and ask him to summon the police? Quietly? Thank you."

The old campaigner was game. "I'll see to it, sah!" he promised, bringing up a neat salute to his peaked cap.

Holmes and I proceeded to the lost property office. At this time of night it was closed and shuttered but Holmes made short work of the lock on the side-door. "This is it," he announced to me. "The final point in our little search. Let us discover what the devious Professor intended to direct us to all those years ago!"

As soon as we entered the darkened room we took to the shadows, Holmes on one side of the door, me behind one of the shelving racks that filled the interior of the space. We waited silently for our pursuers to venture after us.

The delay was long enough for me to begin to doubt our plan but Holmes remained like a statue—or perhaps like a hovering bird of prey stationary in the sky ready to pounce. Then I apprehended stealthy movement outside,

A hand curled round the edge of the door that we had left very slightly ajar. The portal was eased open and a squat, thuggish figure slipped inside. Even in the dim light from the concourse I recognised the watcher from the bridge. He peered about him but did not think to look behind the door he had opened, where Holmes stood concealed.

The brute paused and reached into his frayed jacket. He withdrew a brutal-looking gat and secured it in his fist. He gestured to someone behind him and moved into the interior.

A second low fellow appeared. He bore a long hunting knife and a knobkerrie. He joined the first and whispered, "Where are they?"

The thug with the gat gestured irritably for absolute silence. He indicated that his comrade should search further down the row between the wooden lost luggage shelves.

Holmes still did not move. He was waiting for the third watcher to arrive and was not disappointed. The newcomer peered in and was ordered by gesture to stand in the doorway and keep watch.

That was enough. "Now, Watson!" Holmes cried. He slammed the door hard, closing it with a bone-cracking force on the watchman's arm. The felon yelped and dropped the firearm he was holding.

I had no time to take in more detail. I simply heaved my weight against the rack behind which I was concealed and toppled the whole shelving and all its contents down on the two thugs in the next aisle.

They went down with yelps of surprise. I added to their discomfort by jumping atop the fallen furniture to pin them.

Holmes dropped the man in the doorway with his usual scientific command of martial manoeuvres. He hastened to join me in containing the other rogues as they squirmed loose from the pile of luggage and fallen shelving.

It was no time for Queensbury rules.[31] I reverted to Maiwand rules[32] and stamped down hard on the fellow with the knobkerrie as he climbed free. By the time the gat-wielder was on his feet, Holmes was ready to disarm him and lay him out with a well-placed uppercut.

Holmes and I paused for a moment to catch our breath. "This was easier when we were younger," I managed to gasp.

"Effective all the same," my friend assured me. "And now we have some suspects to question regarding this murky affair."

I eyed the ruin we had made of the lost luggage office. I hoped the station manager was an aficionado of my Holmes stories.

More movement outside set us on alert again, but it was two constables in company with our one-armed cloakroom fellow and the senior platform master. "Here are the ruffians," I told the officers of the law. "Concealed weapons including a firearm are somewhere under that mess."

"Pull them out and hold them close. I will wish to question them," Holmes instructed.

"If they give any trouble they'll get what the Burman got!" the cloakroom attendant promised, brandishing a walking cane.

We peeled aside from the growing furore and the stood a little way off as the three men were hauled from Lost Property. It was now fully dark, the great glassed interior of the concourse now lit only by little flares of gas lamp from the chandeliers over the entranceway and ticket booths and in forlorn rows out along the lengths of the platforms. Curious night passengers stopped to watch as the prisoners were dragged out and taken into charge.

---

31 John Graham Chambers' boxing regulations were published by John Douglas, the 9th Marquis of Queensbury in 1861 and became the standard for fair-play matches across the British Empire and in the United States. It famously asserted that, "you must not fight simply to win; no holds barred is not the way; you must win by the rules".

32 The Battle of Maiwand, 27th July 1880, was a key confrontation in the Second Afghan War, in which 2,746 British and Indian troops were decimated by 25,000 Afghans under Ayub Khan. The subsequent British retreat cost many more lives, with some regiments taking losses of more than 60%. It was during this brutal and desperate confrontation that military doctor John Watson took the "Jezail bullet" that invalided him from army service and sent him back to London and his first meeting with Holmes.

"Now, Watson!"

"We shall start with the fellow who had the gun," Holmes suggested. "See what you can do to revive him, Watson, and we'll enquire as to who engaged him for his surveillance and possible assault."

The unsavoury thug was dressed in a thick sea-sweater and oilskins, suggesting to me that he was one of the many loafers who arrive on boats and hang around the docklands causing trouble until they can next secure a berth. He had a grizzled beard and weathered skin.

I moved up to him as he hung limply in the constables' grasp. I intended to examine his eyes and see if he was concussed or merely feigning. As I approached him I heard the unmistakeable sound of a rifle-shot. The prisoner's head exploded as a .303 bullet passed through it.

More shots followed. A policeman cried out and fell, clutching a leg that now spurted blood. Another of the thugs, rising to flee, took a bullet in the hip.

The curious passengers who had stopped to spectate the arrests cried out and scattered, panicking under fire. Holmes and I dived for cover through the door of the lost luggage office. Holmes rolled as he moved, making it to the doorway holding the dead criminal's firearm that the wounded constable had dropped.

I counted ten shots fired at us, a full magazine for most rifles. Holmes had done the same. He reached out and fired back in the direction of the bridge over the platforms.

No return shots were offered. I took the risk of crawling out to stanch the policeman's leg wound, using the lanyard of his whistle as a tourniquet. The other officer was making good use of his own police whistle to summon assistance.

Holmes darted from shadow to shadow with three shots remaining in his borrowed weapon. He threaded across the terminal using what cover he could find, making his way to the stairs that took travellers up the ornate metal bridge to the further platforms.

His stealth was in vain. The assassin had departed.

I joined my friend as soon as I was able to leave the injured. "The constable and the thug are stable, Holmes. I take it the gunman has departed?"

Holmes nodded. "This is the spot where the rifle was rested. As you can see from the discarded shells, it used a .303 cartridge, but not the standard mark VI now customary to our British soldiers. These are the older Mark III expanding bullets that were outlawed three years back at the Hague Convention. I'll have to examine the rifling to be sure but an initial examination of the casings suggests the weapon was a Magazine Lee Enfield.

That would be hard to trace. The MLE, or 'Emily' as our troops like to call them, was the standard-issue infantry weapon of the British and Colonial Armies and popular with private marksmen. It could fire twenty or thirty targeted shots per minute with an accurate range of five hundred and fifty yards.

"The assailant was quite short, choosing the lower rail on which to steady the rifle," Holmes went on. "He withdrew along the bridge in the direction of the outer platforms. We would have seen anyone descending the way we approached. Pursuit is impossible. Once on the darkened tracks he might escape in any direction."

"Or else lie in wait for us and make another attempt on our lives," I pointed out.

Holmes was thoughtful. "I think not. Consider, Watson. The shot that took down the felon we were about to question was deadly accurate, a marksman's shot, right through the cranium. A shooter of that skill might have taken both you and I down before we ever reached shelter. The subsequent discharge that wounded the constable and his prisoner and sent us all scattering for cover served only to distract us for a getaway."

"Our tail was the target? The other shots were to delay us as we tended to the wounded?"

"We will question his fellows, but I warrant that the dead man was the only one of the trio who knew his employer's identity and orders. That bullet was to silence him and deny us a trail—and it succeeded."

I need not document the next two hours of tedious police interviews. Inspector Lestrade arrived, bad-tempered at having been dragged from his slumbers by a firearms offence at a major London railway station. His mood was little improved to find that Holmes and I were involved and at the scene.

Holmes insisted on speaking with the other prisoners before the one was confined in Victoria Road Police Station and the other transported under guard to Charing Cross Hospital. When we could at last slip away from Scotland Yard's questioning, my friend hastened out along platform 11 so we could speak privately.

"The dead man was a sailor, probably Dutch judging by the technique of the obscene tattoo on his forearm. The five sovereigns[33] in his pocket were most likely advance payment for his work. He had been watching the station for some time, as evidenced by the newsprint on his hands from the racing paper in his hind pocket. His weapon was a Mark I Webley that has not been well maintained. Its serial number suggests old army issue. Enquiries will probably reveal it was lost to the black market some years ago."

"How would he and his comrades know to wait and watch for us here?"

"Ah, there's the thing! From remarks his fellows made it looks as though they have been but one shift in a constant roster of watchers given our descriptions and told to look out for us at Victoria Station. I have alerted Lestrade that more such spies might turn up later, ignorant of what has passed. The question therefore becomes not 'how did our adversaries know we were going to Victoria tonight?' but 'how did they know we were going sometime?'"

"The stolen death-mask?"

"Possibly." Holmes gestured for me to accompany him right to the end of the platform, past the marked grating he had discovered. I realised he was pacing out distances again. "Ah," he breathed as we came to the end of the passenger walk, "of course."

We climbed down onto the rails. Beyond the platform the various lines came together at points, merging into the double track of the LC&DR line and four tracks of the GWR with their distinctive twin rails allowing trains of narrower and wider gauge to use the route. Twenty yards beyond the furthest points was the wooden frame of a signal box.

Holmes approached it. There was a light burning in the windowed upper storey cabin but we made no attempt to use the outside steps and enter the room where huge levers controlled signals and junctions. The detective simply traced round the perimeter, slashing aside weeds to inspect the base of the box.

"Here, Watson," he indicated, squatting to examine a tiny metal plate riveted to the wood on the bottom-most plank of the foundation. The painted-over stud bore the sickle and cross symbol of Ceres, goddess of agriculture; of course she would be close down to the soil, obscured by vegetation.

Holmes produced a pocket knife and scraped at the thick tar-paint that had been slathered across the wood to preserve it. He traced out the

33 At Holmes' time, a coin to the value of £1. An average workman's annual income was £100.

obscured joints where a panel had been cut in the otherwise complete joinery. After a few minutes work he was able to prise it loose.

"Hold a match close, Watson. There is a tin box within the compartment."

Holmes gently drew out an oilskin that wrapped a shallow metal caddy. The whole was roughly the size and shape of a pulpit bible. Age had corroded the hinges but my friend's blade was able to ease the lid free.

"It looks to have been undisturbed for a long time," I ventured.

"The rust patterns and mildew are consistent with it having been placed here twenty-two years ago at the site's refurbishment," my friend agreed. "We should really take this back to Baker Street to open properly, but I confess to an insatiable curiosity as to its contents." He cautiously lifted the lid.

Inside the box was a thick bundle of handwritten pages tied with string. The paper was yellowed, the ink faded but legible. The front page read:

The Dynamics of An Asteroid
By Professor James Moriarty, PhD, FRS, RAS
Finished Draft

"The handwriting is unmistakably his," Holmes declared.

I could not see why even the old spider Moriarty had gone to so much trouble to conceal a manuscript of a volume that was available from any second-hand book dealer and said as much.

Holmes chuckled. "Oh, my dear doctor, you are forgetting your history. Moriarty's first book, his *Treatise on the Binomial Theorem*, made his reputation at only twenty-one and won him his professor's chair. *Dynamics of an Asteroid* was the book that destroyed his reputation, earning him the outrage and ire of the scientific and academic communities—and that was only the expurgated version that his publisher consented to print! This," Holmes gestured to the bundle he now cradled, "this is the original, unedited holographic manuscript with all its darkest content intact."

"I fail to see how a book on physics to do with asteroids could cause such ire," I confessed. "Did Moriarty fake his data or something?"

"Those charges were brought against him, unjustly I believe, by men who would later regret crossing him. I rather suspect that this document contains information expurgated because it was dangerous. Some calculation, some technique, some scientific blasphemy from the fevered mind of that dark genius. A secret that someone suspects and will go to considerable lengths to possess."

A shudder ran through me. I was suddenly aware that Holmes and I were alone in the dark, carrying a document that provoked murder, where only recently armed men had sought to find our treasure before us. At least one adversary, with a deadly aim to rival that of Colonel Moran, was out there in the night.

"Perhaps we should continue our conversation at Baker Street?" I suggested.

Holmes evidently shared the same prickling between his shoulder blades. "An excellent suggestion," he agreed.

—⁊⁊⁁—

The cab pulled up outside 221B a little after two in the morning. A lamp still burned above our doorway, and by its light we were easily able to see the cloaked figure who awaited us on the step.

"Watson—beware," Holmes murmured. His eyes flicked to the other side of the road where a coach stood waiting. At this time of the night there was no good reason that such a private carriage would be there.

It occurred to me that having missed us at the station our escaped assassin would easily surmise we might return to Baker Street.

"Wait here with the box," Holmes cautioned. He opened the door of the brougham and dropped to the pavement.

The cloaked figure shifted, and by her movements I was suddenly convinced that it was a woman swathed inside that dark mantle. When she spoke it was confirmed. Her voice was feminine, low, and strangely accented. "Mr Holmes. Congratulations on solving the Moriarty riddle. I require you to yield his manuscript to me."

"And why should I do that, madam?" the detective enquired. I knew that he would already be analysing her speech, her appearance, her posture for clues to this business. "You do not appear to be carrying the rifle with which you committed murder earlier tonight."

Powder marks on her gloves? Some trace of gun oil about her person? She was of the height that Holmes had calculated our bridge marksman to have been, and of the stature of the burglar he had described.

"I have other weapons," the woman responded. "I direct your attention to the carriage you have doubtless already noted there across the road. Consider its occupants."

I looked too. There, behind the rolled-up windows, I could now discern three terrified faces, mere children by the looks of them, each pressed close to the glass with a knife held to his or her throat. The cruel men who so threatened them were swathed in shadow.

"I have no idea who they are, those infants," the woman on our step went on. "They were snatched today from some gutter-alley in your East End, completely at random. They are of little worth and less consequence— to me. If you do not give me the Moriarty draft I will order their throats slashed and cast their lifeless bodies out onto Baker Street for you to deal with."

I stifled a cry of outrage. I have seldom encountered such casual cruelty or conscienceless evil.

The hooded woman shifted position. For a moment the street lamp reflected off a pale porcelain mask that obscured her face.

"May I ask why you want the document so greatly?" Holmes replied to her. "You have gone to a lot of trouble, even silencing your own subordinate, for a manuscript that has lain hidden for so very long."

"You seek to engage me in talk while you think of a solution to your problem," the cloaked figure declared. "You hope I will betray information by my responses. Well, I am not as clever as Sherlock Holmes or I would have found the papers myself, but I am more ruthless. That is what will count. You have ten seconds before the first child dies."

Holmes' glare might have melted steel. "Very well, madam. Watson, the box."

"Open it first, doctor," she insisted. "I wish to check that the manuscript is complete. Return the pages you have just slipped out of it."

I grimaced and put back the handful of sheets I had just palmed from the back of the pile. The woman was ruthless *and* sharp.

She moved cautiously past Holmes and collected the tin from me.

"The children," I prompted.

"In good time." She paused and inspected the contents of the box, checking that it was complete. "Very well. I'll leave you with this reflection, gentlemen. You smug conquerors in your capital of empire are more than happy to reap the benefits of the misery you sow elsewhere, ignorant of the venal and brutal world beyond. The time is coming when you will all learn firsthand what it is that you have ignored for so long. Sherlock Holmes is very effective in a civilised world where almost everyone follows the rules. He is nothing when society crumbles and that corrupt civilisation is shattered. Think on that—and despair."

She climbed up beside the driver atop the carriage and thumped a distinctive sequence of knocks on the vehicle's roof. The door opened and a bound child was hurled harshly onto the cobbles. The second, a girl of no more than seven or eight, was propelled after him.

I rose to get them, but before I could even quit the brougham the third child was tossed to the street too—bleeding from a slashed throat! The brutes who had ejected her had sliced her windpipe as they did so. The girl landed atop her siblings, spraying blood, gasping for life's breath.

I leaped from our cab, sensible only of the need to clamp that wound and give it immediate attention. The carriage-driver whipped up his pair and the horses leaped to action, dragging the heavy closed carriage away towards Marylebone Road.

Holmes sprang forward too, aiming for the back of the retreating vehicle, but it moved too quickly for even him to vault aboard. His grasping fingers failed to find purchase. He rolled in the dust as the carriage galloped away.

I shouted up to our shocked brougham cabbie. "Hammer at the door of 221, man. Have someone bring out my medical bag. Hurry!"

Holmes loped over to see if I needed assistance. I waved him off at the other children. Two other shocked, terrified, grazed and bruised urchins were in need of care.

I stabilised the girl with the gashed throat and cobbled an emergency tracheotomy. The wound had not been intended to kill, I realised; merely to occupy our full attention while our enemy got away. The brutal tactic had worked perfectly.

"They got the manuscript and they have escaped!" I remarked, furious at the ruthlessness that might inflict such wounds on innocent children for calculated criminal gain.

Holmes was enraged too. "They have got the manuscript," he agreed darkly. "They will not escape."

2. THE DROWNING AND THE DROWNED

A report about Mr Harry Houdini:

The performer commanded the auditorium with his sheer presence. He stood uplit by the limelights, manly frame outlined in skin-tight costume as he cast aside his short cape. "Ladies and gentlemen… Tonight on this very stage you will witness a feat which you will remember for the rest of your lives. A feat so extraordinary, so daring, that no other student of the science of escape would dare it. Here, with your own eyes, you will witness the impossible!"

He swept his gaze round the rapt theatre, drawing in every eye with his hypnotic stare. "You see behind me a platform. Observe, it is raised now on hydraulic jacks, which bring it some three feet above the ground. I pass my hand beneath it for you all to see that it is open, clear of all obstruction save for these four small pillars that support it."

He moved downstage. "Now, I will seek out four members of the audience—strong competent men, please—to assist me in the next step of my venture. You, sir, and you and you—and you, please. Come up onto the stage and help me to fold this hinged platform into a box. Don't be afraid. It is not you who will face certain doom."

The four volunteers were shepherded onto stage by an attractive assistant in fishnet stockings and a feathered corset. She arrayed the men behind the raised platform so as not to obscure the audience's view of the casket that would be constructed, or of the escape artist that would enter it.

"Now sirs," the performer instructed, "you will see that what appears to be a flat surface actually hinges and fastens together into a box. Or shall we call it a coffin? Assemble it, clip in into shape, yes. No need for the lid yet, for I am not confined within. There is other work for you still to do. Delilah?"

The lovely Delilah wheeled out a trolley on which an array of handcuffs and firearms were laid on silken cushions.

"Inspect these closely, my friends," the showman told his volunteers. "You will see that the bonds are police-issue handcuffs, certified only this morning by Inspector Merivale of Scotland Yard. You will see how he has signed the tags on the seals that demonstrate they have not been tampered with. It is these shackles with which you will immobilise me when you place me in the casket of death. Examine them freely. You are satisfied that they are the genuine article? Splendid."

His assistant proffered the four single-shot pistols to be checked.

"Note that these have also been verified by the custodians of the law. Genuine weapons. Genuine ammunition. A single shot from one of these can kill a man dead. You are convinced? Speak up so everyone in the auditorium can hear you."

The showman smoothed his moustaches. "Now ladies and gentleman, you may have heard much of a self-publicising American who goes by the stage name of Harry Houdini. He has a gift of making his feats seem remarkable and unrepeatable. I am here tonight to demonstrate that he is nothing—nothing—compared to the talents of myself, Apollonius the Amazing. Everything Houdini claims to have done, I can *really* do—and better."

He gestured to the box behind him. "In a moment, members drawn at random from your own number will bind me with chains they have inspected on your behalf, will seal me in a box you have seen constructed before your own eyes. That box stands clear of all surfaces, making exit from it impossible. I will be locked inside it, helplessly bound. But that is not all."

Three soldiers marched onto the stage, right wheeled, and took up parade positions.

"These three heroes are members of His Majesty's armed forces. They are off-duty tonight, but here with permission to discharge the weapons you have seen. Their orders are clear. Five minutes after I am sealed inside the casket they will fire their shots into it—through it—destroying the man who lies within. These infantrymen will each fire a round into the crate—away from the audience, please. You need not fear. I have signed legal waivers exculpating you all from all blame should your gunfire terminate my existence!"

The volunteers looked uncertain, the soldiers wooden, but Apollonius did not wait for their consent. "Only the greatest of all practitioners of our sacred art of escapology could hope to survive such a test. Tonight, before you all, I undertake that challenge—and claim the crown which is rightfully mine!"

The audience thundered their applause, led along by the showman's conviction. Apollonius suffered himself to be fastened into the hand and leg-cuffs and hoisted into the box. The lid was closed and bolted. A giant clock was lowered on wires to tick off a countdown of five minutes.

"Remember," were Apollonius' last words before being closed away, "when the time is up, each of you may discharge your weapon into the coffin of death."

The volunteers checked the box was sealed and were dismissed from the stage. Delilah and the waiting soldiery remained.

Someone started a countdown. A drummer in the orchestra pit took up the beat.

So rapt was the audience that they failed to notice a disturbance at the rear, where Martin Beck struggled at the ticket office.

"Let me in, I say!" the portly impresario demanded. "Stop the performance! I need to see the manager!"

"I'm in charge of front of 'ouse," a bewhiskered operator in a red-piped waistcoat identified himself. "I'm afraid there's no h'admittance after the performance 'as started."

"Performance?" snorted Beck. "Apollonius' whole act is a direct copy of Houdini's show at the Alhambra the last time he toured London—except for shoddier sets and a hammier presentation!"

The foyer manager recognised the agitated interloper now. "You're Houdini's fellow, ain't ya? Came down 'ere a couple of days ago waving legal papers and the like and went off with a flea in yer ear? Well you can bug off again, mister. We 'ave a full 'ouse and there's naught you can do about it!"

"I'm not trying to stop your performance," Beck warned. "I'm trying to prevent..." He glanced through the glazed interior doors to the countdown clock sweeping to four minutes. "Oh, never mind. It's too late now anyhow."

"What d'yer mean? 'Ave you ben drinking?"

"Not yet. The time will come." Beck allowed himself to be ushered onto the pavement where he settled on a bench. "I'll just wait here for the inevitable," he told the confused front-of-house staff.

At that same moment on stage, a concealed trapdoor behind the raised platform's mirrored undercarriage was opened from beneath and Apollonius' accomplices handled him down to the space beneath. Making the box appear to have clear air beneath it was easy on a darkened set; it allowed plenty of time for the performer to be dropped to where his attendants awaited him with spare keys for the chains that bound him.

"Good house tonight, Reg," one of them commented to the man who named himself after the first century magician.[34]

"Never mind that," the showman growled. "Get me out of these bloody chains. One o' them audience bastards closed 'em so tight I can 'ardly feel my 'ands and feet!"

"Got the key right here, Reg. 'Old on. This won't take a…"

"What? Get on with it Ramsay!"

"I'm trying, Reg. There's something up with the locks."

"Up with 'em? Whadda you mean? Let me see."

"Stop messing about you idiots an' get me out of 'ere."

"There's something in the 'oles, Reg. Some sort of glue, maybe?"

"Drag 'im over to the light, lads, so we can get a better look."

"Ouch! 'Ave a care, you berks! And 'urry up. They'll be firing their guns in no time and then I'll have to climb up for my big appearance."

"I'm trying, boss. But there's something gumming up the tumblers something rotten."

"Get cutters then. Clip these things off me."

"I'll 'ave a go, Reg, but these is police issue. I'd need a saw and a couple of hours. If I go at it all rough like I'll take your 'ands off."

"That countdown's got less'n a minute. Come on, lads, get them chains loose!"

"'Ow did this sticky stuff get in there anyways? It weren't there when I laid the shackles out on the trolley. 'Ave you been doing Delilah a mischief, Reg?"

"She won't give me the time of day. Just…get these off! They hurt! Agh!"

A round of shots echoed from above. The open trapdoor back up to the coffin of death emitted a trace of gunsmoke and half a dozen pinpricks of dusty light where bullets had passed.

---

34 Apollonius of Tyana is best known from Flavius Philostratus' second century A.D. *Life of Apollonius*. Christ's contemporary, and likewise ascribed with miraculous powers and deeds, he is mentioned and refuted in passing by Christian writers Jerome and Augustine and may have been promoted by Julia Domna, Emperor Severus' wife and mother of Emperor Caracalla, as a "rival" for Jesus. He was "rediscovered" in modern literature in Keats' poem *Lamia*, wherein he warns a bride-groom about his vampire bride. He has since found a place in occult lore, beginning with 19th century occultist Eliphas Levi's attempt to raise Apollonius' spirit.

An early Christian legend describes an encounter between Apollonius and St Paul wherein Apollonius demonstrated his ability to fly high above an arena and challenged Paul to perform any miracle that matched it. Paul responded by commanding Apollonius to fall, ending the magician's life.

"They'll be expecting 'im back up there soon. Much longer and the 'ouse'll be getting nervy."

"Well we can't very well stick 'im back in like this, can we? Get me a fire 'atchet. Let's see if we can't break those links that way."

"You're not swinging a flamin' axe between my wrists, you dunce! Get hot water to melt this glue out. Quickly!"

"I still don't see how as it could get in there in the first place, boss."

"One of them fellows who handled the chains, checking them," Apollonius reasoned. "Sabotage! I tell you, it was..."

They were interrupted by the grinding of the counterweights that raised the bottom of the containment box back into place. While they had argued someone had slipped in and activated the mechanism. Someone was vanishing up into the bullet-ridden box.

"Stop 'im!" Apollonius called out uselessly. It was too late.

In the auditorium the drums clashed to a climax as the substitute slipped the release latch and rose triumphant from the collapsing box. The audience went silent for a moment as they realised this was not the man they had expected to see.

"Good evening, ladies and gentleman," the grinning king of handcuffs greeted his audience. "I am Harry Houdini!"

The crowd went wild.

Houdini blew a kiss to the astonished Delilah and took a bow. "I'm interrupting this rather feeble little attempt to emulate my performances to offer you a real night out. Instead of having to sit through Reg Winters' tedious and derivative conjuring and lock-turning act, why not enjoy a real performance with me at the Lyceum on Wellington Road? I'm sure by now my manager—yes, there he is, the puce-coloured fellah at the back of the stalls, there—my manager Mr Beck has arrived. See him on your way out and he will give you a note of hand good to redeem half the ticket price at any one of my shows. Call it my way of apologising for Apollonius' dismal attempts tonight."

Houdini jumped from the platform. He hooked his toe round one of the support stands and brought the whole apparatus crashing down with a splintering of hidden mirrors and snapping of wood spars.

"It has been a genuine pleasure to appear on this stage tonight and meet you all," Houdini told his usurped audience. His charisma crackled round the theatre, blasting out brilliance a magnitude greater than the pretender he had humiliated. It wiped away any spell the unfortunate Apollonius might have cast. "It's a shame my unfortunate rival couldn't be with us. He is rather tied up."

That got a huge laugh from the house. Houdini bowed again.

A huge doorman bouncer appeared on the boards. "You! Off there. Ahout-of-it!" He moved forward with fists closed to ham-like mounds.

"Or you'll use force?" Houdini scorned. "Tell you what, big fellah. You can take a free shot at me, anywhere you like between neck and waist. But then I get a free shot at you? Agreed?"

The bruiser didn't wait to negotiate. He swung one meaty fist right at Houdini's stomach.

The fist slammed into the escape artist's belly with devastating force. Houdini hardly flinched. "My turn, then," he declared, his grin turning fell and vicious. Before the bouncer could react a piston-blow smashed into his solar plexus, folding him over and dropping him to all fours. The big man quivered for a moment and then spewed onto the stage.

"Ladies and gentleman, thank you for your time," Houdini announced. He jumped over the orchestra pit, landed neatly in the central isle of the stalls, and stalked away towards the rear bar.

The applause began, as he had calculated, before he got half way there. He raised one hand in acknowledgement as he made his exit.

"What... what did you *do?*" demanded the front of house manager.

"I livened up your show a bit," Houdini replied. "Next time book a better act."

Martin Beck was there too, trying to keep his calm. "Harry, we talked about this. I thought we agreed no more of these stunts."

"You agreed. I listened. Besides, the guy was challenging me. You heard him."

"We'll be lucky to escape a lawsuit."

"We'll be luckier if we get one. The publicity alone will bring in more box office than any compensation and costs—and you know it."

"Well yes, but... all the same..."

"There's a few folks in the crowd here who'd like discounted tickets," Houdini told the unfortunate Beck. "This is him, ladies and gents. Choleric fellah here! Form an orderly queue."

There was no chance of that. Somehow Houdini slipped away as Martin Back was surrounded by eager theatregoers.

About two hours later Apollonius got out of his cuffs.

─/|\─

Houdini whistled to himself as he returned to his rooms at the Bridge House Hotel.[35] He'd behaved himself for far too long. It felt good to deliver a little natural justice, even if it was to a preening minor rival who had been too broad in his public scorn of the American showman.

He felt a moment's guilt for poor Martin Beck, besieged by people wanting to attend performances of the upcoming show, but only a moment; Beck was never really unhappy when he was selling tickets.

Houdini reviewed his evening's work. His disguise had been easy enough, and once he'd procured a seat in the lovely Delilah's sight-line it had been simple to draw her attention into selecting him as a stage volunteer. Introducing the paste to the cuff locks had been child's play, requiring only basic slight-of-hand. Apollonius had assisted beautifully, demanding the audience's attention at all times, jealous even of their watching the volunteers he had called on stage.

There was a hotel room key in Houdini's pocket but he didn't reach for it. Instead he slipped a thin curved metal tine from his cuff. It paid to stay in practice.

He paused. There were tell-tale scratches on the doorplate around the keyhole which betrayed another, less skilful slipping of the lock. Someone had gained access to his room since the last time he had been here.

The door to the suite opposite opened. Two masked men with guns levelled their weapons at him.

It was too soon for any reprisal from Reg Winters. This had to be something else.

"Are you guys looking for room service?" Houdini asked.

"Go inside," one of the gunmen answered, gesturing for the showman to enter his lodgings.

Houdini turned the handle and opened the door. He used the motion to obscure slipping a small scalpel-blade into his left palm.

Two more people with firearms waited inside the suite's sitting room. Houdini revised his plan to gash the wrist of his first assailant and use

---

35 The Bridge House Hotel on Montague Close took its name from its proximity with the southern end of London Bridge, but also boasted that it was "Opposite the South Eastern, London, Brighton & South Coast, Crystal Palace, and North and Mid Kent Railways," and of its "Coffee room for Gentleman in which Dining is unsurpassed." A special coffee room was provided for ladies and families, French and German were spoken, and there were night porters on duty. The Assembly Room was "capable of seating upwards of six hundred persons" with "great facilities for large or small Parties, Meetings, Charitable Institutions, Wedding Breakfasts, Public Dinners, Balls. Soirees, &c." *Source*: 1870 Advertising Flyer, available online at http://commons.wikimedia.org/wiki/File:1870_Bridge_House_Hotel_advertisement_London.png

In short, the Bridge House was a major but not exclusive hotel of the kind where a successful showman and his retinue might be most welcome.

that man's dropped weapon to stop the other. The odds had just become much worse.

He looked at the interlopers in his chambers with a degree of surprise. The additional gunmen were actually gunwomen. Two females in dark male suits with white shirts and cravats carried their weapons like they knew how to use them. They had blonde, bound-back hair but their faces were obscured with white pottery masks shaped into sweetly smiling female features.

"Did I miss the invitation to the costume party?" Houdini asked.

"Sit in that chair," he was told.

Houdini lowered himself into the wide armchair, cursing its plush comfort that cradled him too deeply for an easy spring from its depths.

"Hands open on the arms. Move and we shoot."

"How can I sign autographs for you if I can't move?"

The door to Houdini's bedroom opened. Another intruder emerged, casually tossing down items of Houdini's personal correspondence as he flicked through them. Unlike the uniformly-clad dark-jacketed gunmen, this intruder wore elegant evening dress. His face was also masked, but with black silk, and when he spoke his accents betrayed him as English upper class.

"You were born Erik Weisz, I believe, in Budapest, Hungary," he enquired.

"I go by Houdini now."

"So you do." The gentleman deliberately tore a photograph of Houdini's mother in two and discarded it with the rest. "A grub can call itself a tiger but it's still a grub."

"I always find that little guys talk big when they've brought goons with guns to hide behind," Houdini snarled.

"Oh, *so* American! One step up from those monkeys that Darwin chap keeps going on about. Maybe half a step."

"You got some reason taking up my time, or are you just souvenir hunting?"

The evening-garbed intruder took the chair opposite Houdini. "No time for the niceties, eh, colonial? We really lost nothing when we cut you loose, did we?"

"You lost taking a licking like I'm gonna give you soon, buddy. Cut to the chase. What's your game?"

"Ah. Now that's an interesting question. It is a game, yes. Fascinating that you should pick up on that so quickly." The masked gentleman helped himself to a drink from the decanter on the side-table next to him, sipped the brandy, then poured it onto the carpet in contempt. "Here's the thing—Harry. Do you happen to remember a little soiree you attended in Paris given by the Far Edge Club?"

"The Marquis de Confontaine and his chinless drinking buddies the *Club de Bord Lointain*? Sure I recall them. It ended badly for them."

"Did you imagine we would forget you?"

Houdini suppressed a shiver. The Far Edge Club was a collection of rich, privileged thrill-seekers who amused themselves facing dangerous situations and forcing others to do the same. Confontaine and his Paris sycophants had nearly killed the escape artist in the catacombs under the city. Others had not escaped alive.

"If you know about those guys then you know what happened when they crossed me," Houdini warned.

The masked gent snorted. "Did you not understand that we are an *international* organisation—Harry? Inconvenience one of us and there are many others who will avenge the slight."

"Pathetic playboys with no reason to live and no regard for their lives or others?" Houdini scorned. "Shoot me now and I've still beaten you all hollow!"

The masked women stirred dangerously. For a moment the escape artist expected them to fire. He braced himself to overturn the chair and try and dodge the shots, but the gentleman in evening dress continued the conversation.

"We hold competitions, you know, Harry. We try to top each other in providing stimulating spectacles. Confontaine thought you might bring him a cachet within our set. He proved to be overambitious—for his levels of ability."

"You better plug me here and now, because otherwise I'm going to enjoy wiping that smug smile off your unmasked face."

"Games, Harry Houdini. It is all about games of life and death. So here is the game, and here are the rules. Several of the Far Edge Club have gathered in London. We have business here. *You* are the light entertainment. Within the next week you will die."

"It's been tried before."

"You will die. That's the competition, you see. Each of us will plot your death. The one who succeeds wins. Open season on annoying American conjurers. Sniper, poison, trap, blade, who can say whence the end will come? But come it will. One of us will claim the laurel. And possibly your head, for a trophy room wall."

Houdini glowered at the smug gentleman.

"We are not barbarians, though, Harry. We are giving you due warning so you can defend yourself as best you can. And if you stick to the rules we will ensure that no innocent bystander is killed in our game. You cannot leave London. You cannot cancel any public appearance. You cannot let anyone know you are hunted. Even your friend Beck is safe, so long as you do not tell him what is happening. If he knows then he is fair game too."

"You intend to hunt me and I have to keep it secret?" Houdini understood.

"Exactly. The game begins at dawn tomorrow. If you somehow survive long enough to complete your debut at the Lyceum next Monday then we will withdraw and you can survive. That's your incentive, though I caution you now that no one has ever lasted the full week in our manhunts. And I should warn you that a crate of decent claret is at stake, so we are very motivated to see you dead."

"Anything else?"

"No, I think that covers it, Harry. Be a good little Yank and provide us with a decent chase, won't you? Some of my guests have come a long way to kill you."

"Like the girls wearing the pottery there? Or your bag-wearing heavies?"

"My muses dress that like for… other reasons. All here are my servants. Other competitors have minions of their own."

"And I'm not the first you've hunted down like this?"

"Oh no. Far from it. It's one of our old favourites. We might choose a famous soldier or a wealthy tycoon, a famous actress or a penniless street-whore. The result is always the same. We have high hopes for a good chase from you though."

Houdini shrugged. "You've said your piece, now I'll say mine. I don't like you. You've just confessed to being murderers and you're trying to kill me. So you need to know the kid gloves are off. You're coming after me? I'm coming after you. And it won't be prison for you. You guys get thrilled by near-death encounters? Let's see how thrilled you are by the real thing!"

"My, such conviction!"

"Yeah, you might not recognise what this is. It's integrity. It's real."

The gentleman rose. "Then we shall leave you to your… integrity. Enjoy your last night of peace, Harry. From tomorrow morning you are the fox—and the pack is hunting you."

The gunmen waited for ten minutes after their employer and his masked muses has slipped out before they too withdrew from Houdini's rooms.

—›‹—

"You seem preoccupied, Houdini," Beck commented over the breakfast that had just been delivered to their hotel suite. "No appetite?"

Not when every item might be laced with arsenic, Houdini considered. He allowed himself some coffee from the common pot, deciding to trust that the Far Edge Club would stick to their agreement about keeping Beck from harm so long as the agent remained ignorant of the challenge.

"I've a few things I'm trying to work through, that's all," he told his friend and manager.

"A new trick?"

"Perhaps. I need one."

Houdini wondered how the hunters would know if he alerted Beck to the danger. A listening tube concealed somewhere, perhaps? If so that could work to his advantage.

"Could you run through my schedule for the next few days?" he asked his manager. "Rehearsals, public appearances, that kind of thing?"

"Well, everything's gearing up to your new show opening next Monday night," Beck reminded him. "That'll be a gala event. You have rehearsals every day from two till six and a number of society functions. Tonight it's the Lord Mayor's reception, then tomorrow the Locksmith's Guild challenge. Thursday we're dining with Baxter and Norris, the businessmen sponsoring the Tower Bridge stunt. Friday will include some check-ups on the apparatus there, and then the Duke's ball in the evening. I still can't quite get my head around us going to a Duke's ball, like something out of the Brontes or something. We've come a long way from Minnesota, Harry!"

"We've a lot further to go get, Beck—I hope."

"Saturday is the Tower Bridge show. That'll get the papers in a tizzy and grab us the headlines we need to make sure opening night goes with a bang. Sunday's final dress rehearsal and then some free time before the big event. Have you got something else you need to fit in before then? Please don't let it be another interruption like last night!"

"Relax, Beck. If I pull that too often folks'll start buying tickets to my rivals shows just in the hopes I show up to knock 'em down. Winters had it coming. He got it. That'll keep the peace for a while."

"Listen, I took lunch yesterday with someone who might interest you. Dr John Watson, the guy who works with Sherlock Holmes. I met him at that affair of Doyle's in Bloomsbury—the one you ducked out of."

"I try to avoid Doyle these days. He's convinced I have supernatural powers that will prove his spiritualist beliefs. It's embarrassing. But I'm sorry to have missed Watson."

"Yeah, well you might get your chance. That's what I'm trying to tell you. I've sent him and Mr Holmes tickets to the opening, and passes to the London Bridge event too. So it's possible you'll have the world's greatest detective in your audience. *Do not* invite him up on stage to check your ropes."

"Well Martin, you know I like a challenge."

"Do. Not."

Houdini snorted good-humouredly. "Fine. So here's what I intend to do this week. I'm going into strict training. I'll prepare my own food and drink—a special diet. I'll take regular walks to get fittened up for the show. Breathing exercises and such. Don't worry if I disappear off at odd hours of the day and night, it'll all be part of the method. I'm getting my head into the game."

"I'm glad you're taking it seriously—not that you don't always—but why these special preparations?"

"You know me. Always wanting to go one better. So I'll see you at the theatre at two?"

—◦—

Houdini did not know London well, so he instructed the cabbie to take him where he could ask questions about art. A short ride later he was in Trafalgar Square on the steps of the National Gallery. He strode between the stately white columns of the portico and forged inside to discover someone who could answer his questions.

The name of Harry Houdini was familiar to some of the attendants inside. Not long later the showman was consulting with Mr Pixley, a timid-looking man in a twill jacket who was the institution's expert on pottery casts.

"I'm doing some research—for a show," Houdini began. "I'm interested in a particular plaster face I saw recently. Something I've seen more than once, here and in Paris."

"A female face, perhaps?" Pixley enquired. "I think I know of what you speak. You will not find it here in these august halls. If you would accompany me to my basement office, however...?"

Houdini followed the scholar, alert for ambush. The masked women might have been a subtle trap, although the showman could not envisage how his enemies might guess he would choose to chase the lead here. Perhaps the cab driver had been a plant?

Houdini's suspicions were allayed somewhat when Pixley led him into a crowded, book-filled office and gestured to a wall where a carved moulded mask was displayed. "Is that the lady?"

"That very one," Houdini agreed. "Who...?"

"Who is she? Nobody knows. It is a very strange story, Mr Houdini."

Houdini settled on a chair. "I'd like to hear it. I saw a couple of masks like that under some very odd circumstances. Tell me what you can about the lady."

Pixley unhooked the image from the wall. It was a representation of a young woman, possibly only in her teens, with closed eyes and a faint sad smile. So realistic was the casting that Houdini half expected her to blink and look at him.

"This is the Mona Lisa of the Seine," the expert introduced her. "So she has been dubbed, at least. The French call her *l'Inconnu*—the unknown."

He handed the mask to Houdini to inspect. "The legend is that sometime in the dying years of the last century a poor girl was taken up out of the Seine where she had drowned. It is not uncommon for corpses to be taken from that river, as I understand it. Whether her death was suicide or murder was never discovered.

"As is routine with unidentified bodies in that city she was placed on display at the Paris morgue so that those who sought lost loved ones might attend and determine whether their missing kin was found. Nobody ever came forward.

"The victim's beauty, and particularly the serenity of her face with eyes closed as in sleep and lips slightly curved into a gentle smile, caught the attention of the duty pathologist. He commissioned a moulder to create a plaster death-mask of her face, either for aesthetic purposes or to retain some likeness of her for future criminal investigation. The craftsman, in possession of so attractive a template, cast masks of the mystery girl and sold them from his workshop. The images found favour with the artists and bohemians of Fin de Siecle Paris. Production has never ceased."[36]

"This is the death-mask of an unknown suicide or murdered girl?" Houdini checked.

"Indeed. It is also the most popular decoration of every artist's study

---

36 This is still true today. A thriving West Bank industry still exists making plaster casts of *l'Inconnu*'s face.

Nobody is quite sure when the plaster masks and busts of *l'Inconnu* first appeared, but by 1899 they were well known enough to be the central theme of a novella by Richard le Gallienne. In *The Worshipper of the Image*, a young poet gains inspiration from the moulded face, but its evil influence eventually drives him to madness and death. *L'Inconnu*'s many likenesses were commonly held to be echoes of the muse.

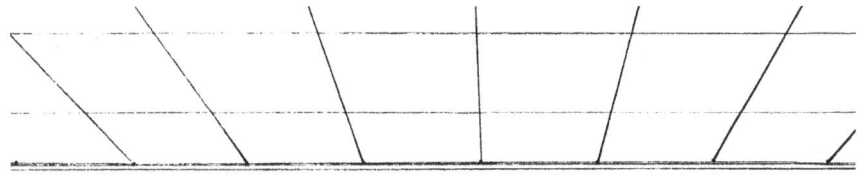

"The French call her *l'Inconnu*—the unknown."

and studio on the Continent. In a few short years, *l'Inconnu* has become the mystery muse of artists and writers across Europe."

"A muse?" That was the term Houdini's late-night visitor had chosen. *My muses dress like that for... other reasons*, he had said. Was Houdini's tormentor another romantic caught in the mystery girl's spell or did he have a more direct connection? Was he proud that his wicked handiwork was commemorated on every studio wall?

Pixley retrieved the mask and replaced it in its display. "Many have speculated over the identity of *l'Inconnu* and the circumstances that might have led to her untimely end. Popular accounts are mostly romantic, full of passion and betrayal. A cruel noble lover, sometimes a disavowed pregnancy, or sometimes she died for lost true love. I doubt now that the truth will ever be known."[37]

"Surely someone has tried to solve the case? Houdini insisted. "Considering how many people hang masks of this girl's face on their walls there has to have been some interest in solving her death."

"*Monsieur* Dubugue of the Parisian police once reviewed the evidence, I understand," Pixley revealed. "Interest was also shown by the enquiry agent LeBrun.[38] It is from his published monograph that I have drawn much of what I just told you. Unfortunately both investigations came well after the unfortunate girl from the Seine was buried in the Cemetery of the Innocents. The trail was cold."

"She had a pauper's grave?"

"I believe she was interred decently by public subscription."

"And no list of the subscribers, I suppose?"

Pixley shrugged apologetically. "None that I ever heard of. Donations of that kind are usually anonymous."

Houdini tried another tack. "You said that lots of people were obsessed with *l'Inconnu* as a muse. Have you ever heard of anyone dressing up their servants as her, masks and all?"

The museum expert shook his head with mild distaste. "Nothing would surprise me, though, where that angelic face is concerned."[39]

---

37 As recently as the last decade artist John Goto created an entirely fictional backstory with facsimile evidence. The "discovered information" is online at http://www.johngoto. org.uk/framer/9text.htm and though Goto acknowledges it as fiction, his identification of *l'Inconnu*e as a Hungarian actress called Ewa Lazlo now appears as fact in several careless secondary sources.

38 These two experts are previously referenced in "The Naval Treaty" and "The Illustrious Client" respectively.

39 Even Mr Pixley might have been amazed by later real-life events of *l'Inconnu*'s fame. In

Houdini sighed. He had hoped for some clue as to his Far Edge Club visitor but had only found additional mystery. He glanced at his watch. "I have to go," he told Pixley, rising and shaking the man's hand. "I've got a rehearsal this afternoon."

"It has been a great pleasure to talk with you, Mr Houdini," the curator assured the famous escape artist. "I'm sorry I wasn't able to assist you more."

"Maybe you can. Let me know if anyone else comes asking about this. Send a wire to me at the Bridge House Hotel. And check with any of your colleagues and contemporaries who might have had enquiries."

"That… might be possible," the earnest museum scholar admitted. "I shall see what may be done."

Houdini thanked him and left by a back exit. He had other preparations to make. A man for whom traps had been set was entitled to prepare a few snares of his own.

The venerable Lyceum Theatre stood on the left side of Wellington Street up from the Strand, hard by Covent Garden. The current 'Theatre Royal Lyceum and English Opera House' dated from 1834, famous in turn for championing English composers like Barnett and Balfe, for its long-running productions of Dickens stories, for its 'fairy extravaganzas' with their spectacular stage effects, and for the turbulent, brilliant early creative years of actors Irving and Terry. Writer Bram Stoker stage managed there

---

addition to being inspiration for one of the most reproduced art images of all time, she can also nowadays claim the title of "most kissed face of all time".

In 1955, Norwegian schoolboy Tore Laerdal fell into deep water. His father Asmund rescued the boy and restarted his breathing with CPR, saving his life. The senior Laerdal was a toy manufacturer who had made his fortune from dolls and cars moulded from the new plastics that were just then becoming popular.

When Laerdal's kiss of life became public knowledge he was approached by the medical community with an unusual request. Would he design and manufacture a training aid for teaching cardio-pulmonary respiration? The toymaker obliged, creating both torso and whole-body mannequins suitable for practicing cardiopulmonary resuscitation. He tried to make them as lifelike as possible. He decided a female "patient" would be least threatening to learners. She was named Resusci Anne. She became the standard CPR dummy used globally for the last half-century. And she needed a face.

Asmund Laerdal recalled his childhood visits to his grandparents' house and the mask that hung on their wall. He borrowed l'Inconnu's appearance for Resusci Anne. A girl who died by drowning has now been resuscitated millions of times across the world. She has trained thousands of people to save others who have stopped breathing. And l'Inconnu, the most kissed girl in history, still remains anonymous, mysterious, and inspiring—forever.

from 1878, and though a stage adaptation of *Dracula* had been put on, the author could never convince Irving, after whom he had modelled the vampire count, to take the lead role.[40]

The theatre had been extensively restored and refurbished since Houdini's visit there earlier in his European tour. There was no sign of fire damage. The new management had set all in order again.[41]

Audiences that filled the venue's two thousand seats entered via Samuel Beazley's impressive pillared portico. Actors and crew used the stage door to the rear on Burleigh Street. The best line of sniper fire would be from the top of the building itself, aimed to cover anyone heading for the private entrance whether they came from Exeter Street or the Strand.

Houdini strode boldly through the front of house and gained access by way of the ticket office. Once inside the building he doffed his overcoat disguise and slipped quickly up the stairs to the upper galleries, to the 'gods' where holders of the cheapest tickets stood above even the balcony that overlooked the circle. From there a small trapdoor led to a service ladder which opened out onto the roof.

Houdini was not surprised to discover that the padlock securing the roof-hatch had been forced.

He smiled grimly. His first scheduled appointment had been almost certain to bring out at least one of the most impatient or ambitious of the Far Edgers, eager to beat fellow competitors to their prize. Houdini hoped that a man so predictable in that way would be as obvious in his other preparations.

He slipped out onto the slick leads of the theatre's flat top. The huge building had three roof levels, of which the escape artist had selected the highest. A lower section over the main auditorium led back towards Burleigh Street where another raised part allowed space for lifting and hauling equipment over the stage. A narrow catwalk joined the two higher sections, and that was where Houdini scurried, aware that a really clever

---

40 Only the façade and portico of the original building were retained. The old Lyceum Theatre before the Samuel Beazley-designed version that Houdini visited dated back to 1765 through two previous buildings on an adjacent site. In 1904, two years after our present narrative, the theatre was substantially rebuilt again in rococo style.
The Lyceum hosted talents like Sir John Geilgud (Ellen Terry's great-nephew) up to its closure for World War II. The post-war auditorium eventually became a venue for concerts from The Grateful Dead, The Clash, Bob Marley & The Wailers, Led Zeppelin, The Who, Emerson, Lake & Palmer, Colosseum, U2, The Smiths and Culture Club. Since 1999 it has been home to the musical production of *The Lion King*.

41 The theatre was extensively damaged in Jim Beard's story, "Houdini Brings the Curtain Down". That Jim Beard is such a vandal.

enemy might have anticipated his investigation and covered that approach.

No such attack came. He reached the rear roof and was gratified to spot a pair of men laid full-length by the edge over the back road. The snipers checked left and right along the route they expected their prey to pass, their long-barrelled hunting rifles ready beside them.

Houdini made no sound as he crept up on them. So intent were they on their vigil that the second man did not notice as Houdini downed the first with a nerve pinch. He first became aware of his quarry's presence when a scientific kidney-punch took him in the small of the back. By the time he reacted he had been hauled up by his assailant and hurled over the parapet.

And held there, head downwards, dangling, with a pair of strong hands folded round his left ankle to prevent his immediate fall to the distant pavement below.

"I guess you were looking for me?" Houdini supposed.

The assassin screamed.

"You know the best thing about there being two of you?" the escape artist suggested. "If you're not smart enough to tell me what I want to know then I can drop you and start again with your buddy. I'm betting the view of you spread out on the sidewalk down there would convince him to talk pretty fast."

"Please... no...!"

"Don't worry. I've trained myself to have a really strong grip. If I let go of you it'll be entirely deliberate."

"What... what do you want?"

"Let's start with who you are. And before you answer, think on this. I might already know things. I might be testing you to see if you're speaking the truth. If I catch you in a lie you'll need to develop powers of flight pretty damn quick."

The hanging sniper trembled. He was utterly helpless, dependent on Houdini's hold to preserve his life. "I'm Corrigan. He's Mumby. We were hired to...to shoot you."

"Who by?"

Corrigan shivered more. "No names, I swear. A cove who's called on us before when there's work to be done, that's all. He sends someone to the Wellington's Arms—that's the pub in Reigate—to find us there."

"Who?"

The sniper hesitated. Houdini jerked his hands down a little.

"No! I'll tell! Some posh flunkey. That's all I know. Pays in cash, on the nose. Gave us a poster with your picture on it. Told us you'd be down there about now. Ten guineas if we got you. Three just to try."

"You've been sent out before?"

"A couple of times, yeah. You have to understand, it was just business. We was dismissed from the regiment. There's no other work for blokes like us."

Houdini extracted a description of the 'posh flunkey' but knew there was little chance of finding him. "Okay, I guess I'm done with you now, Corrigan."

"No! Please! You said…"

While the assassin was still screaming, Houdini hauled him in, slammed his head on the parapet to quieten him down, and applied two pairs of cuffs from his pockets, hogtieing Corrigan with hands and feet shackled together behind his back. He pinioned Mumby likewise before reviving and questioning the second sniper.

"I doubt you'll survive long enough to get to trial," Houdini advised the captives, "but when they come for you, tell 'em that I'm after them as much as they're after me. It's not a game to me. I'm taking it personally. Got that?"

He left them there on the lead flats where he could direct that irascible bulldog of the London constabulary Sergeant Bolt[42] to find them. For the sake of Beck's blood pressure he managed to make it to his rehearsal on time.

━╱╲━

The great Houdini was somewhat distracted at the Lord Mayor's banquet. He and eighty other guests feasted beneath the high timbered roof of the medieval Guildhall that headquartered the Corporation of London, but the escape artist was alert to the many ways attempts might be made on his life as he sat at table.

"You seem preoccupied, Mr Houdini," the society beauty seated next to him observed.

"I guess I'm not used to all this pomp and circumstance," replied the man who'd arrived in America on the immigrant boat at the age of four.

"Is that why you are palming your meal off into a hidden bag under the tablecloth?"

Houdini winced. "I'd hoped I was being discreet," he admitted.

"You are. You could not have employed a more unobtrusive and

---

[42] Police sergeant Bolt met and reluctantly worked with Houdini and Bram Stoker in "Houdini Brings The Curtain Down"

gentlemanly way of avoiding your vittles. I am sorry if my mentioning it has upset you."

The escape king looked again at the woman beside him. She'd been introduced as Lady Sabine Saxhallow, wife of the soldier who sat a few places up on the opposite side of the trestle chatting animatedly with one of the city fathers. She was dressed elegantly, with restrained but expensive jewellery, and her corn-blonde hair was perfectly coiffured. Only her eyes betrayed a sparkle of mischief.

An adventuress? Ladies were often intrigued by the dangerous American performer.

"I'm in training," Houdini explained to her. "A special diet is part of my preparation for my upcoming show. I didn't want to offend my host so I was trying to be covert about avoiding the menu."

"And so you have been, except for my shocking breach of etiquette in mentioning it," Lady Saxhallow assured him. She gestured round the old stone walls with their many flags and plaques, at the stained glass windows of the oldest non-ecclesiastical building in London. "You seem very interested in all this. I've noticed you looking around."

Searching for an assassin, Houdini could not answer. There were no suitable sniper-points here, and he was not eating the food or drinking the wine. There were other ways to get at him. The lady beside him, perhaps?

"It's a curse of my profession," he replied instead. "In my line of work one has to always be looking for an angle. A way out. A tell. A detail that could be used. After a while it gets so you can't switch it off."

"It is an impressive building, if you like that sort of thing," Lady Saxhallow conceded. "The architecture dates from the early fifteenth century, I'm told. It was almost a hundred years old before rich men dining in this room just like us decided to finance a trip to what became Jamestown, Virginia. The Guildhall itself goes back to before the Norman Conquest. The Romans built on this spot even before that, with one of their amphitheatres out back. So I've been lectured, anyhow." She flicked a rueful glance across the table at a scholar who was currently engaged in debate with a colleague about the laws of swanupping on the higher Thames.[43] "It's my first time here too."

---

43 A royal charter of King James IV in 1482 formalised 12th century tradition that all unmarked mute swans on open water belonged to the crown, and could therefore not be caught and claimed by "yeoman and husbandmen, and other persons of little reputation." This led to swan censuses each third week of June, wherein these unclaimed birds were captured, marked on the bill, and loosed again. The tradition continues to this day, although it is only asserted on certain stretches of the Thames and the swans are ringed around the leg rather than cut; nowadays this is a method of checking on the health and breeding

Houdini had detected something of a well-disguised Dutch accent in the lady's speech. "You're not from round here?"

She pressed a finger to her lips. "Sssh. I'm a controversial figure as it is," she confided. "Best not to alarm the natives, eh?"

"Sure. Alarmed natives are the last thing we want." She'd won a smile off him. She was good.

"I'm one of those dreadful Boers, don't you know," she murmured.

Houdini raised a brow. "Aren't the Brits at war with you?"

"Well, not with me personally, I hope. I sold out, you see. I married the enemy." She gestured down the table to the man in military dress uniform.

"Your husband was in South Africa?"

"Worse than that. Major Sir Horace Saxhallow commanded one of those dreadful concentration camps everyone is arguing about, at Viljoensdrift on the Breede River."

Houdini tried to read the lady's cues. Women who attempted to seduce him rarely discussed their husbands or revealed themselves to be collaborators. On the other hand, this seemed beyond his understanding of polite English dinner-table conversation.

"That was how we met," Lady Saxhallow went on. "I was interned at Viljoensdrift, you see, one of many people marched there by the British troops who swept through our territory. They claimed it was for our own safety, and I suppose there was some truth to that. Our menfolk were dead or fled by then, and there had been some Kaffir outrages against undefended farms and the people left on them. Only the administration utterly failed to plan for the numbers of women and children who were gathered up. Poor supply lines bringing bad rations from unscrupulous dealers who knew there could be no complaint at rotten meat or sawdust-stuffed flour. Little sanitation and less fresh water. Virtually no medical care. Ignorance more than malice, I'd say, but a killing ignorance all the same. That was why I complained to Horace—and how we came to know each other."

It all seemed a long way from the glittering bustle of a Guildhall dinner. "I guess people do come together under extraordinary circumstances," Houdini owned.

"Society gossip in London would have it that I latched onto a rich and famous soldier to escape poverty and imprisonment. I try not to be insulted by the opinions of vapid clothes-horses who have never missed

patterns of the declining species. Three ancient Worshipful Companies of 'swan uppers', the Queens, Vintners, and Dyers, take skiffs onto the river to undertake the count. The Queen, whose titles include "seignior of the swans", attended a swan-upping ceremony in 2009, the first time a British monarch has done so for many centuries.

a meal in their lives and live cocooned in wealth and privilege. But you see, Mr Houdini, that we are both explorers in a strange alien culture; and neither of us is quite ready to swallow the feast down whole."

The banquet continued. The Right Honourable the Lord Mayor of London made a flattering allusion to Houdini's presence that brought a smattering of polite applause from the tables. But Lady Saxhallow offered no further personal revelations and did not require Houdini to utilise the polite rebuffs he had half-prepared had she suggested a more intimate acquaintance.

When he got home and tested the food for arsenic, however, he found that the pulled beef would have killed him outright.

On Wednesday, Houdini looked for Sergeant Bolt at the Locksmiths Guild Challenge, but received a telegram warning that the policeman had been suddenly dispatched with an inspector of the detective branch on an urgent investigation to the north of the country. The escape artist found that rather too convenient. He'd wanted to see what Bolt had discovered about Corrigan and Mumby. He wondered who had arranged to send the only officer of the law he trusted to distant Lancashire to deny him aid.

It had occurred to Houdini, somewhat belatedly, that whoever had hired the rooftop assassins was probably nearby when they were caught. Their employer was a member of the Far Edge Club, after all, that elite collection of thrill-seekers who were excited by the nearness of their own death or that of others. Which amongst them would deploy killers and not be present to observe the consequences? But there were too many carriages on the Strand, even rattling past Burleigh Street, to identify one lurker from so many.

How many Far Edge Club members had come to London to kill Houdini anyhow? Was that the whole reason for their visit here, or was something else afoot? How far did their influence go? Would they really stick to their self-imposed sporting rules if the game turned against them? Houdini was eager to find out.

"Harry," Martin Beck prompted. Houdini belatedly realised that he had been announced and was expected on the platform. He strode out onto the walkway that had been set up as a stage at one end of the hall where the Worshipful Company of Locksmiths met.

He stopped and made an unexpected bow to the assembled guests, sufficiently sudden that any gunman aiming a rifle might fire over his head as the target stooped.

When no shot betrayed a killer's presence, Houdini joined the Guild President at the podium and posed for photographs. Thanks to Beck's diligent preparation the press was out in force.

The President waited until the fuss calmed a little then made his introductions. "Gentleman, Mr Harry Houdini has become famous—we lock-makers might say notorious—for thwarting the best attempts of honest craftsmen to keep him confined. He's agreed to come here today to try himself against the best we have to offer. Members of the guild have competed for the chance to baffle the Handcuff King, and we have hopes today of doing it."

There was a welter of applause and more explosions from flash-pans.

"Our agreed rules are these: Mr Houdini will be restrained by three different sets of shackles devised by our best designers. All of the mechanisms are non-standard double-locks that can't be opened with a conventional duplicate key. Mr Houdini will be searched for shims that might slip the pawl[44] and similar tools. He'll be fastened into a hood so there's no question he could regurgitate a lockpick. I'll apply the cuffs myself, and I know how to position them so they can't be slipped using muscle techniques or dislocations. Mr Houdini will be placed into this box you see here behind us, and he will have ten minutes to release himself from all three fetters. Is that the deal, Mr Houdini?"

The showman nodded soberly. "I hope you're not going to make me regret coming to Blighty, Mister President," he answered. His cheeky wink won a round of clapping.

Houdini watched the crowd as his hands were cuffed behind him. He was alert for a sudden movement, a hastily-produced blowpipe or fast-drawn dagger. His keen eyes picked out the face of Sabine Saxhallow somewhere at the back of the crowd.

Then the locks were affixed and he was dragged behind a curtain for a body search by guild members who knew the tricks of the trade. Soon after, wearing only trunks, vest, and the threatened hood, he was bundled into the tall box and the countdown clock started.

Houdini relaxed. Experts were always the easiest to fool.

They'd been so keen to prevent him taking tools into this wardrobe-sized crate, so clever positioning his restraints where he could not simply slip his arms under his legs and bring his hands before him to manoeuvre free. They had concentrated so hard on him that they had never even

---

44 That is, small tapered instruments that might be used to slip a ratchet.

considered the box that Martin Beck had provided for the performance.

Houdini slipped open the hidden compartment in it where his tools were concealed.

The lock he considered easiest was the one on his actual wrists. It had been easy to influence the President to apply the cuffs in order, so that the hardest was highest up his developed biceps. With the easier shackles removed he could slip the most difficult down and simply dislocate his thumbs to scrape free. He need conquer only one patented lock, working by touch alone since he was hooded and his hands were caught behind him.

Houdini applied a torsion wrench and half-diamond pick to probe the keyhole of the simplest cuffs—and froze.

There was something odd about the lock mechanism; something more than a new patent system of holding the tumblers in place. Houdini suppressed a shiver that rippled along his spine.

His sensitive fingers tested the interior rim of the metal hoop that bound him. Yes, *there* and *there*, on the inside of the fetter, were tiny holes, such as might conceal a tiny needle to be sprung when the cuff was opened.

The handcuffs were the trap. His own cleverness was intended to spring it.

Houdini fingered a pair of thin steel spatulas from his kit and slid them carefully between the hidden holes and the flesh of his wrist. Only then did he return with hook and ball picks to conquer the lock. The triggered tines blunted themselves on the metal plates, wasting their expensive foreign venom on unfeeling iron. A minute later Houdini was free.

And the game continued.

❧

On Thursday, a wildly-driven carriage failed to run him down in the street. It was no difficult matter for a man who had debuted on stage at the age of nine as trapeze performer 'Erhich, Prince of the Air'. The trap careened away down Exeter Street and could not be traced.

❧

On Friday morning, Houdini found a scorpion dead in the mousetrap he had placed as a precaution in the ventilation shaft of his hotel bedroom. Later that day a bullet chipped brickwork off the portico of Lawrence Norris' townhouse, where Houdini had jinked suddenly on exiting the premises. If the investor who was backing Houdini's forthcoming Tower Bridge stunt noticed the damage he said nothing.

—⁄❭❬—

Friday also required Houdini to visit Tower Bridge with Beck, to inspect the arrangements for Saturday's publicity stunt. There was no way to avoid appearing in public, in an open venue with lots of overlooking buildings with excellent lines of fire.

"May I ask why you are dressed as a navvy?" Beck ventured as they walked past the Tower of London and made for the bridge.

"I don't want to be recognised. I have no time for rubberneckers today."

"And that's the only reason, is it? Only I've noticed some odd things you've been doing this week, Harry. Anything you want to tell me?"

"Nothing I'd want to worry you with. Just me being me, I guess. Aren't you used to it by now?"

"Some things you don't get used to, Harry."

They reached the span of the new river crossing[45] and passed across the city-side suspension section towards the bascule in the centre. Only the middle third of the bridge could be raised to allow river traffic to pass. Past the first of the two distinctive towers, Houdini's technical crew were gathered to discuss the crane and pulley that would be required tomorrow.

"This is where we'll put it, if that's alright with you, sir."

Beck pointed out the arrangements. "The dignitaries will go on a stepped scaffold there. We have constables to maintain the rope-lines keeping back the public, roughly where the chalk marks are. You'll be taken into the bridge tower here to be searched as usual. That'll be by the Thames harbour-master and some Scotland Yard detective called Lestrade. The chest will be positioned over where Jackson and Bright are measuring up for the crane, so when you're locked inside we can hoist it over the railing and lower you down into the river."

Houdini peered above him, at the high-level walkways that overlooked the span. Those long foot-bridges, freely accessible by staircases in the towers, had already gained a bad reputation as the haunt of prostitutes and

---

45 Tower Bridge was erected in 1894, eight years before the time of our present narrative, as a relief for the overcrowded London Bridge. It had to include a raiseable middle section to allow tall-ship access to the Pool of London docking facilities. At the time of our story the bridge was still painted in its original greenish blue livery; it was not decorated in its present red, white, and blue until Queen Elizabeth II's silver jubilee in 1977.

footpads. They were open to the air, a fine place for a sniper to set a rifle. Fortunately they would be packed with spectators tomorrow if Beck had done his job, reducing the chance of a killer using those vantage points for a fatal shot.

"It'll take about three minutes to lower you into the water," Beck went on. "We're dropping you at low tide, so when you settle on the bed you'll be under about eighteen feet of river. The box will be locked, of course, but we'll seal the outer keyhole off before dropping you so the water can't flood the crate very quickly. We've tested it at… Jackson?"

"It leaks slowly, sir," the mechanic confirmed. "Fills up in about fifteen minutes."

"If you're not out in twelve minutes I'll be hauling you up," Beck warned Houdini.

"Make it seventeen minutes," the showman advised. "I can hold my breath longer than that."

His manager nodded reluctantly. "To win Baxter and Norris' challenge you'll need to break out of your chains, break out of the box, and swim up to the surface. Then the band will play *Dixie*."

"Well," breathed the escape artist. "I wouldn't want to miss that."

━✦━

"Men are moving into position to kill you," Lady Saxhallow told Harry Houdini. "Ask me to dance."

"Would you dance with me, Lady Saxhallow?" the escape artist responded gallantly. He glanced around the crowded ballroom and spotted several liveried footmen angling to be near him.

"Call me Sabine," his unexpected partner instructed him. They escaped onto the dance floor into an elaborate Viennese waltz.

"You have an interesting way of getting a fellah to ask you for a spin," Houdini commented.

"You are already wondering if I am one of the assassins sent to murder you," the blonde in his arms retorted. "No-one sent me. I don't want you dead."

The array of dancers swirled round the tiled dance floor. The Duke of Devonshire's ball was full of the most glittering people in London, the titled and entitled, gathered only a month into the social season. Many of the debutantes who had been presented to the king at court that year were now being displayed for suitable marriage alliances.

"What do you know about assassins?" Houdini asked Sabine.

"We didn't meet for the first time at the Guildhall, Mr Houdini. On the first occasion I was masked."

The escape artist's brows rose. "*L'Inconnu* of the Seine?"

"I'm *l'Inconnu* of the Breede."

"Your husband was the guy who threatened me in my hotel room?"

Sabine missed a step and almost stumbled. "Actually he was not. On that occasion I was working for someone else. Please don't ask me who. I don't want to lie to you."

"So what's your angle now?"

"I want you to survive. I want you to kill the men who are hunting you. I do not like the Far Edge Club."

"And why is that?"

"I didn't like what they did at Viljoensdrift. Imagine what entertainment bastards like that could find at a desperate ill-regulated internment camp? What sport was available?"

"The Far Edge Club was in South Africa?"

"The Far Edge Club goes wherever their games take them. Sometimes they gather in the war-stricken margins where they can prey on the helpless for their cruel amusements. Other times they prefer the capitals of empire where they can strike at even the richest and most powerful of enemies through treachery and sudden murder. But yes, several of them found things to do at Viljoensdrift for a time."

"Your husband…?"

"Let us agree that marriage to him was preferable to playing the games of the Far Edge Club. He protected me as he did not protect others."

Houdini heard the bitterness under Sabine's practiced tones. "You do not like him."

"I hate him—but a bargain was made. I will not be the one to break it."

"Is Sir Horace Saxhallow one of the Far Edgers, then?"

"I cannot say. Draw your own conclusion."

"And you cannot, or will not, tell me who you were with when you visited me before? Can you say why you were one of his gun-gals?"

"I am loaned to him upon request. Often. As I said, I made a bargain."

The dance ended. Sabine pulled away.

"What do you want?" Houdini asked her as she made to leave.

"I will tell you, but not here and now. You are watched. If you can find me when and where we are not observed, then I will answer you." She made a little curtsey to thank him for the dance. "You should escape now, escape master," she advised.

Houdini watched her thread her way back into the colourful throng. She found the cluster of socialites where her husband was holding forth on his military experiences.

The showman dodged those unsettling footmen and slipped unnoticed beneath the white cloth covers of the buffet trestle. He exited via the kitchen and slipped away into the brisk London night before he could be murdered.[46]

—/|\—

A mighty cheer rose from the waiting weekend crowd as Houdini leaped down from the growler and ducked to greet the Portmaster of London. The bewhiskered dignitary had dragged out some archaic uniform for the occasion, but he was outshone by the Pearly King and Queen who flanked him working the audience.[46] The band struck up *God Save the King* and then generously followed it with *The Star Spangled Banner* and *Camptown Races*. The good-natured throng, in a holiday mood and amenable to anything, clapped and stamped along.

At 2:04 the last of the tall-masted sailing ships glided between the raised halves of Tower Bridge's central section and passed downriver towards the North Sea. Massive hydraulic systems lowered the counterweighted flaps back into place so that Houdini's staff could quickly assemble their pulley apparatus for the performance.

"Quite a turnout," Beck shouted to Houdini over the noise of the occasion. "If this doesn't fill seats then I don't know what will."

"Let's see if we can give 'em a proper show, then," the escape artist agreed. "Martin... remember that I never want to worry you, please."

That was enough to worry Beck. "What's going on?" he demanded. "Have you got into one of your crusades again? Tell me the worst."

"Can't say anything now, but I promise to spill the beans after Monday's curtain—if I can. Until then, just have faith in me, please."

---

46 1902 was the year that the first Pearly Guild was founded, formalising a charitable London working-class tradition begun by orphan street-sweeper Henry Croft, who like many such cleaners saved discarded mother-of-pearl buttons to sew onto his trouser seams. Eventually he had a whole set of clothing covered in the shining studs and wore it as he collected money for local churches and care institutions. At his death over 400 followers, similarly dressed, carried on his work. Button-bedecked Pearly Kings and Queens continue to do charity work to the present day

"Any stunt works better with an accomplice."

Houdini nodded to agree the point, but he was already being dragged across to the VIP stand to meet the quality. Beck pushed after him but halted when he spotted Dr Watson by the bridge tower.

"Glad you could make it," he told the tweed-jacketed medical man. "No Mr Holmes?"

"I'm expecting him," Watson admitted. "We've had a week of intensive and exhausting investigation. He needs to finish some business off but he'll be here."

"Do me a favour and keep him away from inspecting the apparatus, will you?"

Watson snorted. "If we got Holmes and Houdini in a room together I suspect it'd be harder to part them than if we used all the locks that have ever tied your chap up to join them."

"You think they'd hit it off then."

"Hmph. That's not what I said," Watson considered with a twinkle.

Beck gestured for Houdini to come over. "Harry, this is Dr Watson, Sherlock Holmes' chronicler. Holmes will be along shortly."

"How do you do, doctor?" the great escapologist greeted Watson. They shook hands. "I look forward to our future acquaintance," Houdini assured Holmes' amanuensis.

"Thank you. Good luck on your stunt. Or does luck play no part in it?"

"Today it might," Houdini admitted honestly. "Ah, I see the speeches are about to begin. There's no escaping them."

Houdini and Beck were dragged over to hear welcoming remarks from several important dignitaries. Fortunately the high-spirited crowd was in no mood for lengthy oration but were inclined to reward brevity. A short while later, Houdini was led away to be searched while his box was hauled into position by the crane. The Locksmiths' Guild assisted again in authenticating the lock that would seal it shut.

Beck made sure of every detail. Houdini had seemed a little distracted. Perhaps it was the lady he had danced with last night? That happened sometimes. All the more reason that his manager and business partner had to attend to every detail.

He checked the chains and the rope on which the chest would be lowered. He ran the winch to be sure it functioned. He tried the footing of the lifting gear that would winch the box up and down.

He was intent on the equipment. He had no reason to notice one pale face amongst the familiar attendants around the crane.

Houdini emerged from the tower's engine room to lusty applause. The London poor who were massed up on the footpath walkway waved bunting as the showman strode to his fate. The band struck up a jaunty march that Beck didn't recognise, then fell silent as Houdini reached the box.

The Portmaster enjoyed his role as master of ceremonies. The Scotland Yard man who accompanied him seemed to shrink back from the spotlight, sweating unhappily under a battered derby. Portmaster and Lestrade publicly affirmed that Houdini carried no equipment. They further verified the chest before applying the shackles that fastened the escape artist at wrist, ankles, and neck into a helpless squat inside the metal crate.

Satisfied at last that Houdini was secure, the Portmaster allowed the lid to be closed. The Locksmith Guild President turned the key and made great show of pocketing it. The lock-hole was covered up by a metal plate that bolted into position, and that plate was sealed with glue and tar to make it watertight.

Chains were wrapped about the outside of the container, fastening it like a parcel with loops around each of its six faces and pinioned on the top with a padlock. The chain ended in a loop, and it was to this that the crane hook was attached so that the box could be lifted and pivoted out over the Thames. Another cry came from the audience as the chest was swung into position over the water.

Silence fell as the pulley lowered the box into the waves.

The Portmaster lifted out his pocketwatch and began the countdown. "Mr Houdini has seventeen minutes," he announced. "Starting now."

While all eyes were on the bubbles that rose from the showman's submerged chest, the pasty-countenanced attendant was able to spike the winching gear without anyone noticing. It would not be lifting Houdini out of the water again any time soon.

Houdini felt the thump as his chest landed in the silt of the river bottom. The trickles of water that already covered the base of the container were cold and uncomfortable. Luckily the Thames was much cleaner now that Sir Joseph Bazalgette's innovative London sewer system diverted the capital's effluence much further downstream.[47] The water here was not now rife with cholera; fish were returning to the Thames.

Houdini turned his attention to escape. He had been naked when an intimate search had been conducted of his person. Neither of his examiners, embarrassed by their duties, had thought to inspect the bathing costume into which he had climbed afterwards. Diversion was all part of the act. Houdini slipped the lockpicks he needed from the waistband of his shorts.

The wrist locks were the first to go. They were modified Hyatt cuffs, whose tumblers had been sawn down to prevent easy turning. Houdini opened them in the wet pitch darkness and laughed as they dropped away, freeing his hands to work on his other gyves.

The box shifted. Something bumped it. River debris? Or something else?

Houdini frowned and went to work on his leg irons. The larger shackles allowed for more complex locks and took longer to conquer. The crate was half-filled by the time he sprung them loose.

Three heavy knocks sounded through the metal box, regular and planned. Someone was out there, under the water.

Houdini grimly turned his attention to the padlock that held his neck-collar in place. The water was up to his shoulders by the time the shank sprang loose of the locking bar—but he was free.

As free as a man could be, inside a locked, chained box beneath eighteen feet of water, menaced by an underwater assassin.

The rim-lock on the metal crate was a very complex one, supplied again by the Locksmith's Guild. Given more space for refinements, the smiths had crafted a key and combination amalgam that would have proved challenging under the best of conditions. Houdini had expected them to concentrate their attention upon it.

He reached for the end of the box, its narrowest side. His fingers found the loose rivets that popped out easily. A simple metal tine pressed into the hole released the mechanism that held that side of the chest in place.

---

47 "The Great Stink" of untreated sewage in the river Thames in summer 1858 brought London to a standstill. Lime-soaked curtains had to be hung in the Palace of Westminster so that Parliament could meet. The event sharply focussed attention on the problems of sewage in the world's largest city. The pollution was also associated with London's cholera epidemics, although that association was later questioned.

The response was to build a massive network of 1,100 miles of parallel sewers to carry the effluent to a vent far downstream. At first sewage poured untreated into the river estuary but later pumping and treatment plants were established. Sir Joseph Bazalgette was the engineer who designed and delivered this engineering marvel. With remarkable foresight he calculated the most generous possible sewer size that might be required then doubled it, which is why his elegant and effective system still serves modern London without having reached its capacity.

Houdini took twenty deep breaths, filling his lungs. He hoped that his diver assailant would be expecting him to work on the lock and come out of the hinged top of the trunk. He folded the end-wall inward, flooding the container. He slipped past the useless chain that wrapped around the box and kicked out into the cold brown water beyond.

There were two men, dressed in rubber diving suits with helms attached to oxygen bottles on their backs. Each carried a spear-gun of the kind that was used to kill sharks.

As Houdini hoped, they had not expected him to slither free yet. He grappled the nearer man before they could react, yanking the air-pipe from his helmet so that water would flood it, hoisting him round as a shield from the other diver's weapon.

The second assassin reacted unthinkingly, firing his shaft at Houdini but burying it in his own comrade's abdomen. The silted water became suddenly red.

Houdini dropped his human shield but kept hold of the man's spear-gun. As the second killer splashed away for time to reload his own weapon, Houdini took precise aim and discharged a bolt into the man's leg.

The shaft took the assailant high in the thigh close to the groin. He fell back, dragged to the weedy bottom by the leaded weight of his diving belt. He fumbled for a moment more with his own weapon before dropping it from nerveless fingers.

Houdini swam down and found the first killer. The man was dead, either from blood loss or by drowning. The escape artist ruthlessly stripped the diver of his oxygen cylinder and pressed the hose into his own mouth. He sucked fresh oxygen into his screaming lungs.

Only then was he able to paddle across to the second attacker. The water around this man was far too clouded with blood for a mere leg wound. Even before Houdini could confirm that his shot had severed the femoral artery he knew the killer must be dead.

He dragged the helmets off his assassins and took as good a look at their faces as the clouded deep water allowed. He replaced the bowl-helms afterwards and removed the bolts from their bodies.

Very little searching was required to find the small white-painted box that lay close to where the trap-crate had been lowered. Houdini had calculated very carefully where he would emerge and had dropped the sealed weighted package very precisely two days earlier. He opened it and removed the air cylinder and face-plate it contained.

Houdini replaced the dead diver's tank where it had been, even reattaching the severed hose. He manoeuvred the loose side of his prison crate back into position until it snapped into place again. He left the defeated shackles inside the box. When seventeen minutes was up and the container was winched back by the worried Martin Beck all that would be found was a still-sealed chest with Houdini's handcuffs inside—and no Houdini!

That had been the plan all along, of course, to vanish at the very moment his enemies were most likely to strike, to become invisible so he could make his own plans and set snares for those who had thought to hunt him. The underwater assassins had been a complication, but their lead-weighted bodies would lie down here until another diver search discovered them. The corpses could offer no clue to how Houdini had escaped.

He tipped the weights out of the white supply box and buried them in the silt of the river bed. The little cube itself dismantled into six simple sides, which Houdini took with him when he swam away beneath the water.

He vanished downstream, unsuspected and free.

He had an appointment with a lady.

"Seventeen minutes," declared Beck. His face betrayed his concern that the stunt had gone wrong. "Haul him up. Now."

The Harbourmaster exchanged a concerned glance with the President of the Locksmith's Guild. "Something is amiss," he discerned. "Houdini should have swum to the surface by now."

Beck nodded grimly.

There was an unpleasant crunching of gears as the pulley engine started up and then seized. The metal intrusion that had been slipped in there earlier had jammed the whole works.

"What is it?" Beck demanded of Jackson.

The stage technician shook his head. "Something in the gears, I think," he puzzled. "I'll need to strip out the wheels."

"Houdini needs hauling up now."

"I'll need a good hour to take this to bits, sir. There's no quicker way."

Beck thought of his friend, trapped down there in the wet darkness, gasping his last breath. He turned to Lestrade, to Watson, to the watching crowd. "Strong men!" he called out. "I need strong men on that rope, pulling it up. Twenty of us, all hauling. Right now!"

He vanished downstream, unsuspected and free.

Alert to the possibility of disaster, spectators surged forward. The cable was pulled free of the fouled winch and taken to pull as if it was a tug-of-war.

It still took too long. The time was eighteen and a half minutes by Beck's stopwatch before the grunting helpers raised the chain-bound box enough to top the surface of the cruel Thames. Another half minute's struggle saw it dangling free of the water. When it came almost to the bridge parapet Beck had the rope tied off so the dripping crate dangled within reach.

"The key!" he demanded of the Locksmith's President, "And someone get me a spanner and a crowbar." The plate that covered the lock had to be removed.

He doffed his jacket and clambered over the rail to dangle precariously on the top of the chest. He felt someone behind him reach over and loop a rope over his torso; John Watson was there, attaching the safety cord, and a gaunt hook-nosed man beside him was assisting.

Beck reached down and unscrewed the cover plate, then pried it loose so it fell into the river. He fumbled down to unlock the chest then hesitated. The binding chains would still hold the lid shut, and the cord that suspended the box depended from the end of that chain.

"Ignore the lock, man," Watson's companion called down to him. "Break through at the end panel where secret studs hold the fake wall in place."

Beck understood. He jimmied the hidden hatch. It broke open, spilling more water. The business manager would have been tipped off into the river by the shifting weight had it not been for the safety rope that supported him. Instead only Houdini's discarded chains slid down to splash into the Thames below.

A cry of shock went up from the pressing crowd. The sealed crate was opened—but Harry Houdini had disappeared!

INTERLUDE: A MAN WHO PAYS HIS DUES

The warder who checked the iron doors of Newgate's cells at lock-up time was disconcerted when one opened at his touch.

The prisoner had not escaped, however. He was still inside. "Come in, Kelly," Colonel Sebastian Moran told the guard. "Quickly now."

The next thing the warder realised was that the best shot in London once again had a pistol in his hand. He swallowed hard and entered the cell.

"Sit there," Moriarty's right-hand man instructed him. "Are you going to be foolish?"

"No, Colonel. Please, I have a wife an' kids…"

"I am well aware of it. Bessie, I'm told, and Ron, Stan, Patty, Walt, and Alwin. You live at 11 Allardyce Street with your elderly father Jack." Moran smiled humourlessly. "I was taught by a very clever man to always do my homework."

Kelly swallowed hard. "Colonel…"

"You are still alive, Kelly, because you have always been decent and respectful to me. If it had been McLeish or Barrow on patrol tonight they would be dead already. Connolly would have been bleeding out his life from a painful belly shot. But you, Kelly, a churchgoing family man, you I am giving a chance."

The warder eyed the gun in the prisoner's unwavering hand. Moran's eyes seemed like chips of ice in the glow from the watchman's lantern. "How did you get a gun? Who opened the door?"

"I still have friends—or at least men who owe me a favour and know better than to deny me."

"You have been a model prisoner here, for eight years."

"I have not before had reason to leave. Tonight I do."

Kelly noticed that Moran's table contained a folded newspaper proclaiming the sensational events of today's drama at Tower Bridge. "You can't get out."

"I can. I will. The chance you have is to make it easier for me. Escort me to the gate and let me depart in peace and I will not kill you. Nothing untoward will happen to any of your family. If you are dismissed, some short time later a package will arrive through your letter-box containing adequate compensation for your loss. Or…" Moran gestured to his firearm, "You may choose a hero's funeral."

"Colonel, you have to understand…"

"I do understand, Kelly. I understand exactly. Whichever choice you make I will respect you for it, dead or alive. But I intend to leave this prison tonight. I have business to attend to."

"There are twenty men between you and freedom."

"And yet I will be free. If they elect to oppose me they will not live to regret it. I know them all." The soldier rose, never taking his gaze off the warder. "You need to decide now what you intend to do."

And so Sebastian Moran walked free from Newgate.

3. THE FACE OF THE UNKNOWN

From the account of John Watson MD
Thursday, 8th May, two days before Houdini's disappearance:

I am often asked by those familiar with my chronicling of Sherlock Holmes' investigations what the great detective really thinks of my accounts. Some readers have expressed scepticism that my friend can be so critical of the summaries of his cases. I explain that Holmes' objections to my narratives are more to do with presentational methods than with reporting the adventures themselves.

"Sensationalist and popular," he described *The Hound of the Baskervilles*, handing back the new volume I had presented to him at breakfast four days before. "You revel in the Guignol aspects of the enquiry, record with sentimental detail the characters and interactions of the principals, and yet omit the minutiae of evidence that render the investigation useful to students of criminal science."

As he spoke, Holmes was on hands and knees crawling across the floor of our living room, shuffling stacks of files, maps, papers, and scribbled notes as he tried to order the very kind of minutiae of which he spoke.

"You would prefer me to spend chapters on the details of mud and the measurement of footprints," I recognised. "Those are elements of importance in the story, of course, but lengthy technical discussion might exhaust the common reader. Any writer must select from the range of things he might include in his narrative those elements which work best to convey the sweep of that story."

"A painter on a canvass rather than a photographer recording all," Holmes summarised. "Why must an account be made in the first place?"

I bristled a little. "When I first began my records it was purely as a private memoir, to aid me in understanding the strange new world in which I had found myself at Baker Street. Later, issuing some few of those testimonies seemed like a fitting tribute to record the courage and skills of a fallen hero—a great man and great friend who had allowed me to believe him dead for many months."

Holmes had the grace to wince. That three-year deceit was an old wound between us, but still ached sometimes. "You know the reasons for that deception, Watson. Our recent visit to the deadly Moran is a chilling reminder of how you were closely watched by the remnant of Moriarty's agents for any sign that I was alive. However, I was flattered by your literary tribute to me, obfuscated and stylised as it necessarily was. Why, though, since I have returned hale and whole, have you continued with your publications?"

"You are no less worthy of recognition for your work now than when I thought you gone," I replied honestly. "As for couching your exploits in the form of detective stories, my reasoning at first was that the method would serve well to conceal those details which confidentiality or good taste would require reserving from the public; and later I came to understand the power of the format."

Holmes pulled half a dozen foolscap sheets from a manila file and laid them out before the hearth, weighting them down with the poker. I noticed the papers were shipping crew manifests. He made a gesture with his long, expressive hand to indicate that I should develop my theme.

"We live in the heart of the most civilised, developed, city on Earth, the capital of the largest empire the world has ever known," I began. "We have access to science undreamed-of by our ancestors, to sophistications and understandings unavailable to most in our present day. And yet London, and the nation it rules, is still beset with the poison of crime and the infection of injustice. We know ourselves to be imperfect, and the civilisation we have built to be imperfect also." Perhaps I was remembering Mrs Kent's outrage at Doyle regarding the Boer camps.

"You see our meagre efforts at addressing criminal activity as relevant to society," my friend ventured.

"I see it as of first importance. When you use logic and deduction to shine light on some dark forgotten wrong, when your diligent efforts or untrammelled brilliance defeat another predator who stalks the world we are creating, you remind us all of an ideal of justice. Have you never wondered at the popularity of my accounts? Surely it is because society wants to know that crime is not impossible to destroy, that men of intellect and conscience can overcome greed, hatred, and brutality? One story of Sherlock Holmes doing that speaks to the heart of our race. It is a small reminder..."

"That no effort is wasted in seeking out truth or thwarting evil," Holmes understood, finishing my thought for me as I faltered. "An interesting theory, my friend, and one worthy of Dr John Watson."

"That is why I continue with my chronicles," I owned. "Criminals must learn to fear Sherlock Holmes and the process of the law. Society must understand that justice requires application, as diligent an effort and expertise as engineering a bridge or administering a colony." I felt suddenly abashed at my idealism. "It is perhaps arrogant of me to assume my flawed accounts might add to those ends," I admitted.

Holmes clapped me on the back. "You contend in an area beyond my capacity, Watson—but I can understand why you seek to contend there."

"Those atrocities last Sunday," I offered example, "The shootings at Victoria, and that vile assault on the child outside our own front door…" My thoughts returned to that girl, now slowly recovering at Bart's hospital.

"Indeed," my friend agreed. "It was my contemplation of the evidence left by those events that led me to express my concern about recording minutiae."

I glanced at the volume of my novel that Holmes had returned. Many margins were filled with scribbled amendments, hundreds of footnotes and comments adding in the chemical analyses and character profiles he had undertaken during that old case.

"You have made progress regarding the identity of the woman who demanded the Moriarty manuscript from us?" I enquired.

Holmes gestured to the stack of notes and documents that currently obscured the rugs and carpet of our lodgings. "It is in the detail, Watson. I pity you having to summarise for your readers the painstaking links of a hundred minute fragments of evidence that I have studied."

"Perhaps you might assist me by first explaining to your poor chronicler what it is you have unearthed in this mountain of calculations?"

Holmes snorted. "Our problem with this case is not the lack of evidence but rather the deluge of it." He held up a set of statements scrawled in untutored juvenile hands. "Accounts from our Baker Street Irregulars of what witnesses have said of the covered carriage that cruised the poor quarters of London seeking children to snatch as hostages. A strange carriage in those quarters will be observed even at night, by those who would consider it a source of illicit income or an opportunity for larceny. We have descriptions of the masked thugs and a slender cloaked figure who supervised them from the vehicle's interior."

He indicated a set of sketches that I recognised as wheel tracks. "The prints of the coach in which our mystery assailant departed. I have identified the carriage as being hired from the stables on Cromwell Street, paid for by cash by a brute of a man whose boot-size and gait match descriptions of one of the kidnappers. A substantial deposit was forfeited when the coach was not returned on time. It and its horse were found abandoned at the Embankment."

Next he proffered a crumpled and stained envelope, retrieved from some rubbish bin. It bore in neat woman's script the address of the shipping company that had brought us Moriarty's mask. "Note the glue on the transverse, Watson. This is the accompanying envelope that bore instructions for bearing the parcel to us. The interior note has alas gone to light someone's pipe. Still, the handwriting is telling, of an educated right-handed female of middle years and scholarly habits. She was nervous as she addressed the message. She is not the same woman who signed the Newgate register."

He held up a canvas-backed ledger filled with crabbed tiny script. The contents were coded with numbers and strange symbols. "One of Moriarty's pay-books," Holmes explained. "It covers a number of transactions to some of his field operatives for the years 1887 to 1891, the time of his demise. Some are quite telling. This payment to one Anton Naudé, for example, and passage for him to Capetown aboard the steamer *Palmyra* in January '88…"

"The very boat from which poor Jack Douglas was lost overboard!" I recognised.[48]

"The same. But of relevance to our current investigation, this payment to a funerary mask-maker in February of 1891, mere weeks before Reichenbach, is a telling lead."

I was torn between Holmes' discovery of the likely origin of the stolen death mask and news of the identification of Douglas' assassin. "But if you now know who killed…"

Holmes raised a cautionary finger. "Anton Naudé is no longer with us, Watson. His work aboard *Palmyra* was evidently his retirement piece. He remained in South Africa at its conclusion, and thereafter his payment was reduced to the honorarium with which Moriarty retained the services of many hidden agents across the world who remained inactive save for rendering occasional reports."

"Still, a note from Mr Sherlock Holmes to the colonial officers of the law…"

"When this slim ledger came into my possession I of course made enquiries after Naudé. Upon his master's fall he disappeared into the veldt and was not heard from again for several years. The enquiry agent whom I engaged finally discovered that Naudé had settled down somewhere near a village called Bethulie, close by Trompsburg. By then it was too late to

---

48 This event, attributed to Moriarty's agent, concluded *The Valley of Fear*.

chase the felon. He had sided with the Boers in their uprising, either as mercenary or partisan, and was shot dead on Christmas Day 1900 in a skirmish with our infantry. His remains were identified by those who knew him. There is nothing else to be done there, Watson. He was a bad man who came to a bad end."

"Not bad enough," I grumbled, remembering our last parting with Mr and Mrs Douglas as they fled England for refuge in South Africa. "What then of this mask-maker whom Moriarty paid?"

"A specialist on the West Bank of the Seine," Holmes reported. He passed me a promotional pamphlet for *Monsieur* Pape of Avenue Laplace, Arcuil, advertising a variety of facemasks and plaster busts, including custom death masks, made in life or posthumously.

"People still buy such things?" I wondered.

"Evidently so. My own timeline of Moriarty's movements has a gap for 8th and 9th February 1891, with indications that he may have crossed the channel to France. That corresponds to the payment entry in this notebook. I have wired *Monsieur* Dubugue of the Paris constabulary to enquire of Pape's whether they retain any record of purchase or collection of the item."

Holmes had not yet finished illustrating the wealth of evidence in our case. "Next we come to statements collected by the police at the Victoria incident. Here are the usual conflicting set of witnesses and would-be witnesses, recorded by Lestrade's ham-fisted officers of the law. Even so, there is enough testimony here to adduce that our murderous rifleman was actually a riflewoman, likely the same female who accosted us in Baker Street."

"Were those ruffians at the luggage office working for her, then? Why did she shoot her own man?"

Holmes tapped his next bundle of papers. "Interrogation of the low-life whom we captured reveals that they did not know the identity of their employer. All assumed it was a man. The seafaring bravo who took a .303 to the cranium was the one who hired the rest and the only intermediary with whomever funded their activities."

"Which is why his employer killed him," I surmised. "To silence him when he was captured."

"Just so, Watson. It was he who instructed the others to look for us, to search the station. We were expected."

"And he is silenced."

Holmes made an expressive moue. "His voice is stilled but he still has much to tell us. My examination offers much more useful information to add to our stacks." He took up a lithograph and coroners report. "The man's tattoos, for example, are a history of his travels. The oldest suggest he first sailed in the Tropics, probably the Caribbean, but the style of his newer disfigurements suggest he worked the Gold Coast and then the Cape. His faded tan indicates an approximate time of his return to England, around two months ago. Calluses on his hands and feet suggest his role as a sailor was a humble one."

I knew my friend by now. "You have identified him."

Holmes nodded acknowledgement. He tapped the shipping manifests he had lately laid out. "Our dead seaman is Edward Clark, although he has employed other travelling names. He returned to England as a hand on the packet *Ariadne* from Capetown, arriving and cashing out at Southampton on 17th March. His whereabouts between then and his reappearance to interrupt our treasure hunt are still unknown."

"How did he become recruited by our adversary, then?" I puzzled.

"How indeed? A gunny-sack in his lodgings contained £40 in bank-notes when he died, presumably to pay his confederates. I have asked that the numbers on the notes be traced but I have no great hope of our opponent being careless enough to allow such a trail to be followed. A woman who is ruthless and resourceful enough to shoot her own minion, who would seize random innocent boys and girls from the streets as a back-up plan, and who would slice one child's throat as a mere distraction to prevent pursuit, is unlikely to make so rudimentary a mistake as to leave a cash trail."

"A woman dispatched the mask to us in the first place," I remembered.

"It may be the same person," Holmes considered, "but then who burgled Baker Street to steal the item? Someone undoubtedly wanted me to trace Moriarty's buried manuscript and was prepared to follow up and relieve us of it, but did the murderess act for herself or on another's behalf?"

He returned to his listing of the hundred or more details he had gleaned in his investigation so far, and the forensic detail with which he prosecuted each. He was right that such myriad data made for poor storytelling. Suffice that Holmes had inspected the dead and the living; had traced and examined the carriage that had snatched the children; had investigated the circumstances under which Moriarty's package had come to us; had reviewed the likely time and method by which the manuscript had come to be concealed beneath the signal box; had pieced together a partial chart of movements of the late Edward Clark; had initiated enquires into the commissioning and collection of the death mask at Pape's; had chased the identity of Moran's feminine visitor; and had in short turned that vast intellect and unstoppable logic to grind the myriad elements of the disturbing events into some irrreductable truth.

For my part, less methodical and inspired creature that I am, I had only one original idea. "Holmes," I ventured. "I have recently encountered a lady newly returned from South Africa, like Clark, who may have travelled on the *Ariadne*. She struck me as a formidable and capable woman."

Holmes regarded me with amusement. "You wish to know more of the woman who made such an impression on you at Doyle's event," he teased. "Well, who knows whether she might have some insight into the case that may be useful?"

"I am not in the habit of tracking down widows," I insisted.

"Then it is probably significant that you are considering tracking this one," Holmes suggested.

I left Holmes to further cover our floor with his investigation.

—／｜＼—

A Report About Mr Martin Beck
Thursday, 8th May, two days before Houdini's disappearance:

Beck was the first to admit that being manager and promoter of Mr Harry Houdini was not a typical job. Most men behind successful stage acts had to worry about venue bookings, crew discipline, receipts, returns, staging, publicity. Many had to try and rein in their difficult principals, cover up their star's indiscretions and mistakes, fend off angry creditors or outraged spouses.

Few had to worry about their client solving murders, exposing criminals, uncovering supernatural frauds, and taking on rich, powerful fanatics; in-between designing new ways to risk their life before a paying audience.

No other manager had to try and keep up with such a fertile, brilliant, and devious mind as that of Houdini.

Over the time since Beck had first wired Houdini to hire him in Chicago, 1889, the impresario had developed a catalogue of methods to make the attempt.

"Well?" he asked the page at the Bridge House Hotel, slipping one of the odd heavy British half-crowns to the lad wearing the pillbox hat.

"What you said," Bobby answered, pocketing the tip. "Your bloke, 'e slipped out using the fire escape. Odd, it were. He dodged out there and crouched down right sudden, like 'e didn't want to be seen, or else like 'e thought someone would throw somefink at 'im. Then 'e scuttles down the stairs right sharpish, ducking and weaving all over. Not drunk, like. Real slick, like a boxer on his toes. He vanishes off down the back alley and disappears across London Bridge."

"What time was this?"

"About oneish this morning by the reception clock."

"How long was he gone?"

The page boy was used to certain residents slipping out by night to enjoy the pleasures of London. He wasn't comfortable with those same guests returning unseen. "I'm sorry, sir. I di'n't see 'im come back. I don't know 'ow he got in. I thought 'e was still out this morning 'till he rang for 'is paper."

Beck proffered an additional sixpence and asked to be shown the roof. There, on the flat part nearest to the adjacent building, lay the thirty-foot plank that Houdini had used to return to his chambers. The agent saw no need to share his deduction with his informant.

"I want to know if my friend slips up to here, too," he amended his instructions.

"Right you are, sir," Bobby replied cheerfully, pleased at the prospect of additional remuneration. He hesitated, though. "Um… if someone else was wanting to know about your friend's movements an' all, what should I tell 'em?"

Beck frowned. "Who else has been asking?"

The page blushed. "Couple of coves, at different times. A toff slipped some silver to Jenny as changes the beds, and there were a bloke in a bowler as 'ad a word wi' Stan 'oo does the day shift. And there were this ugly-lookin' bruiser what 'as 'ad his nose busted for 'im sometime, what gave me a clip round the ear for my sauce and wanted to know which room Mr 'Oudini were in. I told 'im wrong, though."

"Thanks for that," Beck responded. "Let me know if anyone else comes asking, with a good description and anything else you can get on them." He dug into his waistcoat and proffered another silver half-crown bearing the head of the old queen on it. "Be careful though. Sounds like these folks are up to no good." He thought again and drew a printed cardboard slip out too. "Here. Couple of free passes for Mr Houdini's gala show on Monday night. Bring your best girl."

Bobby beamed in delight. "I'll keep a real special eye out, Mister Beck, I promise yer!"

"You do that. We've got to watch Mr Houdini's back, after all."

The lad pelted back down the stairs to resume his station. Beck leaned against the brick wall of the stairwell stack and sighed. "Harry, what have you gotten yourself into this time? And why don't you want me to know?"

He descended to find a cab to the Strand, knowing that when he finally worked out what was happening it was bound to be worse than he expected.

From the account of John Watson MD:
Thursday, 8ᵗʰ May, two days before Houdini's disappearance:

Beck and I met again that afternoon at the Savoy Bar and Grill. He greeted me heartily in the American manner to which I had become accustomed during my stay in San Francisco. "Good to see you again, Watson. Your friend makes headlines even easier than mine does!"

He referred to the articles recounting the Victoria Station shooting that had been quick to report the presence of the great detective. "We could have done without the press interest," I admitted. "Fortunately our housekeeper has a talent for shooing away reporters. With a broom, on occasion."

"That's a difference between us," Beck chuckled. "Column inches equal seats filled for Harry Houdini. That's why he's appearing at a challenge from the Locksmith's Guild tonight, to tweak a few noses and keep the presses rolling towards our Tower Bridge stunt on Saturday."

"Holmes is indifferent to pressmen," I responded. "They have learned to their cost not to press him too hard. He is not above reeling off analyses of their personal habits and indiscretions in front of their colleagues."

Beck snorted. We were interrupted by the arrival of our food, this time a splendid chop with green vegetables and a dollop of French mustard. For a time our conversation halted in salute to the chef's efforts.[49]

---

49 The Savoy's manager from 1890 had been César Ritz, who with chef Auguste Escoffier had established it as a fashionable venue for fine dining. However, these men were dismissed in 1897 over the disappearance of £3,400 of fine wines ($500,000 in modern money) and for "receiving gifts" from suppliers. They subsequently purchased Simpson's-in-the-Strand and established the Ritz Hotel. At the time of our story the Savoy was managed by George Reeves-Smith, who held the post from 1900 for a remarkable forty-one years.

We chatted companionably. I mentioned some details of the reason Holmes and I had left London so quickly two days before, although of course I did not identify Sir Robert Norberton or Shoscombe Old Place. Beck listened fascinated to the details of our enquiry and its eventual solution thanks to a frightened black spaniel.[50]

At last my dining companion set aside his knife and fork and asked, "Do you happen to know any good private detectives? Not Holmes, I mean. Regular enquiry agents, like the Pinkertons we have in the States."

"There are a few men that Holmes calls upon for routine investigations. It depends upon the character of the case to which he might turn." I viewed Beck speculatively. "Have you some need of such a man?"

"Perhaps. Or a bodyguard, maybe. I'm just not sure."

The waiter cleared our plates. Another glided in with the sorbet.

"Can you tell me the nature of your concern?" I ventured.

Beck hesitated. He fidgeted with the pince-nez spectacles that perched on his rounded nose, and prodded his dessert with a spoon. "Houdini can sometimes be secretive," he admitted at last. "That's part of the nature of a showman like him. He loves to deliver the grand surprises."

"I know what that's like," I admitted with feeling. Holmes' taste for the theatrical had not left him when he had retired from the stage.

"An illusionist must be a master of misdirection. Often Houdini undertakes ventures that require deception or discretion. He sometimes gets involved in...not cases like those of your great friend, Watson, but Houdini has a keen sense of natural justice. He cannot abide fraud, or bullying, or misuse of trust. When he encounters those things he tends to...respond."

"I'm aware from the papers that he has been instrumental in exposing some very shoddy practices and people."

"Yes. I'm proud that he does that. Not just because the publicity helps fill seats but because, well, a man of Houdini's limitless talent *should* employ it for the public good. But sometimes I worry that he'll get in over his head."

I nodded. "I know what that is like."

"Of course. Holmes went missing, presumed dead, for two-three years, didn't he? You must understand exactly the anxiety a man might feel when a friend is endangered by doing the right thing."

---

50 On 6th May 1902, Holmes took a case presented by the head trainer John Mason from the racing stables at Shoscombe Old Place, Berkshire, which required a sudden trip to discover the truth about the behaviour of the owner of champion horse Shoscombe Prince. The investigation is chronicled in "The Adventure of Shoscombe Old Place" in *The Case-Book of Sherlock Holmes*.

"You have some special concern for Houdini just now?" I surmised.

"Well, usually when he gets up to some shenanigans he fills me in eventually, lets me know what he's up to—or at least what he's into. Right now he's cut me out, and I'm certain there's something amiss. I want to help but I don't know how."

"That's only natural. The problem is that sometimes well-meaning interference can cause more problems than it solves. I've learned to be careful blundering into Holmes' work, for fear of upsetting some plan he's laid."

"And I have confidence in Harry, for sure. But I can't help this feeling that maybe he's in trouble and he can't tell me for some reason."

We paid attention to the sorbet and awaited the Turkish coffee. "What would you ask an enquiry agent to do? Follow Houdini?" I was thinking of Mercer, the enquiry agent whom Holmes used as a general utility investigator.[51]

"Keeping up with Harry would require an extraordinary talent," Beck cautioned. "No, I was wondering if perhaps he might check up on a couple of other points."

"Such as?"

"Well, first off, some folks have been buying information about Houdini's movements from the staff at our hotel. Different people, I think, at least three of them. I'd like to know who they are and what they're up to. And then there's this."

Beck produced a telegram flimsy from his inner pocket and passed it over to me.

++ ANOTHER PERSON ENQUIRED ABOUT L'INCONNU TODAY STOP INFORMING YOU AS AGREED STOP ARRANGED MEETING 3PM AT GALLERY STOP ATTEND? STOP PIXLEY ++

"Who is this Pixley?" I asked.

"No idea," the impresario replied. "I've never heard of him and I've no idea how Houdini knows him. This wire came for Houdini just before I left, but he's already at rehearsal and he won't be back till after four. I don't want to pull him away from his practise time anyhow."

I glanced at my watch. "It's quarter to two. There's no time to call an investigator to chase down this Pixley."

"I know," Beck replied. "I was kind of hoping you might be free to accompany me."

"I should be glad to. But to which gallery and to what unknown might we be attending?"

---

51 Mercer is mentioned in canon in "The Adventure of the Creeping Man" from *The Case-Book of Sherlock Holmes*.

There Beck was uncertain.

I applied Holmes' methods as best I could. "This telegram's office of origin is Trafalgar Square," I pointed out. "That's right across from the National Gallery. It was sent at 10:41 today, which was probably someone's morning break. I suggest we find out if there's a Pixley works at that Gallery."

"Makes sense. How can we do that?"

I called over a waiter and asked if they had a telephone line. Thereafter it was a simple matter to place a call to the National Gallery and confirm that their staff included a Mr Pixley who catalogued their pottery collection.

"Amazing," Beck marvelled. "In less than ten minutes you have cleared up half the mystery."

"This is simple routine," I assured him. "By now Holmes would be telling you what Pixley had for breakfast yesterday. Let's finish our meal and go over to see what this fellow can tell us."

━╱╲╮╾

Pixley had one of the basement offices beneath the National Gallery, far away from William Wilkins' columned façade and the marbled entrance foyer.[52] A porter shepherded us down dusty brick corridors to a cluttered room.

A lady waited there. She stood uncertainly as we entered. "Mr Pixley…?" she began, then paused and paled as she recognised us. "Dr Watson?"

"Mrs Kent," Beck responded, recovering quicker than me. "What a pleasure to encounter you again."

The visitor awaiting the pottery expert was indeed the same firebrand who had accosted Doyle at his launch, the very woman whom I had determined to track down regarding her possible travel on the *Ariadne*. "Ma'am," I greeted her, fumbling to catch my wits.

"How did you find me?" she asked, taking a step back then forcing herself to stand still. "How did Holmes know?"

"Know what?" I puzzled.

"About…" She hesitated and clamped her mouth shut. "What brings you here?"

---

52 The National Gallery on Trafalgar Square is the third building to house the collection. It was designed by William Watkins in 1832-7 and was at the time criticised for its lack of space and "aesthetic deficiencies". Only the façade of that building now remains fronting a building that has been modified and expanded many times.

"We have some questions for Mr Pixley," Beck told her, smiling charmingly. "About *l'Inconnu*."

Mrs Kent looked at him sharply. "What do you know of her?"

"Her?" I was still struggling to keep up.

"My friend Mr Houdini has an interest," Beck replied. "But perhaps you already know about that?"

"Houdini?" Mrs Kent's brows furrowed. "The stage performer?"

"The same."

"Why would he wish to know about…"? Again the widow halted mid-speech. "My appointment is with Mr Pixley."

I would have asked the porter where the curator had gone but the fellow had vanished. "We were hoping to speak with Pixley also, Mrs Kent. It was not our intention to disturb you."

She looked sceptical. "Really? You just happen to be here, now, by mere coincidence?"

"Mr Pixley knew of Houdini's interest in *l'Inconnu*," Beck explained. I had to admire the chap's cheek and bluff. "He tipped off Houdini that you wanted a chat about…her. Houdini wasn't available so I popped along instead. Dr Watson was good enough to be my native guide."

"Pardon my curiosity, Mrs Kent," I chimed in. "You seemed distinctly unhappy to see me just now. I trust I did not offend you at our earlier meeting."

She turned her gaze back to me. "No. Nothing like that. I just…hadn't expected to see you, Dr Watson. Not here."

"You seemed to expect Sherlock Holmes might have tracked you down," Beck pressed. "Any special reason why a detective might be hunting you?"

"Any reason why that might be your business?" the lady flared at Beck.

I stepped between them before Houdini's manager had his eyes scratched out. "Again, my apologies for intruding, Mrs Kent. We came to Pixley hoping to learn something of *l'Inconnu*. He seemed to think you wanted to pick his brain on the same subject. May we know the reason for your interest?"

"For *my* interest?" Mrs Kent hissed. She was a splendid figure of woman when she was angry. She gestured to one of the casts on Pixley's wall, that common muse mask of the innocent-looking young lady one sees on studio walls everywhere these days. "Why should I not care about her?"

"*That* is *l'Inconnu*?" I realised. I looked more closely at the plaster face. I had seen that mask recently—beneath the hood of the mystery woman who had taken Moriarty's manuscript.

"Of course it is," Mrs Kent scorned, as if it were self-evident.

"And what is she to you?" Beck demanded.

Mrs Kent glared at the impresario. "She is my sister."

"Your sister?" I echoed. "Do you know where she was last Sunday night?"

The lady turned that angry stare on me. "Do you mock me now?" she demanded. "My sister has been dead these fifteen years!"

Her anger crumbled to grief. I was appalled to see my clumsy enquiry had brought her to tears. "Mrs Kent, please accept my abject apology. I perceive that I have stumbled ignorantly into some deep and complicated sorrow, and am doing harm where I intend none. Please do not be upset by my colossal bumbling. I promise you it was not intended to offend or hurt."

Beck also looked at the cast. "I've seen dozens of these," he muttered to himself. "I never knew who she was meant to be."

"No-one knows who she was," Mrs Kent told him. "No-one except me."

I held out a chair so the lady could sit down. "You said she was your sister. Would you tell us the circumstances of your story? Please?"

"Why should I?" Mrs Kent asked defiantly.

"For several reasons. You know who I am, and of my association with Holmes. We are currently working on a case which involves a mask such as the one you call *l'Inconnu*, so any information you have might be helpful. A man has been killed, several others injured, and a child nearly died from a cut throat. You will see why whatever data you can offer would be important. Also, Mr Beck is following-up on his friend Houdini's interest and earlier visit to Mr Pixley regarding *l'Inconnu*. Finally, if you will pardon the impertinence, you appear to be in distress, and it offends my better instincts to encounter a lady in need and not proffer what aid I may. Mrs Kent, please confide in us so we can clarify this murky affair and assist you."

"At least until Pixley shows up," Beck added.

Mrs Kent quickly composed herself. She sat rigid in her seat, her eyes turned towards the sweet-faced mask that hung over Pixley's desk. "I was married in '85," she began. "Giles Kent was a geological surveyor by profession and a social reformer by temperament. His political leanings sometimes got in the way of lucrative employment, so shortly after our wedding he accepted a position with a mining engineering company in their Paris office and we moved to live there. Giles' mother was from Normandy so his French was excellent. Giles' orphaned sisters Amile and Yve, then thirteen and seven years old, lived in our household."

The lady's expression tightened. "Amile was fifteen when she ran away from home; eloped, her parting note claimed. Giles and I were desperate, but appeals to the police, to my family, to the British embassy were all useless. Then, on November 3rd 1887, some four weeks after Amile's disappearance, Giles told me that he had discovered information about her whereabouts. He left home to find her and never returned. I was told that his horse threw him and he broke his neck."

Beck whistled softly.

"You can perhaps imagine the difficulty of my position," Mrs Kent went on. "Alone in Paris except for little Yve, suddenly bereaved, friendless and somewhat short of funds. It was only by the financial kindness of an uncle that I was able to survive. It was almost four months later when I recognised a plaster cast on a studio wall as the face of Giles' missing sister."

My heart heaved in sympathy for the lady. "What did you do?" I ventured.

"I tracked down the potter, of course. He had a crate of the masks ready for shipping. They were evidently his most popular line. He told me they were a death-mask he was commissioned to take of a suicide who had been lifted from the Seine the previous year, only three days after Giles' fatal fall. By the time I spoke with him the girl had been buried in a common grave for three months. I could not even trace which pauper's plot she was interred in. But I am certain that it—the mask, the dead girl—was Amile Kent.

"I tried everything I could to discover what had happened to her. Where had she gone, and with whom? All to no avail. For fifteen years I have had to live with the mystery, while Amile's image hangs on every artist's wall to remind me of her loss."

"Yet you kept l'Inconnu's identity secret," Beck noted.

"What business is it of the world, of those sentimental poets who call her their muse, who she really was? But even now I am striving to discover what really happened. After all this time I have a thread to follow. Now I can…"

We were interrupted by the door slamming open. Two rough fellows in balaclava helmets stood there, pointing pistols. "Come with us, Mrs Kent!" one of them called before he registered that she was not alone in the room.

I hurled a chair at his head and closed the distance to knock aside his pistol and grapple him. "Look to the other, Beck!" I shouted out.

"Oh, for sure!" the rounded impresario replied unhappily. But he pressed forward all the same, intercepting the second man who was trying to get a clear shot at me as I wrestled his partner in crime.

Mrs Kent waded in, shouldering Beck's thug into a high stack of box files that tumbled down around him.

The distraction proved helpful. I managed to get a firm grip on my assailant's wrist and I'm certain I snapped something there, carpal or ulna. In any case he yelped and shied back.

At the same time, the porter must have recognised that something was happening downstairs and began to raise a fuss.

Beck's ruffian caught him a good stomach-punch, folding the manager over wheezing. The criminal looked for a moment at Mrs Kent, correctly calculated that he was unlikely to be able to extract her from the building as planned, and instead buffeted me aside to haul my injured opponent away.

Both men had lost their guns by now. Mrs Kent retrieved one of them and fired after the retreating attackers with inexpert enthusiasm.

I picked up the other revolver. "Come on, man!" I called out, heaving Beck to his feet. "After 'em!"

The poor chap staggered after me gamely, winded as he was. Two middle-aged fellows chased a pair of masked thugs along the under-corridors of the National Gallery.

A third balaclavad man lurked by the stairs, presumably to help with Mrs Kent's abduction. He raised a handgun and fired down at us, forcing Beck and I to take cover.

The three kidnappers retreated away and escaped into the throng of Trafalgar Square. By the time I was able to summon a constable it was too late to find them. All they need do to disappear was to pull off their masks and climb into any one of the two-score carriages parked around the monument.

"I regret that excellent lunch now," panted Beck. "What was that all about? Does any of this make sense to you? Could these be the people Houdini has upset?"

"Looks as if we've stumbled into something, at any rate," I admitted. "While the police arrive we had better look to Mrs Kent and see what she can tell us."

We were delayed for a moment by the porters' discovery of Mr Pixley, knocked unconscious and trussed in a broom cupboard close by his office. Whilst I examined the ambushed curator Beck hurried on to see to the lady.

He emerged from Pixley's office stricken. "Watson! Mrs Kent is gone!"

A Report About Mr Martin Beck
Thursday, 8th May, two days before Houdini's disappearance:

"Houdini, what aren't you telling me?"

The great escapologist looked up from studying the papers of John Henry Anderson, 'the Great Wizard of the North'.[53] "Did you have a particular secret in mind, Beck?"

The manager considered confronting Houdini with what he knew of the escapologist's secret entrances and exits from the hotel, or about the men who seemed so interested in his movements. He particularly wanted to bring up *l'Inconnu*, Houdini's interest in the mask or the girl it depicted. He hoped to discuss with his friend the events of that afternoon at the National Gallery, and the revelations and subsequent disappearance of Mrs Morgaine Kent.

He chose instead to say, "I'm just concerned that you seem under a lot of pressure, Harry. Is there anything you need me to help out with?"

"You mean apart from you arranging the tour, booking the venues, dealing with management, hiring the crew, shifting the props, handling the press, fending off the insurers, arranging travel, getting us permits, and calming down Mrs DuGrasse the mad costumier? I thought that was all pretty helpful."

"Yes. Anything else? Any... problem you haven't mentioned."

Houdini shook his head. "Nothing I need bother you with, Beck."

"No side-adventure that I might need filling in about?"

"Nothing." Houdini produced a flask from his inner jacket pocket and sipped the water it contained.

"You're not eating or drinking what the hotel supplies," Beck observed.

Houdini held up the silver flask. "This is healthier for me. I'm in training."

"Harry, you *would* let me know if you were in some kind of jam, wouldn't you?"

"Beck, I promise you that if there was anything I should be telling you about, I'd tell you. Don't let pre-show jitters eat you up, man."

"So everything is fine for Saturday?"

"Saturday, Beck, is going to be very memorable."

---

53 John Henry Anderson (1814-1874), whom Sir Walter Scott dubbed "the Great Wizard of the North", was one of the first stage-magicians and a pioneer in the field of magical illusion. Houdini, born the same year as Anderson died, cited him as one of his heroes and inspirations. When Houdini discovered that Anderson's grave at Aberdeen was in disrepair he paid for its regular upkeep.

In twenty-one years of association with Mr Sherlock Holmes one inevitably picks up something of his methods.

From the account of John Watson MD
Thursday, 8th May, two days before Houdini's disappearance:

In twenty-one years of association with Mr Sherlock Holmes one inevitably picks up something of his methods. I had not previously bent that experience to tracking down a distressed young widow in teeming London but I now discovered that I was well-suited for such a task.

I might have asked Holmes for his assistance. I would have laid before him the whole perplexing matter of the attempted abduction at the National Gallery and that strange account of the eloped sister had it not been for my friend's sudden absence from Baker Street. A hasty note left warning for Mrs Hudson of his intentions to be away again for "a night or so". It averted our housekeeper's intense frustration but did little to supply us with information about why the great detective might choose to abscond. It was not, however, atypical of Holmes to disappear without trace into the criminal underworld on some subtle investigation.

Even without Holmes I was able to acquire the lodging address of Mrs Kent, not from the charitable society where she volunteered, not from Doyle and his officious secretary Galpin, but rather from the steamer company who had forwarded on her trunks; Mrs Kent had indeed returned to England upon the *Ariadne*.

Unfortunately, according to testimony of a landlady who had been compensated for two weeks' accommodation in advance, the lady had quit her Seymour Street rooms "rather abruptly not these two hours since".

From what I could gather, Mrs Kent must have slipped away while Beck and I were chasing down would-be kidnappers in balaclava helmets, returned immediately to her neat, modest rooms on Seymour Street, and made a hasty departure before any pursuer could find her again.

A shilling gained me access to the lady's former accommodation. Holmes might have vented that the place had been cleaned (although cleaned imperfectly in my opinion; Mrs Hudson would certainly not have passed it). I was interested more in seeing where the lady had chosen to live on her return to England.

The abandoned lodgings were a three-room affair, a suite of sitting room, bedroom, and somewhat paltry kitchen, with a bathroom down a hall landing. It was the digs of someone who was passing through, or perhaps of someone so busy as to not care or have time for finding a more congenial home.

Nor was it a place where Yve, tragic Amile's younger sibling who would now be twenty-four years old, might stay with her widowed sister-in-law. I wondered what had become of that other orphan in Mrs Kent's care.

The vanished tenant had left no forwarding address, bundling her things into a hired trap and disappearing without any explanation. I examined the grate for ashes of burned correspondence, at first irritated that it may have been cleaned away, then embarrassed to realise that it was May and there would have been no hearth-fire to dispose of paperwork.

Instead I checked the house's dust-bin, which stood unemptied in the yard at the rear of the premises. This messy business won me a pair of discarded envelopes, the one stamped by the National Union of Women's Suffrage Societies, the other a private correspondence in a woman's hand on which there was no return address.

Also discarded was a quite mundane shopping list of grocery items in Mrs Kent's own hand—and that handwriting was familiar to me!

I had seen a script like that before, neat, cultured, and feminine. Holmes would have been able to make a definitive judgement, but I could only note that the fist looked very much like that on the envelope directing Moriarty's death mask to us.

I remembered again those lively green eyes widening in dismay as she recognised me in Pixley's office. How had Holmes discovered her, she had wondered, that women who had posted that strange souvenir to us five days before.

I confess to a pang of disappointment that the splendid Morgaine Kent might be the villain of the piece.

I was unwilling to give up the trail, however. The second envelope, though devoid of any return address, did have a franked stamp that offered a date and location for the post office from which it had been sent. The letter had arrived only two days ago, posted at Stratton Street beside Berkley Square.

I considered Mrs Kent's position: newly returned to England without any close friend with whom she might stay, hunted for some reason by ruthless masked men, setting in motion events leading to the recovery of a manuscript hidden by the late Professor Moriarty. Where might she turn in need if not to the only personal correspondent of whom I was aware?

Lumm was the man I needed. It was to that grizzled cabbie that Holmes most often turned to discover the movements of those who had used public Hackney carriages for their London journeys. Lumm would check the travel logs of the major companies and could usually, given a start time and date and a general end destination, discover the address to which a cab might have delivered its passenger.

The old coachman was happy to take my money and research me an answer. I did not correct his assumption that the enquiry actually came from Holmes. Word from him reached me within an hour, of a journey starting at 5:15 pm on Seymour Street, conveying a well-dressed woman with half a dozen suitcases and bags and a travel trunk to a particular address in Berkley Square.

The *London Gazetteer* supplied the owner of the townhouse in question. This was the first time I heard of Major Sir Horace Saxhallow.

It was eight o'clock when I called upon the address. The lamplighters were just progressing through the streets igniting the gas mantles before dusk. I approached the Berkley Square townhouse and presented my card. "I am seeking Mrs Kent," I explained to the superior footman who answered the door.

It was late for a social visit, especially from an uninvited stranger. For a moment I expected to be tossed down the steps onto the pavement. The servant was certainly large enough to do it. It was that momentary hesitation that gave me pause, before he replied, "I will enquire whether Mrs Kent is at home."

I was left on the doorstep while he vanished inside. Through the partly-open door I was able to see a black and white tiled floor and a sweeping staircase. The layout was thin and long like all London townhouses, but no expense had been spared on the home. I was intrigued to see several pieces of African origin mounted along the stairwell wall.

Presently the footman returned. "Mrs Kent regrets that she is unable to receive you at this hour. She asks if you would be so good as to return tomorrow at the hour of eleven."

"I shall," I agreed. "Please convey to the lady that I only wish to assure myself of her wellbeing after her unpleasant experience at the National Gallery and to render what assistance I can in resolving the situation which prompted it."

The footman nodded noncommittally and closed the door.

Holmes' influence on me told, though. Before I left, I engaged the lamplighter in conversation. From that old infantryman I learned that the Saxhallows had only recently returned to London from the Major's service in South Africa.

─୬|៶─

A Report About Mr Martin Beck
Friday, 9th May, one day before Houdini's disappearance:

Mr Galpin set aside his coffee, trying to disguise his distaste for the beverage, and gestured to the documents on the table before him. "Consider the proposal, Mr Beck. I cannot see how a man of your considerable business acumen can fail to be attracted by the proposition."

Martin Beck sighed. "Look, Galpin, I'll be straight with you. Harry Houdini is not shy of publicity, and he's very happy making money. But if we decide to go into the publishing business and tell stories about him, we don't really need you or Mr Doyle to handle it for us."

"Who better?" Galpin challenged. "You've seen what we have done for Sherlock Holmes. When Dr Watson's latest account came out last week they were queuing down the block for copies. Imagine the publicity a Harry Houdini series might generate. Imagine the income."

"Sure. And Harry likes Doyle, I know. But that doesn't make this a smart option, Galpin. Watson doesn't really care about the money. He only wants to show the world how his buddy does good things, so he doesn't read the small print as long as Doyle doesn't mess up the stories too much. Me, I'm Houdini's manager, and it's my job to read the small print."

Galpin sat back in the stuffed armchair in the Bridge House Coffee Lounge. "We can finesse the detail, Mr Beck. I'm talking about the principle here. A series of adventures featuring Harry Houdini, running first in one of the weekly periodicals then collected in book form. The material doesn't have to be from life. We can find any number of decent ghost-writers desperate for a commission who can offer some kind of fictional narrative."

"I'm not saying it's a bad idea," Beck responded, "I'm saying that if we go for it then there's really no need for us to involve you or Mr Doyle. Houdini is keen to retain final oversight over everything with his name on it. While we're travelling round Europe he can hardly keep a track on a story a week in some Brit publication, can he? For that matter, why would we set up using the London press? We'd go to New York or Chicago or San Francisco or somewhere, to catch the U.S. market.[54] Sorry, Galpin, but you've got to tell Doyle 'no' on this one. I hope there's no hard feelings."

Doyle's personal secretary pursed his lips. "You've been candid with me, Mr Beck, so let me return the compliment."

---

54 J.C. Henneberger eventually commissioned a fictional adventure featuring Harry Houdini for seminal American pulp magazine *Weird Tales*. "Imprisoned With the Pharaohs", ghost-written by H.P. Lovecraft, appeared in the May-June 1924 edition.

Beck breathed hard. "Oh boy!"

"Mr Houdini has become something of a success with his European tour. He is presently better known here and on the Continent than in the United States. You have signalled your intention to continue your grand tour eastwards, into Hungary and Russia and who knows where before returning in what you hope will be triumph and a blaze of publicity to launch yourselves back in your homeland. But there are risks. The biggest risk is Houdini himself."

"How do you figure that?"

"Mr Beck, your principal lives a very dangerous lifestyle. He risks his life nightly on stage for the entertainment of the masses. One slip, one error, and your meal ticket is gone. One miscalculation and you are back to booking vaudeville acts for second-rate theatres in your Midwest dustbowl. It is hubris to turn down a solid contract now and gamble on some future success depending on your client's survival."

Beck reddened in anger. "Is that so? Well that client is also my best friend, buster. He's a helluva lot more than a meal ticket. I'd drop every contract I ever won rather than see him hurt, and I'd sure drop *you* like an apple with a maggot in it. I don't play the odds on his living or dying to line my pocket and I don't like guys who think I do—or whose minds work that way. So maybe we'd better call this meeting done, Galpin, as a punch in the teeth often offends."

━ノ\ヾ━

From the account of John Watson MD
Friday, 9th May, one day before Houdini's disappearance:

I called upon Mrs Kent as instructed, only to be told that she was no longer resident with the Saxhallows at Berkley Square. "Mrs Kent regrets being unable to keep her appointment," a different large retainer told me at the doorstep. "Good day."

"Might I see the master of the house?" I enquired.

"The Major is not at home."

"The lady, then?"

"Lady Saxhallow is preparing for a social function this evening. She is not available to speak with strangers."

When the door was closed on me again I sauntered across the road to where a boot-black urchin was squatting beside the railing to the private garden in the middle of the square.

"Well, Wallace?" I asked him.

"You wus right, Dr Watson," the young rascal of Holmes' 'Baker Street Irregulars' told me with a cheeky grin. "About 'alf past nine this mornin' it'd be, by the chimes, when this big coach comes up to collect the lady. Posh job, it were, not a hire cab, wiv a coat-of-arms an' that. Nice pair of 'orses too. I likes 'orses."

"I don't suppose you happened to overhear where the driver was directed?" I prompted Wallace.

"Nossir. But I did perch meself on the board at the back an' go wiv 'em, like."

Holmes picks his street lads well. "That was a bit of smart thinking, lad," I congratulated him.

"Thanks, guv. Anyways, we went down 'cross Piccadilly, past Queen's Park and the Palace, then dahn to the river and over Lambeth Bridge. I wus startin' to get a bit worried that we'd go right off my patch out into the countryside or sumfing, but we jest ran along the Albert Embankment for a bit and turned left 'afore Vauxhall Bridge. When the coach rattled towards some big black wooden gates in this 'igh wall I decided it was time for me to 'op off, so I did 'afore it disappeared inside."

"Where was the place?"

"Dunno. No marking on, but I took the street address. Jonathan Road, it were, off of Vauxhall Walk."

"What then?"

"I waited a bit to see if aught 'else 'appened. I wus just thinking I'd better leg it back 'ere to meet you at eleven when the gates opened again and out comes that posh carriage, only this time wiv a fellah in the back. Geezer in morning dress. So when the wagon goes past I nips back on and cops a free lift back 'ere, see? And 'ere I am."

I smiled back at the rascal and dropped a half crown into his hands. "I'll be sure to tell Holmes how well you did," I promised.

"'Fanks, boss!" Wallace called out before he sped away back to his own streets. My precautionary deployment of a useful idler had been well worth it.

I hailed a cab to take me south of the Thames to hunt down Wallace's black gates.

━╱╎╲━

A Report About Mr Martin Beck
Friday, 9th May, one day before Houdini's disappearance:

Clifford was the man recommended by Mercer, the enquiry agent that Holmes occasionally used for routine investigations. Clifford was a phlegmatic fellow of middle years with a growing paunch and a comic red nose, but he knew his business.

"You was asking about them blokes what was asking about Mr Houdini," the investigator told Beck.

"That's why I engaged you, yes."

"Well, I think I might have something for you. Quite a few interesting bits."

"Spill them then. Don't keep me in suspense."

Since Beck wasn't taking the hint to offer him a drink from the Scotch bottle on the dresser, Clifford got on with his report. "First off, this hotel is being watched. *Seriously* watched. And not just by one person or even one team. I reckon there must be two or three outfits, each separately keeping an eye on the place."

"The Bridge House is under observation? By who? What for?"

"Well, I reckon it's got to be Mr Houdini they're set on. There's one bunch with field glasses in a flat over the ironmonger's business across the way. There's another lot who seem to like pretending to be cabbies, which makes me think they're not local because the actual cabbies fingered them to me right away. I think there might be a third crew who've just booked in here as guests, but it's hard to be sure."

"Can we find one and ask him?"

"Could do, but they look like tough nuts to me. I'd want some company."

"And the people behind these extraordinary spies?"

"Well that's another interesting bit. Did you hear about a couple of thugs named Corrigan and Mumby what were arrested on the roof of the Lyceum Theatre last Tuesday? No, I thought not. There were brought in by a pal of yours, old sour-face Bolt, who doesn't stand for nonsense in his cells. But that night Sergeant Bolt was packed off for a long investigation into racketeering in Manchester and the likely lads was bailed out by a smarmy representative of one of our capital's sleazier solicitors."

This was all news to Beck. "What were they doing on the roof of our theatre?"

"By all accounts they were there for Houdini. He evidently took 'em down and left 'em for Scotland Yard. But then someone managed to pull some very serious strings and get them loose."

"Who? Where did they go?"

"Dunno who. To be honest, that's past my range. Someone rich and important enough to lean on a senior officer, that's for sure. And as for Corrigan and Mumby, the whisper is that they won't be turning up for their hearings on account of being fed to the fishies."

Beck blanched. "Dead?"

"Silenced. So the rumour goes, anyhow."

"Harry, what have you gotten into now?"

Clifford shrugged. "This is all getting a bit beyond me, Mr Beck. There's them fellows in balaclava masks at the National Gallery. There's blokes camped out round this hotel. There's killers for rent on the roof of the Lyceum, and somebody willing to finish them off to shut 'em up. It's all too much." The investigator snapped his notebook shut and made a decision. "I won't be able to follow this up no more. It's too risky."

"Maybe if I upped your per diem?"

"Can't spend it if I'm dead. When you set me on this I was thinking jealous husband or maybe professional rival wanting to pinch secrets. But this runs much deeper than that, Mr Beck. Too deep for me. I'm done."

Beck sighed. "Okay. You're out. But is there anything you can tell me, anything at all about any of the various goons who are stomping around pushing my blood pressure up?"

"The bloke what tried to bribe that page behind the desk? He worked for a lady."

From the account of John Watson MD
Friday, 9th May, one day before Houdini's disappearance:

I was hurled bodily into the cellar, landing heavily sprawled across the cold brick floor.

Mrs Kent rushed over to assist me. "Dr Watson!"

My captors closed the door on us, confining us in the gloomy basement.

"Are... are you all right?" I gasped, struggling to regain my wind.

"As well as might be expected considering my confinement," the lady replied with remarkable calm given our circumstances. "May I enquire how you come to be here?"

"We had an appointment for eleven."

Morgaine Kent was dumbfounded for a heartbeat. "You are a very persistent caller," she acknowledged at last.

"I was concerned that you might require assistance. I had hoped to be more use than this."

I sat up and looked around our prison. The cellar ran the full width of the old bottling factory where Mrs Kent had been taken. The only light came through dirt-crusted glass tiles let into narrow casements at each end of the chamber, far too narrow for anyone to escape through. The only door was metal, bolted from the outside.

"How did you find me?" the lady asked. "Is Mr Holmes close by?"

"Not as far as I know," I admitted. "Although he might turn out to be the janitor or the chimney sweep or anyone else, knowing him. As for locating you, your carriage was followed. I called hoping to be of some aid. I admit to being somewhat confused about what aid to render."

"I understand, doctor. Perhaps it is time for me to clarify matters somewhat. Will you come and sit on one of these crates? There is a little food left from the provisions I was given, and a jug of water. Poor hospitality, but one must still do one's best."

I sat while she solemnly served me a rind of bread and a cup of stale water as if we were taking high tea in a society parlour. Morgaine Kent carried her civilisation with her.

"I disliked you intensely for a long time, Dr Watson," she told me suddenly. "It was unfair of me, of course. I apologise."

"Because of my views on Boer camps?" I puzzled.

"Because of your association with Mr Holmes, and because of your accounts of his stories. One of them rather…upset me."

"For that I am profoundly sorry, Mrs Kent. Which story offended you?"

"The one that first alerted me to the truth about a relative whom I had always respected and admired," she replied. "I did not wish to believe your claims about Uncle James, but after making enquiries I learned that what you wrote in "The Final Problem" was probably true."

My jaw dropped. "Your Uncle James… *Moriarty*?"

"That is correct. Before marriage I was Morgaine Moriarty."

"Then it was you who sent that mask to us at Baker Street!"

"Indeed. Perhaps I should begin at the start?"

That is what Holmes would have wanted. "Of course. Please explain what you think I need to understand, Mrs Kent."

The lady folded her hands on her lap and stared at them. "I met my future husband when I was eleven years old. Giles Kent was then a rising young geologist with a promising future. He was a guest at my Uncle James' university house at a time my parents and I were visiting. This was in the last months before Professor Moriarty fell out with his academic colleagues and quit his tenure."

And began his life as the Napoleon of Crime, I did not add.

"It was almost ten years later that Giles and I met again. By then I was completing my education at Newnham Women's College, Oxford. I was offered an opportunity to remain on as secretary to its co-founder, Mrs Millicent Garrett Fawcett, but instead I married Giles. He seemed very dashing and cosmopolitan to me then, a tireless firebrand pamphleteer, and I was very touched by his care for his young orphaned sisters. We removed to Paris for his work, as I previously intimated."

"Until there were the terrible incidents of Kent and Amile's deaths," I reflected.

"Until then."

A link occurred to me. "You said you were in dire straits and were assisted by an uncle…"

"Uncle James, yes. You knew him as a criminal mastermind, a fearsome adversary who almost claimed the life of Mr Sherlock Holmes. Yet to me, defenceless and friendless in that alien city, against a powerful enemy, he was my salvation."

"A powerful enemy?"

Mrs Kent flushed. "I reveal this only because we are come to grave peril, Dr Watson, and personal secrets must give way to survival. In the months before Giles' death I was portuned by one of his friends, his so-called friends. To be plain, he attempted to seduce me. After Giles' death I feared that this powerful man might seek to press his suit more fiercely."

"Who was this cad?"

"His name was Nestor de Maupassant, of an ancient and rich house. He and his friends were of the highest rank but the lowest morals. When Giles became involved with them it caused… there was strife between us that had not been there before. Indeed, Nestor recounted for me some liaisons he claimed my husband had enjoyed as his guest, as if one infidelity might excuse another."

"You appealed to your uncle for protection against this blaggard," I recognised. For the first time ever I was glad of Moriarty's vindictive genius, for surely no French roué, however powerful, might prevail against the malice of the world's most dangerous criminal.

"Yes. I first wired Uncle when Amile disappeared. I thought for a moment that perhaps Nestor might be responsible for her absconding, but Giles said not. Besides, the age gap between Nestor and Amile was grotesque. Why, Nestor's son was five years her senior. Then Giles had his fall, if it was a fall, and he too was gone."

"What did Moriarty do?"

Mrs Kent hesitated before answering. "He sent an agent to assist us. Mr Naudé came with money to meet the debts that Giles had left and to purchase passage for Yve and I back to England once Giles' affairs were tied up."

I looked up sharply. "Emile Naudé?" That was the name of the assassin who had travelled on the *Palmyra* the following year.

"That is so. You know him?"

"I know of him. Like your uncle the Professor, we never actually met."

"I was so *angry* with your account when I read it," Mrs Kent confessed. "Of course, by then I was back at Newnham, working for Mrs Garrett Fawcett, the job that finally took me to the Boer camps. At first I thought your story sheer malice, but eventually I came to understand that I had not known uncle so well as I had thought."

"How did you come by his death mask?" I wondered.

"It was February 9th, 1891, that I last saw uncle. He visited me and we took tea together. He told me that he would probably be going overseas on business for a while. He was in a strange mood, reflective, even more obscure than usual. He informed me of trust bequests he had established for Yve and I. And then he showed me the mask he had commissioned from some Left Bank potter."

"It surprised you?"

"I thought it morbid and grotesque, but uncle made me promise that if anything happened to him, on the tenth anniversary of his death I would sent it to a colleague of his as a momento."

"Which colleague was that?"

"Sherlock Holmes, of course. I had no idea then that he was speaking ironically of his greatest rival. I agreed to his request, placed the object in storage, and thought no more of it until accounts came back of the accident at the Reichenbach Falls."

That event had painful associations for both of us. I moved the interview on. "You did not send the mask to us last year,"

"No. I knew by then of the enmity between Professor Moriarty and Mr Holmes. I wanted no part in perpetuating that feud. Indeed, last summer

I was so busy with the campaign about the atrocities revealed by Miss Hobhouse and the subsequent Ladies Commission to investigate them that such ancient history seemed quite irrelevant."

I gestured round to the dark basement wherein we were confined. "Something clearly changed."

"Somewhat. Whilst in Pretoria I made a friend. Lady Saxhallow was a most unusual woman, and a woman of unusual conscience too. It was her covert testimony about her husband's governorship of the Boer refugee camp at Viljoensdrift that led to his quiet dismissal and their return to England. When I too returned home she re-established our acquaintance."

"You were close enough that when you needed to flee from masked kidnappers it was to her that you turned."

Mrs Kent nodded assent. "I am certain that this is none of her doing. Rather I think it some revenge of her husband's for his disgrace and discharge."

"Does Sir Horace know of his wife's part in it?"

"I pray not. He is a brutal and vicious man, Dr Watson. There were things we could not prove to include in our report. The stories of his behaviour at Viljoensdrift, of his 'games' and those of his rich guests with the helpless victims in his care… Things I do not care to repeat. I am certain that if he learned of Sabine's betrayal he would destroy her."

"You intimated that she played some part in sending the mask to Baker Street."

"She did. I mentioned those rich friends of Major Saxhallow's. They call themselves the Far Edge Club, a collection of dilettantes who thrill at the closeness of oblivion, their own or others. Amongst the visitors who took their sport at Viljoensdrift was a name familiar to me, although I did not realise he had been there until Sabine told me in England. It was Gabriel de Maupassant, son of the man who had so pressed me in my younger days."

"He sounds as unpleasant as his father," I observed.

"That would be an achievement, but it is possible. Sabine did not like him anyhow, but she learned from him what her father's intention had been all those years before in tangling Giles in his webs of debauchery and in seeking to seduce me. It seemed that my uncle had left behind a manuscript, some unexpurgated copy of his mathematical book. These papers included some secret considered dangerous and potent. It was this hidden document that the older Maupassant had sought, and that search had something to do with Amile's death."

I wished more than ever that Holmes had been present to interpret all of this. "The death mask contained clues to its location that only Holmes could interpret."

"Exactly! Sabine and I reasoned that if we belatedly carried out uncle's wishes then Mr Holmes would retrieve the manuscript. Surely there were no safer hands than his in which to place it? For our protection I took precautions to conceal the identity of the sender. However, it seems as though others now seek the manuscript, presumably including Major Sir Horace Saxhallow. This is hardly the secret lodgings to which Sabine suggested I travel this morning."

"And what is the secret in *Dynamics Of An Asteroid*?" I wondered.

"Dr Watson, I have no idea."

━╱╲━

A Report About Mr Martin Beck
Friday, 9th May, the evening before Houdini's disappearance:

Devonshire House dominated Piccadilly. Its grand Palladian frontage concealed one of the richest and largest private residences in England. No London society calendar was complete without attending the ball there in the first week of May.

When Beck arrived, the forecourt was teeming with expensive private carriages, with attendants, and with dazzling young debutantes being delivered to the ball. This was one of the first events of the Season since these young ladies had been formally presented to the king at court. During the next few months of parties, receptions, and social and sporting occasions, the newest crop of rich and eligible young women would meet bachelors seeking a wife of the right class and breeding.

Houdini was already there, awaiting his friend just inside the dazzling entrance arch, out of line-of-fire by any sniper positioned on a rooftop opposite. "Welcome to the show, Beck," the escape artist grinned. "If you want to study the upper class Englishman in his natural habitat then this is the place."

"It's a cattle market," Beck opined as he watched expensively-gowned girls being escorted by their duennas up the formal stairs to the massive gilted *piano nobile*.[55]

---

55 Literally "noble floor", a formal upper story reception room.

"This is only the start of the rounds, buddy. After this there's events at the Proms and the Royal Academy, the Great Spring Flower Show, the Oxford-Cambridge Boat Race, the Henley Regatta, Royal Ascot, the Grand National, Glorious Goodwood, plus some royal events like Trooping the Colour, and then it all caps off before the 'Glorious Twelfth' of August when the shooting season starts.[56] By then these eligible noble fillies are expected to have made good matches ready for next year's wedding cycle."

"It's another world," Beck observed. He had been born in poverty in the Slovakian town of Liptovský Mikuláš, had made his way to America with an acting troupe at age sixteen, and had made his way as a beer garden waiter in Chicago before joining up with the Schiller Vaudeville Company. If he was now a successful impresario, an American citizen, a man of reputation and influence, it was entirely due to his own efforts. This old world of privilege and inheritance seemed completely alien to him.[57]

"I guess the Brits like their cotillions too," Houdini reflected. "Look at some of these get-ups. Can you imagine what Madame DuGrasse would make of some of these things?"

Beck shivered at the reminder of the company's mad costumier. He still had scissor-marks on his forearm from her last tantrum. He looked around him as Houdini led the way up into the *corps de logis*, the central

---

56 'The Proms' refers to the Promenade Concerts at the Albert Hall, founded in 1895 by Sir Henry Wood to make good music available to the masses. The Royal Academy Summer Exhibition is an open display of all kinds of new artwork; it has been held each year since 1769. The Royal Horticultural Society's Great Spring Flower Show was first held in 1862, and at the time of our story took place at Temple Gardens, between the Embankment and Fleet Street, but it has since been moved to its modern location and become the Chelsea Flower Show. The annual University Boat Race between the Oxford and Cambridge University Rowing Clubs commenced in 1829. The five-day Henley Regatta knockout boat race first debuted in 1839. Royal Ascot is the culmination of racing at the Ascot track founded by Queen Anne in 1711; spectator admittance to the Royal Enclosure there is highly sought and tightly restricted. The Grand National is a challenging handicap steeplechase held at Aintree near Liverpool since around 1836 (opinions vary as to the first "official" race). Glorious Goodwood refers to the key races at the Duke of Richmond's Chichester racecourse. Trooping the Colour is the annual parade of military standards and regimental march-by before the monarch at Horse Guards' Parade by St James' Park. This event also marks the British ruler's official birthday.
The last presentation of debutantes to the monarch was in 1958; thereafter Queen Elizabeth II abolished the ceremony. Later events on the Society calendar include the Glyndebourne Opera, the Royal Windsor Horse Show, and the revived Garter Chapel ceremony.

57 Beck could not know that he was seeing the last glory days of Devonshire House. The 9th Duke of Devonshire who came into the title in 1908 inherited debts left over from the 7th Duke and was the first to have to pay the new Inheritance Tax, a sum of £500,000 ($75 million in modern currency). Devonshire House, already unfashionable in the austerity after the First World War, was closed in 1919 and sold and demolished in 1920. Its loss was eulogised in Siegfried Sassoon's "Monody on the Demolition of Devonshire House."

block where seemingly-endless enfiladed chambers ran off in all directions. "This sure puts our takings into perspective, Harry. What do you reckon this Duke of Devonshire guy must be worth?"

"Well, his family's been in the business for a long time, Beck. This place was put up in the 1730s on the ashes for some earlier pile from the 1660s. The first Devonshire was around in the 1300s. They've had some years to rake the cash in."

A trio of giggling young ingénues hurried past, gossiping and casting long glances at a pair of young guardsman officers in their smart red tunics.

"Listen," Beck told Houdini while they had some anonymity amongst the press of guests, "I know about the guys who are watching you. And about those goons on the theatre roof. What's going on?"

Houdini steered his partner away from the balcony rail to one of the quieter chambers in the long succession of elegant Devonshire House staterooms. "Listen, Beck, you've got to drop it. Please, I mean it. If I could tell you I would, but I can't. All I can ask is that you trust me, Martin."

"Whatever the trouble, Harry, you know I'll stand by you. I engaged a detective to…"

"Beck - I'm deadly serious. Leave it. Not a word more. And no enquiries."

"Hey, I was the one got gut-punched by some hoodlum in a mask when that lady was asking about that death mask you were interested in."

This was the first Houdini had heard of the hushed-up incident at the National Gallery. "Okay, fill me in on that," he conceded.

"Like you're telling me stuff?"

"Beck…!"

"Right." Houdini's manager sketched out his adventure with Mrs Kent and the claims she had made about her sister-in-law Amile.

"Where is Mrs Kent now?"

"Vamoosed. Dr Watson is trying to track her down." Beck eyed his friend speculatively. "Does this *l'Inconnu* have something to do with what you're not telling me? Harry, I'm really worried."

Houdini glanced at the casual passers-by who were circulating through the enfilades. Any one of them might be an agent for the Far Edge Club.

"Martin, honestly, and for the last time…"

"Mr Houdini," called a dazzling blonde woman, "how pleasant to meet you again."

"Lady Saxhallow," the escape artist recognised. "May I present my manager Mr Martin Beck?"

"Charmed," the elegant lady told the impresario. "I would make your acquaintance further, but I am certain that Mr Houdini is about to ask me to dance."

Beck regarded the glorious beauty in the sparkling silk ballgown that must have cost as much as, say, Idaho, and replied, "That would sure be the smart thing to do, ma'am."

"Will you give me a dance?" Houdini asked Lady Saxhallow.

"That much at least," she replied with a simmering smile.

Beck had no further chance to talk to Houdini. The showman and his dancing partner hastened onto the dance floor.

Beck watched them for as long as he could before they vanished in the throng.

━╸╱╿╲╺━

From the account of John Watson MD
Friday, 9th May, the evening before Houdini's disappearance:

Mrs Kent and I remained imprisoned throughout the day. No-one attended to us or even checked on us. We settled ourselves to the disciplines of confinement, even to the etiquettes of sharing a single toilet bucket. As Morgaine pointed out, it was better amenity than many of the women of the South African camps enjoyed.

Mostly we conversed. I have never been locked up with a more congenial companion for that. The lady proved herself erudite and well-informed on whatever topic we discussed.

We moved on from the circumstances leading to our present difficulties to a discussion of the South African situation; to a comparison of the climates and cuisines of Rhodesia and Afghanistan; to reviews of military camping equipment; to consideration of the tyranny of railway timetables; to some comments on modern fashion in Britain and the Continent; to the pitfalls of publishing; to the tendency of heroines and friends of the hero to be kidnapped in contemporary fiction; to the absurdity of being reduced to such roles in the modern age.

In all of this Morgaine Kent proved herself a perfect lady and an informed and compassionate intellect. We grew passionate in our arguments but never angry. We discovered in each other's views a contrast which challenged our own.

It was an enthralling imprisonment, yet some part of my mind warned me of danger. *This* was the niece of James Moriarty. If only a tenth part of the late Professor's twisted genius resided in her then I might be caught in some elaborate and deadly game. Nothing she told me could be relied upon. This could be some plot to gain information about Holmes or to close some trap upon him by manipulating his friend.

"You do not trust me, John," the lady discerned. "You consider that this captivity might be a ruse, and that I am part of some conspiracy against you and Mr Holmes."

"Rather say I have to be cautious, Morgaine. You are too good to be true."

"I will receive that as a compliment, and say in return that I also had certain doubts and fears when you were thrown into my prison. Conversation with you has wholly allayed them. While I am sorry to have drawn you into this danger, I am absurdly comforted that you are present to share it with me."

My old soldier's heart thumped harder as she stirred in me a chivalry drummed into one since school. "Morgaine, I will do my uttermost to protect you in this current circumstance. You will not be harmed while I yet live. My oath on it."

"And me a Moriarty?"

"Yes. Even so. I will not abide a woman being harmed if I can prevent it, and not you especially."

Mrs Kent smiled wanly in the dimming light. "You have come years too late, my gallant protector." She fixed her gaze on me. "What other than my name makes you suspicious of me?"

I reasoned that if she was the murderess in the *l'Inconnu* mask then there was nothing I knew that would assist her. If she was instead some innocent drawn into this murky business by accident or design then she needed to know that the Moriarty manuscript had been taken from us by force. I took a breath and outlined for her the details of the document's discovery and loss.

She crammed her knuckles to her mouth at the point in my tale where the child was harmed. "But is she alive? Did you save her, John?"

"She survived. She is in special care at St Bart's, well tended—and guarded."

"If I was the woman in my murdered sister's mask then you are right to beware me," Morgaine conceded. "A deadly shot with such ruthless amorality... Do you believe me to be her?"

"I find it harder and harder to think that," I admitted. "You are either the most duplicitous and fiendish manipulator alive or else... well, this is not the occasion to speak of that."

"What later occasion to you expect there to be, John? It is clear from our pooled accounts that some enemy has twisted my good intentions so as to gain access to my uncle's papers. That I am now abducted from what I thought a safe haven and held here suggests some villain has further use for me: for further information if the manuscript was obscure, perhaps, or else for the kind of lethal sport that the Far Edge Club enjoyed at Viljoensdrift, hunting human prey."

She lowered her head, dreading her fate yet unwilling to yield to it. In that moment I decided that if Morgaine Moriarty was deceiving me she had utterly won. I surrendered and accepted her as she seemed to be.

"Do not despair, Morgaine. I have faced worse situations than this. Holmes is still free. Tracking us to this place will be child's play to him. Your enemies may have made arrangements they consider sufficient to capture and confine me. No such preparation is adequate to obstruct Sherlock Holmes."

The lady indulged me. "You have great faith in your friend. I am worried sick for mine. If Sir Horace has intervened to have me held here then he must also have moved against his wife. Sabine knew all. She gave me refuge at Berkley Square last night. When I departed from there this morning I thought it was her arrangements that I followed. The Major cannot move against me without also moving against her, yet she is not here in this cellar with us. What has he done with Sabine?"

As if in answer to her question, the bolt creaked back as the basement door was unlocked. I rose and placed myself before Mrs Kent. It was time to keep my word.

The enemy was come.

━╱╿╲━

A Report About Mr Martin Beck
Friday, 9th May, the evening before Houdini's disappearance:

"Y ou are alone?"

Beck turned to find another elegant society beauty regarding him. Her blue silk gown, tasteful jewellery, elaborate Pompadour hairstyle, and general bearing made the Orpheum Circuit entrepreneur feel like he'd crawled out from a sewer. "I guess I don't know anyone here much," he managed to answer. He'd only been invited because of Harry Houdini.

"I too." The lady had a foreign accent, a French way of whispering her hard consonants. "I am come with a gentleman, but he is playing cards."

"That doesn't sound like a smart guy to me."

"As you say." The lady smiled. "I am Sigrette Confontaine."

"Martin Beck. A real pleasure to meet you… miss?"

"Marquise. But mademoiselle passes these days. Sigrette is easier on the tongue, however."

It took Beck a few moments to get past this beguiling introduction to register the lady's surname. "My friend Houdini had a less than pleasant encounter in Paris with a Marquis de Confontaine."

Sigrette nodded acknowledgement. "Le Marquis Etienne-Louis Pierre-Phillipe Saint Jealle de Confontaine et Asnières-de-la-Châtaigneraye. My brother. Shall I dazzle you with all my names too?"

"That confrontation did not end well." *It ended with that cruel member of the Far Edge Club dead*, Beck diplomatically did not say.

"Yes. Thank you for that."

Beck's brows rose. "Your brother was killed."

"Yes. A great service to me. *Merci.*"

"You… didn't get on I guess."

"That is so. I will not explain the details, they are sordid and personal. Enough he is gone and I am free of him. I wished to thank you and M. Houdini for your assistance in that."

Beck reflected that it was usually his heroic client that the pretty dames wanted to thank. "I'll pass it along."

Sigrette linked her arm into his. "You are too modest. Will you not spend time with me?"

"Gladly. But why? I mean, I get you're happy about, well, about your brother, but…"

Houdini and Lady Saxhallow whirled past on the dance floor below the balcony where Beck and the marquise stood. Sigrette Confontaine sniffed. "She is parvenu," she scorned.

"Lady Saxhallow?"

"Sabine Cronjé. A Boer refugee who crawled into the Viljoensdrift camp then crawled into its commander's bed. A wedding ring doesn't hide the dirt. Get close enough and she still has the stink of the veldt on her."

"You… don't like her?"

"I am not a man. What is there to like?"

"I've just met the lady, so I didn't get chance to form an impression."

Sigrette squeezed his arm. "Well here is the difference between Sabine

"Come with me, Sigrette."

and I. She chose to whisk away the brash bold man in the spotlight, the talk of Europe. I came to converse with the person behind his success, a man who is perhaps not conventionally handsome with the chiselled heroic jaw, but a man who has interesting things to say? *Non?*"

Beck swallowed. "I'm sure happy to talk with you."

Sabine whispered something to Houdini. They disappeared from the dance floor.

"So tell me interesting things," Sigrette asked Beck. "You are to do something special tomorrow at the Tower Bridge, are you not?"

"Sure. An escape stunt to drum up some column inches for the show we launch next Monday. You should come along and watch it."

"I will have to check my calendar. What will I miss if I do not attend?"

"Oh, only Houdini packed up in chains in a steamer trunk lowered over the side of the bridge into the Thames, with about seventeen minutes to get out before he drowns."

"There will be a trick. He will not truly be in the box."

"Oh, he'll be in there. But as for the rest, I'm afraid that's all a closely guarded secret."

"I understand. Secrets are important. I sometimes think…"

The marquise was interrupted by someone calling her name. A good-looking Frenchman in perfect evening dress glided through the crowds. "Ah, there you are, Sigrette. I was wondering where you had got to."

The lady did the introductions. "Martin Beck, this is my escort Gabriel de Maupassant. It seems he has finished his hand of *vingt-et-un*."

"It bored me," de Maupassant remarked. He peered down his nose at Beck as if the American bored him too. "Come with me, Sigrette."

"Au revoir, M. Beck," the marquise bade the impresario as she allowed herself to be steered away to dance.

Houdini had disappeared too. There was no sign of the sparkling Lady Saxhallow. Beck had no wish to watch Sigrette being handled around the *piano nobile* by her effete aristocratic swain.

He felt a long way from the Orpheum Circuit in San Francisco, Sacramento, and Los Angeles.

He slipped away early and headed back to his hotel.

—⟩⟨—

From the account of John Watson MD
Friday, 9th May, the evening before Houdini's disappearance:

Major Sir Horace Saxhallow was a military man, with regulation moustache and clipped tones. I took an instant dislike to him, not only from what I knew of him at Viljoensdrift and his behaviour towards Mrs Kent, but because of his superior attitude and cruel sneer. There are some officers one knows from the start are 'bad 'uns'. Saxhallow was one.

He descended the stairs to our cellar prison holding a service revolver aimed not at me but at the lady. Two of the flunkies that had overpowered me on arrival flanked him. A third remained alert by the door.

I took three deliberate paces to keep myself between the gun and Mrs Kent.

"Very gallant," he sneered, unimpressed. "Who the devil are you?"

"Go to the devil yourself and find out," I answered him.

He turned his attention to Morgaine. "You were at the camp. You made your libellous report on me. Tell your gallant protector how discipline was maintained there. Warn him to answer my questions."

"This man tortured the internees whom he thought might have concealed their wealth on their properties," Mrs Kent warned in furious icy tones. "If any of them had lived to give testimony we could have seen him hung."

"I'm not squeamish when it comes to handling the enemy," Saxhallow warned. "You are my enemy, Mrs Kent. You know what I will do to you if you do not tell me what I want to know."

Morgaine clenched her fists. "I will not assist the butcher of Viljoensdrift."

"You shall. It only remains to discover how badly you must be hurt to convince you to comply."

"You could come out from behind your gun and face me like a man, you arrant coward," I suggested.

"Or I could shoot you in the gut and let you bleed out while Mrs Kent confesses all about her uncle's book."

The lady hesitated.

"Tell him nothing on my account," I instructed her. "This man is no officer or gentleman, a disgrace to his uniform." I determined to turn the interrogation around. "Why do you want the manuscript so badly in any case? Why chase Mrs Kent round the National Gallery?"

Saxhallow frowned. "What are you babbling about?" he demanded.

"Mrs Kent, I offer you one final chance to avoid the ordeal that otherwise awaits you. Where is the unexpurgated version of Professor Moriarty's book?"

"I do not know," Morgaine replied.

I saw the look of pleasure in the Major's eyes. It was the answer he had been hoping for.

I decided to test a theory. "The book was hidden before Moriarty's death," I revealed. "Clues were inscribed on a cast of the Professor's visage. This death mask recently fell into the hands of Sherlock Holmes, who interpreted the code and recovered the document."

Saxhallow's scowl deepened. "Sherlock Holmes? The notorious detective?"

"The famous detective. Mrs Kent has never had the document you seek, knows nothing of its contents, and cannot tell you its current whereabouts. Your information is out of date. Her kidnap is pointless."

I had established to my satisfaction that Saxhallow was not the only player in the game. It was not he who had sent the men in balaclavas to Pixley's study. Nor had he been involved in the gunplay at Victoria Station or the subsequent bloody abstraction of the recovered book by the masked woman.

But I had miscalculated too. "You are correct, whoever you are," the Major agreed. "She is no longer any use to me. You never were. You can both die now."

I saw his finger twitch on the revolver's trigger. I lurched forward, knowing that I would be too late to prevent him firing into me.

The hammer fell—and jammed!

I slammed into Saxhallow, knocking him to the ground, and vented my feelings on his face. The pair of thugs who stood guard jumped in to drag me away.

The sentry by the door at the top of the stairs rolled all the way to the bottom and slumped out insensible on the bricks. Holmes slithered down behind him, his own pistol aimed implacably at the pair of felons who wrestled me.

"I suggest that you gentlemen refrain from any further struggles," my friend advised them. "Dr Watson, congratulations on getting to the criminals ahead of me."

"Holmes! I should have known that you would arrive at the most dramatic time."

"Say rather that I required the drama as distraction to neutralise the guard by the door. Your own heroics were most effective."

"His own heroics almost got him killed!" Mrs Kent objected.

The baffled thugs, uncertain what to do whilst covered at gunpoint with their employer battered on the floor, raised their hands so I could relieve them of their firearms.

"You found me through young Wallace, I suppose," I checked with Holmes.

"Indeed. You are fortunate that I caught the fast boat-train back from Paris."

"You have been to France?"

"I felt it necessary to check on the commissioning of Moriarty's death mask and to verify certain other details. This will be Mrs Morgaine Kent, née Moriarty?"

"I am," agreed the brave lady. "I apologise for putting you to unintended trouble."

"I would not miss the case for the world," Holmes told her valiantly. "Now…"

Saxhallow sprung up suddenly. He had a second pistol in his hand, and it was aimed straight at my forehead. "Drop the weapon, Holmes!" he ordered. "Drop it now!"

To my dismay, Holmes laid the gun on the floor.

"Kick it away," Saxhallow instructed. To his henchmen he added, "Well, put your arms down fools, and bring rope to tie them. Must I do everything myself?"

Morgaine Kent was still beside me. I did not realise until she moved that she had seized up one of the weapons I had confiscated from the thugs. She raised it and fired into Major Saxhallow, emptying the entire chamber into him as he fell.

She stood, eyes wide, panting, staring down at the man she had killed. "For Viljoensdrift," she said at last.

Saxhallow's men lost their nerve and fled. We could not stop them without a gun battle. "I will know them again," remarked Holmes.

I approached the trembling lady. "Morgaine? May I take the gun now?" I asked gently, and coaxed the emptied weapon from her grip. "We need to get her out of here, Holmes. Somewhere safe. Let the police clean up here."

The great detective cast a last long gaze around the cellar; he had already completed his investigations above. He searched the Major's pockets but they were empty. Evidently Saxhallow did not wish to risk any personal items being soaked with blood as he pursued his entertainments. Holmes paused to inspect the dead man's boots and nails and then swept towards the stairs.

"Let us find the lady refuge," he agreed.

━╱╽╲━

A Report About Mr Martin Beck
Friday, 9th May, the night before Houdini's disappearance:

The lobby page Bobby had a late report for Houdini's manager. "You arsked me to keep an eye out for rum customers what 'ad checked in after you an' Mr 'Oudini," the excited boy declared. "Well, our Maisie—that's my step-sister what does the laundry an' linens for the top floor—she says there's something really odd going on in rooms 124, 126, and 128."

Beck proffered the expected coin. "What's the story?"

"Three blokes, tough-looking but well-dressed, fit like sportsmen maybe? All German or Bavarian or somefing like that. Speak some foreign lingo anyhow. Hair cropped right short, 'cept for their boss what 'as whiskers. Maisie says she knows he's in charge 'cause of the tone what he speaks to the others in. 'E's the one with all the old scratches on 'is face."

"Scratches? You mean... duelling scars?"

"Dunno. But 'e turned up day after you and Mr 'Oudini. He won't 'ardly let anyone go into his rooms, not even to change the towels an' bedding. Maisie reckons 'e's got a big trunk o' guns and that 'cause of 'ow 'eavy it were carrying up there—She's walking out with Terry, the porter, see? Any'ow, these blokes is comin' an' goin' at all hours and never a decent word for anybody. 'An their rooms are right above yours and Mr 'Oudini's."

Beck whistled softly. "Do you have names for these charmers?"

Bobby sneered. "Names? Shmitt is their boss-man. But anyone can sign 'isself as Shmitt, can't 'e? We 'as lots of Shmitt's in 'ere from time to time. And their companions Mrs Shmitt. Even more of their English cousins."

Beck acknowledged the probable pseudonym. "I'd better go up and see them then." He glanced at his watch. It was well past ten. "Perhaps in the morning?" After all, Maisie thought they had guns.

Beck trudged to his room, troubled, lonely, and with an itch between his shoulder blades.

━╱╽╲━

From the account of John Watson MD
Friday, 9ᵗʰ May, the night before Houdini's disappearance:

Morgaine's safest refuge was Baker Street. I took her there.
"Your detective inspector seemed awfully casual about being called out to a dead soldier and a pair of kidnappers," Mrs Kent noted as she sipped a warm mug of Mrs Hudson's best broth.

"Lestrade knows our ways by now," Holmes responded.

"Will I be charged with some crime?"

"You acted in self defence," I assured Morgaine. "No jury would hold you guilty. No prosecutor would press a charge. You saved our lives."

Her hands shook a little. I steadied them so she should not spill her drink.

Another thought came to her. "Oh! I must tell Sabine that I have killed her husband!"

"Leave that for the police tonight. For now you must hide out. It seems as though Sir Horace Saxhallow was not the only person hunting you."

"Yes. Yes… It is just that… I have never taken a life before. It is…"

"You saved lives too, Morgaine. Our lives. Hold to that."

The lady forced herself to calmness. "Of course. What is required of me now?"

"Your account is helpful to our investigations, Mrs Kent," Holmes declared. "However, there are still many points yet to be resolved; not least the whereabouts of the manuscript."

"Morgaine has told you everything she told me, with remarkable consistency," I assured him.

"I do not doubt it. But there are questions she cannot answer. How did Saxhallow learn of the manuscript? What did he intend for it? How did he intercept Lady Saxhallow's plans to spirit Mrs Kent away?"

"I am equally concerned with the questions that have tormented me for fifteen years," Morgaine interjected. "Who killed Amile? Was Giles' death an accident? Was it really part of some plot to gain my uncle's manuscript? What could demand such terrible deeds?"

"Why would the woman who stole the document wear a mask-image of Morgaine's lost sister?" I wondered.

"All worthy questions," agreed Sherlock Holmes. "Add in one more: why did the Major's gun misfire when he tried to kill you tonight, Watson? That one serendipity saved your life. It is a remarkable coincidence."

"You do not like coincidences," I observed.

"I would not know. I have so rarely encountered them."

I dossed down on our sofa, fretting about the murderers who still ran loose, worrying about a woman wearing the mask of a drowned girl, hoping that Mrs Kent was safe and cosy in my bed above.

A Report About Mr Martin Beck
Saturday 10th May, the morning of Houdini's disappearance:

Beck rose early. It was the day of Houdini's Tower bridge stunt and there were hundreds of details to attend to, from checking off the permits and signing the work dockets to finalising the VIP seating and calming Mrs DuGrasse the mad costumier. Beck dispatched his senior engineer Jackson to begin site preparations, dashed off replies to anxious telegrams from stunt sponsor Baxter, and sent instructions for additional seating to be made available for the brass band; all before the theatrical manager found time to head down to find the breakfast buffet.

At this hour the dining room was still quiet. Half a dozen travelling salesmen munched through their plates of ham and scrambled eggs and nursed their strong teas before a day of work. A fractious family, evidently visiting from the provinces, argued over toast and who had let the baby get his hands on jam. Otherwise Beck had the long food-stuffed side-trestle to himself. He helped himself to crispy bacon and fried bread and cautioned himself not to wolf them down despite his heavy schedule.

He turned as he heard Bavarian-accented German being spoken. Three tall broad men had entered the breakfast hall; Beck recognised them from Bobby's description.

The impresario paused mid-sausage. He inspected the burly strangers, noting their tanned and weathered countenances, their hunters' poise. Maisie had been correct about the whiskered fellow being in charge.

"Morning, fellahs," Beck heard himself call out to them. "What brings you to London town?"

Their leader growled and responded with a Bavarian crudity suggesting what the agent could do with his greeting. Beck responded in fluent German, "I guess there's no room for manners in that bullet head of yours, then?"

He knew it was a mistake even before he'd finished speaking. Each of the trio overtopped him by a head. He'd been warned they were dangerous.

The pair flanking the whiskered bully peeled off to approach Beck.

"Who are your big pals, Martin?" Houdini asked from the doorway.

All three Bavarians turned to face the escape artist. Their leader spoke. "Nicht hier. Nicht jetzt." *Not here. Not now.*

"Morning, Harry," Beck called, relieved that Houdini had made it back from wherever he had vanished with the blonde the night before, more relieved that his entrance had been so timely.

Houdini was clearly aware of the hostilities that had been imminent, even if staff and guests had not picked up on it. He sauntered over past the whiskered stranger, picked up a dish, and said to him, "Sausage?"

The Bavarian reddened. He turned on his heel and marched out, gesturing for his attendants to flank him.

"I don't think his breakfast agreed with him," Houdini observed.

"I don't think Mr Shmitt agrees with anyone," Beck breathed.

"Shmitt? That, Mr Beck, is the big game hunter Graf von Sigren. I've seen his lithograph in the hunting journals. He likes to kill things." Houdini's brows furrowed. "How very interesting that he happens to be here now."

✤

From the account of John Watson MD
Saturday, 10th May, the morning of Houdini's disappearance:

Saturday's papers had nothing to say about the passing of so distinguished a soldier as Major Saxhallow. The old brewery had been cleaned and Sir Horace's body extracted before constables had arrived. Holmes did not seem surprised. Indeed, he looked upon it as a confirmation of some theory that he was formulating in that steel-trap mind of his.

Our case had reached one of those impasses. Affairs were no less urgent, but information needed time to come in and ideas wanted space to develop. Holmes was eager to follow up on Major Saxhallow's contacts and I busied myself ensuring that Morgaine was comfortable and comforted in our rooms. I was gratified at the effort Mrs Hudson made to offer Mrs Kent a warm welcome.

Whilst Morgaine was downstairs consulting with our landlady on domestic matters—Mrs Kent's wardrobe and possessions were presumed still at Belgrave Square—Holmes spoke to me about our case.

He proffered an item from our morning mail. "We wondered what was in the unexpurgated Moriarty manuscript that might cause such interest, Watson. This morning I have received a reply on the subject. My cousin is a promising man of science whose bellicosity belies his expertise. Here is his note."

I inspected the letter. My blood chilled.

Dr George E. Challenger[58]

_____ College

Mr Sherlock Holmes
221b Baker Street
London

8th May, 1902

Sherlock,

I have received your note seeking comment of Professor James Moriarty's out-of-fashion mathematical treatise *Dynamics Of An Asteroid*. Herewith is my summary and interpretation.

It has been theorised that the asteroids which occupy a belt in space between the planets Mars and Jupiter might be remnants of a failed planet, one which never coalesced from its stellar debris; or that they once formed a planet much like our own but were pulled apart by geological, tectonic, or gravitational stresses. *Dynamics* champions the latter view.

Moriarty posits that the asteroids were once united in a significant planetary mass, as occured with the rest from the primordial solar nebula. He asserts that his hypothesised celestial body was broken into fragments by internal or external tectonic and gravitational stresses. Moriarty utilises his mathematical observations of the motion and positions of many contemporary asteroid fragments such as Ceres and Pallas, attempting to back-plot the trauma that separated them into the rubble they are today. I should say that modern astronomy doubts that these asteroids ever formed significant planetesimals, let alone a planet, but such was popular thinking of the 1880s.

Dynamics Of An Asteroid further goes on to model the physics of major mass tectonic disruptions that might destroy such a proto-planet, fitting the mathematics to geological, tidal, and volcanic incidences. The calculations are abstruse but brilliant; I doubt a dozen men on the planet are qualified and capable of verifying them. Fortunately I am one of them.

---

58 By 1912, G.E. Challenger had risen to professorship and his adventures were promoted by Sir Arthur Conan Doyle in *The Lost World* and its sequels. The suggestion that he was Holmes' cousin was first put into print in Baring-Gould's biography, which asserts that Challenger's mother was sister of Siger Holmes, Sherlock's father. Philip José Farmer in *Tarzan Alive* preferred that the relationship be rather through Holmes' mother.

Where Moriarty got himself into trouble was in his questioning of certain Newtonian principles, which are tenets of faith within the so-called scientific community. Rather than hold his corner against the loud voices of orthodoxy he chose to skulk away and sulk, thus losing the chance to develop his argument and win his case.

As to any danger his unexpurgated work might offer, I can only suggest that a set of calculations that models mass terrain disturbance on a continental scale might, if somehow applied practically, offer the means of unprecedented destruction by earthquake, volcano, or tsunami. Indeed, the published volume goes on to discuss those potential cataclysms upon other worlds, including our own Earth, but omits any proof formulae.

My content suggestion is, of course, purely a speculative hypothesis. Who would be so foolish as to test a theory that might consume cities or even shatter our planet?

-- GEC

"The idea is surely fiction," I said.

Holmes frowned. "Think carefully, Watson. Moriarty's mathematical genius allowed him to model, to describe the conditions under which a whole world might tear itself apart to asteroid rubble. Even ours. It made him few scholarly friends."

"I can imagine. Still…"

I halted. If any mad genius could calculate the forces required to shatter our planet it was surely James Moriarty.

"It has long been whispered that the Professor's most pertinent calculations were omitted from the published edition. If George is right then those sections may detail how to destroy great tracts of our globe. Equations about how to set off earthquakes or provoke volcanic activity are rather prone to misuse."[59]

"Equations now in the hands of an unknown adversary."

"Indeed."

"How then to proceed? Whom should we inform? What may be done?"

Holmes cradled his fingers, bent his head forwards, and began to think. When Mrs Kent returned to us he sprang up, made his apologies, and stalked out of Baker Street.

Holmes and I agreed to meet that lunchtime for Houdini's public demonstration at Tower Bridge.

---

59 The idea that it was this content that caused Moriarty's academic shunning and provoked or exacerbated his criminal career does not originate with the Canon but has been mooted in fandom for a long time. Treatments of it appear in Robert Bloch's "The Dynamics of an Asteroid" in *The Baker Street Journal* 1953, in Isaac Asimov's "The Ultimate Crime" from *More Tales of the Black Widowers*, 1976, and elsewhere.

4. THE FARTHEST EDGE

From the account of John Watson MD:

Sherlock Holmes took charge.

Even as the empty sealed steamer trunk was hauled back onto the Tower Bridge parapet, emergency preparations were being activated. Beck had arranged for a reserve diver to be on hand in case the stunt went wrong. He was ordering the man into the Thames after the vanished Houdini when my friend called a halt. "Check your gear before you enter the water," Holmes advised the frogman.

A judicious check of the diver's apparatus revealed a loosened clasp that would have filled his air hose with dirty river water.

"An effective saboteur who could damage a winding mechanism might think to also incapacitate rescue equipment," Holmes warned.

The crowd was becoming restless, picking up on the concern of Houdini's crew that something might have gone wrong.

"Is this part of the show?" the Harbourmaster enquired. "If so I question its taste."

"I wasn't told about this," protested Baxter, one of the rich sponsors who had funded the stunt.

"There has been a difficulty," answered Martin Beck. "You may rely upon Houdini to turn it into part of the performance."

An attractive lady with a French accent squirmed her way through the pressing crowd. "M. Beck? Is everything well? What is happening?"

"You need not concern yourself, Marquise," Houdini's manager assured her. "We are suffering some technical difficulties…"

"Deliberate technical difficulties," Holmes growled. "Gentlemen, I beg you to keep the crowds back so that I can carry out my work."

"Mr Holmes!" recognised the President of the Locksmith's Guild. He turned to the others. "Do as he says!"

"Where has M. Houdini gone?" the young woman that Beck had called Marquise asked. She stared in baffled concern at the dripping empty crate.

"Where are the men who attended to this crane?" Holmes demanded.

"Jackson?" Beck called, gesturing for a fellow in overalls who was consulting with the diver on the matter of his air valve. "Where is everyone?"

The mechanic did a quick check of Houdini's crew. "Everyone's here but Bright, Mr Beck."

"Has this Bright chap any reason to leave the performance?" I asked.

"None at all," Beck replied darkly.

"Bright's a good man," Jackson insisted. "We've hired him before, last time we were in London."

Holmes looked up sharply. "He lives locally? Send round to his house now. Send a constable along. Quickly!"

"A bobby? Why?"

Holmes looked over at me. "We have recently encountered a criminal who is not above threatening the lives of innocents to force others to do her bidding. Bright was the rat-faced man in the leather overall, yes? An habitual tobacco-chewer with a weakness in his left eye, whose mother recently died and whose wife is not so adroit at mending trousers? Several children, including one blonde-haired daughter whom he dandles on his knee? Look to his family, Mr Beck. Look to them now."

"What?" the theatre manager gasped. "How...?"

"Best to marvel later," I advised Beck. "Dispatch people as Holmes suggests."

"I shall go myself," Inspector Lestrade announced. He turned to his harried sergeant. "Keep things in order until support arrives."

Beck had a hurried conference with the Harbourmaster and with the harried policeman that Lestrade had left in charge of crowd control. He offered facile assurances to his sponsors, the Marquise, and other concerned onlookers that Houdini was merely again grabbing the headlines he loved so well. Then he returned to me and asked in a secret undertone, "What is going on?"

"Holmes and I encountered a woman wearing a mask of *l'Inconnu*. To achieve her ends she gashed the throat of an infant stolen at random from the city's streets. We are concerned that your friend Houdini's interest in the death mask might come from some encounter with this lunatic."

"How could one woman plan what has happened here?"

"She had aid. There were a number of brutes working for her. Better to make the precautionary checks that Holmes suggests than be sorry after."

"And what do I tell the crowd here at Tower Bridge?"

"Tell them that the performance is over," Holmes suggested.

Beck straightened his waistcoat, assumed an expression on public confidence, and turned to the assembly.

"Ladies and gentlemen! As you can see, Harry Houdini has amazed us all again—even me, his manager! Trust the greatest escape man in the world to escape from even a malfunction of his apparatus. Nothing can stop the Handcuff King! Now all that remains is to thank you for your attendance. You have seen a marvel of the modern age. Tell your friends!"

"But where is Houdini?" demanded the President of the Locksmiths.

"Where indeed? He is a man of mystery. When he chooses to vanish, none can fathom it. Only be certain that when the curtain rises at the Lyceum Theatre at seven o'clock this Monday, Mr Harry Houdini will appear! Those of you fortunate enough to have gala tickets will see so for yourselves. The rest may still be able to find seats at other performances in our short season, available today and every day at the theatre box office. You have seen a remarkable stunt here, ladies and gents, but I promise you that this is the merest taste of the show Houdini plans!"

He made a theatrical bow to the stand where the dignitaries were arrayed, a second to the crowd thronging the span beyond, and a third to the handsome French lady.

Meanwhile, the diver had repaired his equipment and Jackson had stripped down the winch. "This gear was the problem," he showed Sherlock Holmes. "A nail amidst the teeth for starters, and I'll swear someone has filed down the milling here. See?"

"I can go into the water now," the frogman offered. "I had better go and check for the worst."

"Good man," Holmes told him. To the anxious metropolitan police sergeant who was shooing the crowds away he added, "Send to your station. Have them place men to walk both banks downriver for three or four miles. The tide will be shifting out soon."

"They're looking for a body?" the officer concluded gloomily. "Then you think…"

"A mere precaution, but a necessary one."

As the poor sergeant hastened off to The poor sergeant bustled off to await Lestrade's return so he might foist off his Holmes problem. We watched the diver wade into the Thames from the shallows beside the Tower of London.

"What is going on here, Holmes?" I asked the detective when we could snatch a moment for private conversation. "Do you really believe this incident is part of the same affair as our Moriarty mask case?"

"There is some possibility of it, Watson. I have not yet had the opportunity to outline for you the chain of events that I believe underline this affair. I beg your indulgence until we have time to sit down with the principles and untangle these plots."

"Will Mrs Kent be all right at Baker Street? Might this be some diversion to snatch her again? Should I return and check on her?"

"You may rest easy that the precautions we have set in place for her protection are adequate. It is some time since we found it necessary to set a guard upon our home but our defences are secure." Holmes regarded me curiously. "You are notably solicitous of Mrs Kent's wellbeing, even above and beyond your usual chivalry."

"She is a lady whom I hold in high regard, Holmes. Even in extreme adversity she displays the finest qualities."

My friend gave me a long look, with an expression I could not read.

It was fifteen minutes later when the diver hauled a body out of the river. It was not Houdini.

The response to that ate up much of the rest of our day. More policemen were dispatched, as if they might now prevent any more aquatic murder. Additional frogmen dove into the churning brown Thames, risking themselves in the growing ebb. A couple of hours of diligent searching discovered a second dead diver.

"There was conflict," Holmes reported, examining the corpses and offering up an account of an underwater struggle that later turned out to be accurate in every detail.

"You are saying that these guys were there to try and kill Houdini!" Beck gasped, flushing furious red at the thought of his friend's harm.

"A premeditated assault, Mr Beck."

"You mentioned that Houdini was being watched," I reminded the theatre manager. "You asked me to recommend a good man who might look into it."

Beck summarised the findings of his enquiry agent, and revealed Clifford's abrupt withdrawal from the investigation.

"Useful," Holmes mused, lighting his pipe and puffing it as he stared out over the bridge railings at the riverscape beyond. All of London pressed around that snaking channel, the City to the right with St Paul's dome and two dozen familiar spires, the newer sprawl of the South bank to the left, the crowded wharves of the world's busiest port.

He was disturbed by Lestrade's hasty return. "You were right about trouble at Bright's home," he admitted to Holmes. "Masked men holding the family at gunpoint – in London! They were gone before we arrived to untie the wife and children. But Bright never made it home. He was ridden down by a carriage at the end of his street. He's a goner."

We were interrupted again, by news that a third body had been discovered. This one was washed up beside Lambeth Bridge, close to four miles upriver.[60]

"That's not possible," objected Beck. "The currents..."

That was not the only remarkable news. The body was that of a woman. She was wearing only a white plaster mask.

━╱╎╲━

A report about Mr Harry Houdini:

Houdini was a man of inexhaustible resource. He rose from the Thames under Waterloo Railway Bridge clad in only the bathing trunks that he had worn for his stunt. He had discarded his breathing apparatus to the river bottom to better cover his tracks. He slipped ashore below the iron latticework of the train lines and passed unseen into the knot of dockland warehouses beyond.

Twenty minutes of careful movement got him to a rented lock-up under the viaduct arch. He had no key, but he still had a full set of picks and he was Harry Houdini. He slid into the cramped interior of the space he had leased only days ago as a secret refuge from his pursuers.

He allowed himself half an hour to relax. He consumed a packet of chocolate biscuits for energy. He chose from amongst the packages of clothes he had left there, dressing himself as an unremarkable labourer with a peaked flat cap that came down to shadow his eyes. He hauled out a tin tea-caddy and extracted thirty pounds sterling from the bankroll hidden inside. He added a selection of unique special equipment to his pockets, and finished by sliding a Derringer target pistol into his jacket.

Less than an hour after vanishing at Tower Bridge, Houdini was free, disguised, equipped, and armed.

He had baffled his hunters. Now he began his hunt.

To aid his anonymity, he hopped aboard one of the horse-driven double-

---

60 At the time of our story, the bridges of London from west to east, in downriver order, were Vauxhall Bridge, Lambeth Bridge, Westminster Bridge (by the Houses of Parliament), Waterloo Railway Bridge, Waterloo Bridge, Blackfriars Bridge, Blackfriars Rail Bridge, Southwark Bridge (pronounced Suthurk), Southwark Rail Bridge, London Bridge, and Tower Bridge (by the Tower of London).

decker omnibuses that took passengers into town. The slow passage of the cumbersome vehicle and its frequent stops whenever a traveller held out his hand to be let on or off was offset by the anonymity of the ever-changing crowd that filled it.

The bus took him as far as Oxford Street. Houdini could have hopped off earlier, but then his route would have taken him through the theatre district where there was a greater chance of meeting someone who knew him. Instead he walked as far as Oxford Circus, halting only to dive into a side street to purchase a bucket and a long-handled sweeping brush. A labourer with bucket and brush could pass unremarked almost anywhere.

Whistling to himself, he strode on down Regent Street then cut across Bond Street until he arrived at the elegant green preserve of Berkley Square. He walked past the Saxhallow residence without any pause, but he missed no detail of that elegant frontage.

At the end of the row was a narrow alley, leading to the mews that ran behind the houses as service access to the rich dwellings' coach-houses and stables. Houdini located the rear of the Saxhallow property. It was protected by a locked gate and high spiked iron railings. The Handcuff King smiled at the three-lever mortise that barred his way.

In the privacy of the mews he opened the satchel on his back and shook out a proper longcoat. The addition of formal coat and a tie transformed him from peasant to prince. Exchanging the flat cap for an extendible topper and adding an ostentatious signet ring (that contained another lockpick, purely by routine) completed the change. Houdini strode back to the front door of the residence and pulled on the bell.

An elderly retainer answered after a significant delay. Houdini wondered whether the pause had been to winch him from his death-bed.

The visitor presented his calling card. It proclaimed him to be Morris Mayerfield Jr., Chairman of the Orpheum Entertainment Circuit, O'Farrell St, San Francisco, California. The card was genuine, received by Houdini from the German immigrant entrepreneur who had purchased and renewed the Orpheum Opera House and had expanded the business to a thriving vaudeville empire in a few short years. Martin Beck was Mayerfield's general manager.[61]

"I am here to see Lady Saxhallow," Houdini announced to the butler in the Germanic-American tones of the man whom he impersonated. Morris would have appreciated the attention to detail, Houdini considered.

---

61 The extravagant Orpheum Opera House on O'Farrell St between Stockton and Powell was in significant debt when it passed to Morris Mayerfield Jr in 1897-8, but under his entrepreneurship and the astute management of Martin Beck it quickly prospered to become the first in a rapidly-growing set of theatres that became the Orpheum Circuit.

The aged retainer looked at the visitor with sad rheumy eyes. "This is a house of mourning," he replied. Houdini noticed the black silk armband over the butler's black jacket sleeve. "Major Sir Horace Saxhallow departed this life last night."

"Did he now? What happened?"

"The Major died peacefully of heart failure. Lady Saxhallow has withdrawn to the country."

"I must have missed the obituary. When did all this happen exactly, and where?"

The retainer looked ruefully at the ill-mannered American. "Her ladyship is not at home. The house is closed. Good day, sir."

"Where is she then? Where in the country?"

"I am certain that if you were meant to know then you would," the butler sniffed as he closed the door.

Houdini's mind raced. Was Saxhallow really dead? If so, why and how? A heart attack was far too convenient. Was he one of the Far Edge Club? If so, what had pushed him off that edge?

If you can find me when and where we are not observed, then I will answer you, Sabine Saxhallow had said to Houdini. But she had withdrawn to the country.

There was more going on that just a death-hunt, the showman reflected. He thought back to the detective's report he had picked from Beck's pocket, the account of investigations that his manager had commissioned from a private enquiry agent. Beck was as astute as a representative of a man like Houdini had to be. He had discerned Houdini was hiding something from him and had set out to discover the truth. Those researches had even been of some value to the absconded escape artist in understanding his enemies.

Then there was Graf von Sigren, a rich game hunter who had the resources to afford a much better hotel than the Bridge House. It seemed likely that the brutal Bavarian was either a member of the Far Edge Club or in its hire.

Von Sigren was too bulky to have been the man who had visited Houdini's quarters to announce the lethal game, though. Sabine Saxhallow had claimed it was not her husband—apparently late husband—who had commanded her services that night. There was therefore at least one more player. And who had been the second woman masked like *l'Inconnu*?

How did any of this involve rights campaigner Morgaine Kent, who had apparently been a target of kidnap as she sought answers for her sister's death; a sister who may have been the death-mask's inspiration?

Which woman had been behind the mask when a child's throat had been slashed on the cobbles of Baker Street?

"I guess I need to tug a few more loose ends to know," Houdini muttered to himself.

He sauntered as a man of leisure back to the corner of the square, then retraced his steps into the mews to return to his workman's attire. With brush and bucket in hand he ventured to the rear of the Saxhallow residence. It was a moment's work to shin up the cast-iron drainpipe and gain access to a second storey window—the Brits would undoubtedly insist he had broken into the first floor.

The building was indeed deserted. The staff had left with their mistress, leaving only a tiny skeleton crew of useless retainers to maintain the abandoned townhouse.

Houdini has chosen well. This landing overlooked the reception hall below and led to the principal bedrooms. He found the Major's sleeping accommodation first. Sabine's room was next to it, connected by a private door. He turned the locks on both external doors and set to work to conduct a thorough search.

His first conclusion was that Saxhallow was probably dead. Beneath virgin sheets was a red-stained mattress, marked where blood had seeped from some mortal wound. Saxhallow—or someone—had been laid here the night before, judging by the age of the blemishes. He had not died of heart-failure, unless that heart had failed by being pierced with blade or bullet. Nor did Houdini think that the sinister stains all proceeded from the same injury.

Saxhallow's writing bureau had been cleared out. Its rim-lock was forced.

The other cabinets in the room contained a fine collection of hunting guns, an equally comprehensive selection of whips, canes, lashes, and willow-wands, and a selection of handcuffs, ankle-cuffs, and assorted fetters. A lower drawer contained instruments that left Houdini feeling somewhat queasy.

Lady Saxhallow's chamber was barer. Many gowns and personal items had been removed. Her dresser was devoid of make-up jars, brushes, or other paraphernalia.

Houdini did not like the scratch marks on the posts of her canopy bed, which told of shackles being attached there.

➖〉〈➖

From the account of John Watson MD

Holmes looked up gravely from his examination of the woman drawn from the Thames. "Your conclusions are accurate, Hetteridge," he told the coroner in whose examination room the victim had been laid out. "A young female aged between twenty and thirty years of age, murdered by a right-handed gash across the neck caused by a sharp instrument. She died some days ago and had been in the water since shortly after her demise."

"I would estimate her death as being four to eight days past," I interjected. It depresses me to have become so expert in such matters.

"As you say, Watson. Before her death she was manhandled, I would say by at least two men with handspans of nine and nine-and-a-half inches judging by the bruising. There was sufficient time between their restraining her arms and her death for the marks to form. Although I do not believe she was sexually assaulted before her murder I am compelled to assess that she was a prostitute by trade, albeit no streetwalker. Look for a missing girl from one of the better class of cathouses around Lambeth or Vauxhall. Someone will be missing a valuable asset—unless that owner is the murderer."

I picked up the water-spoiled death-mask that had been tied to the dead woman's face. Someone had a grisly and twisted sense of humour to recreate in part the circumstance under which the original Inconnu had been discovered in the Seine.

There was one aspect of the crime that was evident even to me. "The method of death, Holmes. This kind of slice is exactly the sort of wound that was inflicted on behalf of a woman in a mask like this one upon that kidnapped child."

"What's this?" asked Hetteridge. His domain was south of the river. He had not seen the report of the injured but recovering street urchin who had almost died on Baker Street. I quickly summarised whilst Holmes continued his examination.

"This corpse has the same height and figure as the woman we encountered that night. The mask is the same too," he mused.

"Was the manuscript taken from her even as she took it from us?" I wondered. "Is the form of her death some kind of perverse statement?"

"Let us remain with the facts," Holmes urged me. If he sounded irritable then it was because it had been a long day. Dredging the river, unearthing two slain divers, fending off the questions of the Harbourmaster and

Inspectors Lestrade and Merrivale, then examining the mystery woman of Vauxhall Bridge had made for tedious and unpleasant work. "There are still a number of matters to resolve in this murky tangle," Holmes observed.

The tangle was about to become murkier still; and deadlier yet. A young uniformed constable clattered down the steps to Hetteridge's cellar. "Mister Holmes! Doctor Watson! There you are! Inspector Lestrade has 'ad us looking all over for you! You 'ave to come, quick!"

Holmes glanced at me and asked the flustered young bobby, "What is the matter, Glesson?"

The out-of-breath constable leaned on the stair banister and gave his news. "Colonel Moran, sirs. He's escaped!"

━✦━

A report about Mr Harry Houdini:

Over many centuries the ancient tributary rivers of the Thames had been canalled, then covered, then forgotten. Many of them had been reduced to little more than addenda to the city's Victorian sewer system. Some of their courses had been lost. Now many of the waterways that had been familiar to medieval Londoners were mere street names. The Westbourne, Tyburn, Fleet, Walbrook, and Effra were ghost rivers now, buried and out of mind.

Houdini had no idea if he was progressing along a channel that now drained the Fleet or the Westbourne, or whether this was one of the many lesser waterways that had once made London an attractive place to found a city. Perhaps the sturdy red brick arches were part of Sir Edward Bazalgette's remarkable waste engineering vision, part of the five hundred and fifty miles of sewers that had transformed London after "the Great Stink" of 1858. All the American visitor knew was that the particular passageway along which he edged ran directly beneath the Strand, and therefore under the Lyceum Theatre.

As with many of the old buildings in the theatrical district, the Lyceum was connected to the underground streams. Some of the theatres had once even pumped water from the sources atop which they were built to flood their stages for mock naval battles and other spectacles. In London, everything new was built upon something old.

Houdini was gratified to see them there.

Houdini had scouted the secret approach before the Far Edge Club had ever threatened him in his Bridge House Hotel suite. It was what he did.

It was past midnight by the time Houdini edged out the bolts that held the cellar grating in place. He slipped from the water tunnel, grateful that it was high summer and the stream below was reduced to a mere trickle in the middle channel rather than the cataract it might have been in worse weather. He laid the cover back in place but did not replace the fastenings; he intended to leave as unseen as he had come.

The escape artist made quick work of the locked doors that sealed the deserted lowest basement from the prop stores and stage lifts of the higher cellars. He slipped like a spectre past the decorators' scaffolding where the final restorative touches were being made to the refurbished auditorium. No effort was being spared to have the theatre ready for its gala reopening on Monday night.

A pair of night-watchmen sat on the stage, playing cards by the light of an oil lamp. Houdini was gratified to see them there. Rivals had broken into places where he performed before, eager to steal his tricks. Beck was sententious about ensuring there was proper security on his equipment.

The showman remained in the shadows far from the sentinels. He made his way backstage silently and swiftly then concealed himself until the watchmen had made their appointed rounds. Confident that they would settle again for another half hour, Houdini moved on to make his preparations.

He had a show to put on in two night's time.

From the account of John Watson MD

"John!" Morgaine Kent set her aside her knitting and jumped up when Holmes and I returned. "I was becoming concerned."

"You need not have stayed up," I assured her. It was well past one in the morning by the time Holmes had satisfied himself on the details of Moran's escape and had offered what advice he could to the troubled officers of Scotland Yard. A number of Newgate warders were now being closely questioned.

"I could scarcely have slept. Your telegram warning of your absence left much to be desired."

"The most dangerous killer in London is loose again," Holmes told the lady briskly. "You know Colonel Sebastian Moran?"

Morgaine blanched. "I have met him, just once, in Paris. He was with my uncle when the Professor visited me. I did not care for him."

"You are an excellent judge of character," I assured her.

"You did not, by any chance, visit the Colonel in his gaol confinement?" Holmes checked. I recalled that someone who signed herself Sybella du Plessis had been Moran's sole visitor; but the handwriting did not match that of Mrs Kent.

"No. Why would I?" Morgaine asked. "You are saying that Moran is loose?"

"The arrangements for confining him were utterly inadequate!" Holmes fumed. "They had grown lax in their vigilance, and now we must all pay for it."

"Why would the Colonel escape now? Has it something to do with the other events going on around my uncle's manuscripts?"

"The timing is highly suggestive," Holmes agreed. He moved around the room, drawing the curtains behind the window blinds. I well remembered an air-rifle shot through the glass of Baker Street delivered with absolute precision through the silhouetted head of a Holmes bust. "We must consider moving Mrs Kent to other lodgings. Precautions that would be effective against any other assassin may be insufficient against Moriarty's right hand."

I also recalled that despite Holmes' caution, agents of Moriarty had once managed to infiltrate and set fire to our chambers.

"Should we decant tonight?" I asked my friend.

"No. Such reflex response may be exactly what Moran is hoping for. Nor have we any indication that eliminating us or reaching Mrs Kent are on the Colonel's agenda."

"It seems a fair supposition to me, Holmes."

The detective had already asked the pugilists he had retained to guard the premises to remain on watch through the night. I opened, cleaned, and refreshed my service revolver. Morgaine watched our precautions with well-controlled alarm.

"Is Colonel Moran the secret force behind my troubles?" she wondered. "Was he perhaps allied with his fellow-soldier Major Saxhallow?"

Holmes snorted. "I rather think it was Watson and I who stirred this excursion. We alerted Moran to some plot to gain his old master's manuscript. Moran may well be on the trail of the same killers we are. His methodology will differ to ours."

"You mean he will leave a trail of bodies across London," I translated. "What shall we do?"

"If we pursue the mystery we shall inevitably cross paths with the Colonel. Many of the elements that have baffled us of late are secretly joined. You recall reading of the policeman's death at St Pancras Station? *That* was one of the factions that seeks Moriarty's book, having gleamed that some London rail terminal was involved in the plot. If an officer of the law interrupted them making illegal investigations…"

"He was killed to silence him!" I exclaimed.

"Factions?" Morgaine queried.

"Or partners working competitively to differing ends, perhaps," Holmes allowed. "Saxhallow sought the manuscript but seemed genuinely surprised that an attempt had been made to snatch you in Piccadilly. The methods of the masked woman and the late Major seem to have been distinctively different. And then there is the matter of Houdini."

"You do not suspect the escape man of some part of this plot?" I objected.

"I hope not," the great detective replied. "Houdini would make a supremely competent and dangerous adversary of significant resource. But he is most certainly involved in the tangle. There were the assailants on his theatre roof, common thugs hired by a slightly superior one. There are the watchers set to dog him, each hired by some different master. Either he is now hunted or he is the puppet master behind the hunt."

"I doubt he is a villain, Holmes. Beck is a very decent sort who would not associate with a scoundrel."

Holmes' smile was humourless. "Martin Beck may not know what he is dealing with. You noted the lady with whom he conferred at Tower Bridge. Come, Watson, I know you never miss a striking female."

I winced as this was said in Mrs Kent's presence. Sometimes Holmes is deaf to social nuance. "I saw Beck had a few words with a society beauty."

"I have since identified her. She is La Marqisa Marie Sigressa Alotta Francoise-Claire Saint Sirene de Confontaine et Asnières-de-la-Châtaigneraye, known more commonly as Sigrette. She is the younger sister, or some would maintain the daughter, or possibly both, of the late Le Marquis Etienne-Louis Pierre-Phillipe Saint Jealle de Confontaine, who died last year under mysterious circumstances during an encounter with Mr Harry Houdini."

"Beck… might not know that," I admitted.

Morgaine frowned. "I have heard the name Confontaine. I think that Giles—my husband—may have known him. He was part of that viper

Nestor de Maupassant's rich debauched circle, where my husband was drawn into debt and infidelity."

"Indeed," Holmes confirmed. He flicked through the pile of telegrams that had awaited him on our return. "That same Nestor who sought to influence you, Mrs Kent, to reveal or to uncover the whereabouts of Professor Moriarty's manuscript. The Nestor whose abrupt death coincided with the visit to Paris of a man called Anton Naudé, just before you were visited by your uncle, Naude's employer."

"You are suggesting that Moriarty eliminated a rival who was probing too closely into his affairs?" I recognised. As Morgaine winced I wished I had not spoken.

"The timing is suggestive. It matches perfectly with a significant payment to Nuadé in Moriarty's pay ledger."

"This is the same felon who was aboard the *Palmyra* when poor Jack Douglas was 'lost at sea'."

"What then of Amile?" Mrs Kent asked urgently. "It seems that in invoking my uncle's aid I may have doomed a man. Did I... also provoke my sister-in-law's death?" It had been around the same time that Nestor de Maupassant had died when *l'Inconnu*'s body had been dragged from the Seine.

Holmes hesitated. He looked weary. I remembered that he had endured a gruelling express journey to Paris and had worked through most of the previous night. 'What did you discover in France?' I wondered but did not ask aloud.

Holmes told me later that there had been two payments made to Naudé for his work in Paris, but he did not reveal it to the Professor's distraught niece.

"Mrs Kent, have you ever heard of the *Club de Bord Lointain*?" my friend asked instead.

"The Far Edge Club," the lady translated. "I think Giles mentioned it. A gambling den, I thought." She frowned. "Why mention it now?"

"The Far Edge Club is one of those underworld rumours, a myth whispered between rich roués and spoiled dilettantes, of a wealthy elite who thrill in courting death. This sometimes means risking their own privileged lives for the rush of surviving a near-death experience. Other times the pleasure comes from watching another struggle for life—and sometimes losing that fight."

"Surely not, Holmes," I protested. "If there is such a group then..."

"They meet from time to time across the world," the detective warned. "They rarely stay in one place for long and they do not often venture onto my domain." He referred to his telegrams again. "A number of men whose morals I have reason to question have recently entered the country. At my request my brother Mycroft has the port authorities remain alert for certain passports. Ten days ago several gentlemen whom I suspect to be Far Edgers came to England. Amongst them was Gabriel de Maupassant, Nestor's son and inheritor. Travelling with him was Sigrette de Confontaine."

"And you encountered a woman wearing dead Amile's face," Mrs Kent noted in cold angry tones. "Gabriel would have been around nineteen when Amile eloped with an unknown suitor. The father failed to seduce me to spy on Uncle James. Did the son turn his attentions to her?"

"The use of the death-mask is compelling," Holmes owned, "but hardly conclusive. I must look more closely at the doings of de Maupassant and his friends."

The hour was late but I was outraged at the things I had heard. "What can be done? Where shall we find this de Maupassant to demand answers?"

Holmes held up a long cautionary index finger. "There is nothing more to be accomplished until morning," he instructed me. "There are certain overseas messages yet to receive before I have all the information I require to act. Tomorrow I shall seek to resolve the jumble laid before us. You, Watson, must first question Beck about Houdini's involvement with the *Club de Bord Lointain* in Paris and then look to shifting Mrs Kent to a more remote location. Shall we prevail upon Henry Baskerville for some hospitality?"

"Who is Mr Baskerville?" Morgaine wanted to know. "Ah, your newest book!"

"You have read it?" I asked, absurdly pleased.

"It was most informative, John."

"Then you will know that Sir Henry is an old client and a friend who has a remote estate on Dartmoor," I explained.

"Certified free of monstrous hounds," Holmes added with a wry humour. "A place where every stranger is noted will be a better hiding place for the lady than anything London can offer. We shall make the arrangements tomorrow, Watson. You will escort Mrs Kent down there— with Mrs Kent's consent, of course."

"There is no other man whom I would trust to protect me," Morgaine answered, setting my heart singing.

Holmes pursed his lips. "Ah." He set aside his papers, rose, and clapped his hands. "Sleep," Holmes advised. "We have had a long and stressing day. Let us snatch what relief we can from Morpheus and then face the problem refreshed tomorrow."

"You will not accompany us, Mr Holmes?"

"My work will take me elsewhere. In the morning pray wire Mr Beck and invite him to join you for an early lunch, Watson. Take his testimony on the matter of the late Marquis de Confontaine and the Paris affair."

"Of course," I agreed. "And what will you do?"

Holmes would say no more. Bidding us a good-night he vanished into his chamber. Violin music came from under the door for ten minutes, and then Mr Sherlock Holmes passed into quiet slumber.

⟍⟋⟍

A report about Mr Harry Houdini:

T he *Sunday Times* had a wealth of stories to choose between as its feature articles.[62] Houdini was gratified to note that his Tower Bridge disappearance took the lead, but was less happy about the early discovery of the men he had encountered under the Thames. The retrieval of a woman's body in the river also occupied one and a half columns, enhanced by the salacious detail of her nudity save for a plaster face-mask, and by the obvious signs of her murder. The escape of the notorious Sebastian 'Tiger Jack' Moran[63] from Newgate Prison and warnings from the police about the dangers of approaching him occupied the rest of the front page.

Houdini had no reason to associate the notorious Colonel with his current problems but the incident of the masked women caught his immediate attention. He had met two such creatures less than a week

---

62 British newspapers did not then make use of banner headlines.

The Sunday Times was in no way affiliated to *The Times* newspaper until they came into common ownership in 1966. Founded in 1821 as *The New Observer* (no relation to *The Observer*, founded 1791), it became *The Sunday Times* two years later. In 1893 the paper was acquired to Frederick Beer and came under the editorship of his wife, Rachel Sassoon Beer, who also edited *The Observer*. She was the first woman to edit a national newspaper and continued in both editorial posts up to 1901.

63 This nickname for Colonel Moran comes not from the Holmes canon but from the hunter's next-most-significant appearance in two of George Macdonald Fraser's *Flashman* books, and particularly in *Flashman and the Tiger* (which also includes cameo appearances of Holmes and Watson).

Moran presumably gained his nickname on the occasion when he "crawled down a drain after a wounded man-eating tiger", as reported in "The Adventure of the Empty House". The incident is also referenced in T.S. Eliot's poem "Gus, the Theatre Cat", whose feline thespian "…once played a Tiger - could do it again - Which an Indian Colonel pursued down a drain."

before. Now-missing Lady Sabine Saxhallow had confessed to being one of them. Who was the other? And which of them had got her throat cut?

A rapid scan of the story did something to ease the escape artist's mind. The body had been in the Thames for several days, perhaps as long as a week. Sabine had been pressed up against Houdini on the dance floor just two nights since.

The other masked mystery woman had died, then? Had she too been 'loaned' to the man who had threatened Houdini and explained the rules of the Far Edge Club's sport? Had she also dared to transgress her instructions? Did the same fate now await Lady Saxhallow?

A quick flick to the obituaries confirmed the reported death of Major Sir Horace Saxhallow. "Peacefully, at home," Houdini read, and snorted. The scarlet mattress belied any claim of peaceful passing.

So what now? Houdini had vanished with the intention of throwing his murderous trackers off his trail long enough to discover who they were and to turn the game around on them. Sabine Saxhallow seemed the only lead to those unseen adversaries; yet the beautiful Afrikaner might be the deadliest trap of all.

Before the British Library Reading Room had closed yesterday, Houdini had consulted the Army Lists and found the entry for the former commander of the "Breede River Camp". The paragraphs summarised the Major's military achievements, rank advancements, and his town and country addresses. Sheafward Manor lay near Godshill, Hampshire, in the New Forest, a hundred miles southwest of London.

There were still watchers on the Lyceum and the Bridge House Hotel. Houdini scouted a wide circle round his lodging-place, identifying the men who kept vigil. There was no sign of the Graf or his minions; presumably they had staked our their hunting ground inside the building. The escape artist decided on a different target.

It was still early on Sunday morning so traffic was subdued and footfall was light, but there was enough for the escape artist to shuffle unremarked close to the alley where his selected target was positioned with field-glasses.

"Any sign of him yet?" he asked over the observer's shoulder.

"Nah. Nuthin'," came the reply before the watcher realised he did not know who'd spoken.

He turned round into a Houdini gut-punch. As he folded, the showman attached a handcuff to the cast-iron drainpipe that drew gutter water off the alley roof. The other half of the fetter snapped shut around the snooper's wrist.

"Hey, what…?" the man gasped, winded, before Houdini slammed him back against the dirty bricks of the passage wall.

"Looks like 'he's' shown up," the escape artist told the seedy spy. "What are your orders then?"

The man tried a clumsy left-handed swing. Houdini rewarded him with an ear-box. While the watcher was reeling, Houdini attached another set of cuffs so that both hands were now fettered to the cast-iron pipe. He confiscated a crude handgun, a knife, a gat, and a garrotting cord from his prisoner's pockets.

"Just so we're clear, pal, if you give me any more trouble, try any more tricks, I'll start getting nasty," Houdini warned. He pulled a cigar case from his jacket and held it carefully. "You know what a Peruvian bird-spider looks like?"

The worried captive shook his head.

"Oh, they're great. Arachnid that grows nearly as big as your hand. Bite poisonous enough to paralyse a small bird so it can be eaten alive. Or so it can lay eggs in its prey, which then hatch and eat their way out. Amazing things, Peruvian bird-spiders."

Houdini stroked his cigar case lovingly. The cuffed thug looked worried.

The showman smiled discomfortingly. "A local in Peru, a native, if he happens to disturb a nest of these things, if he gets bitten, he'll go beg a friend to finish him. They call *suparo da mercio*, the mercy stroke. 'Cause it saves the agony, see?" He pressed the stud that released the cigar case lid. "Now I've got this great bit in my upcoming show, a new act, where I get shut up with a bird-spider that could kill me with one bite. It's a trick, of course, because the bird-spider won't attack unless he spots movement or there are loud vibrations like noise. So as long as a guy doesn't move or scream or shout, well then he's just fine."

Houdini twisted the watcher around, slammed him face to the wall, and touched the cigar case to the back of the man's donkey-jacket.

"I'd be real still and quiet now, bud," the escape artist suggested.

The terrified watcher froze in place, sweating, trying not to tremble.

Houdini flicked his cigarette lighter. "I've got a part of the show where I put my arm in fire, too. There are special fluids you coat your skin with that make it flameproof for a few moments. Shame I don't have any of that stuff with me." He shifted the lighter towards his captive's cuffed hands. "You think you'll be able to keep quiet and not flinch while I burn you?"

The snooper tried not to squirm. He was certain he could feel something moving on his back. "Please!" he gasped in a whisper. "Don't. Take it away!"

"Yeah, well that depends on you really. Why are you keeping watch on me?"

"Just a job, boss. Nothing personal. I just got paid."

"Paid to do what? What were you supposed to do if you saw me?"

"I… I can't…"

Houdini raised his lighter.

"If I get a clear shot at you, I take it. Clean an' easy. If I see you but can't plug you, I tell Caddy. That's all."

"Where's Caddy?"

"I-in a Growler parked down the road. Me and Hammond an' Druther report to him. Get this thing off of me!"

"Careful. It's looking disturbed," Houdini advised. "Who hired Caddy to set you on?"

"D-dunno," he promised. "I'm just muscle. I watch where I'm told, rough somebody up if they need it. Nothing too serious usually, I swear. A bit of 'ouse-breaking if there's a search to be done. I don't usually kill people. I wouldn't really 'ave done for you."

Houdini obtained descriptions of Caddy, Hammond, and Druther. He heard about the other gangs who were staking out the hotel. One of the crews had not shown up today; presumably those men had been in the employ of the late Major Saxhallow.

He left the watcher as he was, shackled to a downpipe. "Wait," the thug protested. "What about the b-bird-spider?"

"Looks settled," Houdini admitted. "I don't really fancy trying to get him back in the box. Don't worry. I've got others I can use for the show. You keep that one."

The showman grinned and slipped off to find Caddy's growler. The unfortunate thug stood silent and still, sweating, convinced that some deadly monster clung to the back of his empty jacket.

The mentioned vehicle was parked in Thomas Street, under the shadow of the railway viaduct leading into London Bridge Station. Houdini strolled past then stopped and called to the coachman. "Hey, chum. You know your axel-pin is coming out, right?"

The jarvey climbed down to check the wheel. Houdini scientifically dropped him unconscious to the ground. He rolled the fellow underneath the Growler to avoid attention.

He slipped into the carriage to sit beside the occupant. "Caddy. I hear you've been looking for me?"

The thugs' employer reached for a walking stick that might have been a sword-stick. Houdini discouraged him with a fist to the cheek that bounced Caddy's head off the far side of the compartment.

"Don't swear like that," the showman advised as he cuffed the lowlife to the door of the carriage. "Would you kiss your mother with that mouth? Besides, that was just a light tap. Look what I've got here."

Caddy frowned as he saw the silver cuspidor in the escape artist's hands. "You seen this trick? You stick a cigar into this thing, click it down, and the blade slips the end off the stogie ready to be smoked. Then you stick a finger in there—like this."

Caddy struggled but Houdini was stronger. The thug-master's middle finger was forced into the metal circle.

"So what you do then," the showman explained, "is you snip it down and take off the digit. A good-quality cuspidor will cut right through bone. Very efficient design. Everybody screams, of course. You show the bloody severed finger all round. Then you do some hocus-pocus and you just pop the finger right back on. Tumultuous applause. Bow." He looked doubtfully at Caddy. "You do *know* how to stick your finger back on, right?"

"N-no," the villain confessed.

"Ooh. Well than, that's going to be a bit of a problem for you." Houdini pressed his finger on the clip so that the blade touched Cuddy's flesh.

"Stop! Stop it! What… what'd'you want?"

"I want goons to stop following me around and trying to kill me. Right now I want the name of the guy who sent you after me."

Cuddy blanched. "Then you better cut my fingers off. Nothing you can do to me is worse than what he'll do if I squawk."

"Really? 'Cause I've got a vivid imagination."

Pale-faced Cuddy sneered. "You're not in 'is league. I know. I've seen what 'e does to folks in his power—and to blokes what betray 'im. No, I'm not talking."

Houdini could see it in the man's face: a genuine terror beyond anything the showman might instil with methods he was actually prepared to use. He wondered at the kind of villain who could cause such fear in his minions.

Cuddy was still squirming for a way out. "I won't tell you 'oo the boss is, but… I know 'oo paid one of the other gangs what's after you. I knows about Soapy Venson's outfit."

"Who is Soapy Venson?"

"Why, 'im and 'is crew used to do the dirty for old Milverton back in the day.[64] Look, I'll give you the bloke what paid for Soapy to stalk you. That's got to be worth my fingers, right? Right?"

"Tell me, then."

"It were a Frenchie, a bloke named Maupassant."

Houdini's eyes narrowed. "Gabriel de Maupassant?" The minor aristocrat had been present at the Duke of Devonshire's ball, Houdini recalled, squiring the lady who had so captivated Beck.

"That's 'im. Frilly shirt an' nose in the air. I bet old Milverton once 'ad a whole bunch o' dirt on that stuck-up ponce!"

"Where's Maupassant now?"

"Dunno, I swear. I only knows this much 'cause one of Soapy's lads got a bit too drunk with Doxy Nell and blabbed a bit what 'e shouldn't."

"Then how do you know about Maupassant's shirt-frills?"

Cuddy blanched. "It… I might have done some work for 'im before, last time 'e were in London. Chasin' down this filly what 'e was interested in. That's all. We 'ad a bit of a barney about the price, which is why I guess 'e went to Soapy this time."

Houdini pumped Cuddy on what he knew of the Frenchman before leaving the thug-master in the same state as his coachman.

After that it took the escape artist the best part of an hour to work his way through Soapy Venson's bravos until he could press their leader for an address. The greasy little racketeer—who seemed to have acquired his nickname from an aversion to washing—eventually crumbled and admitted an address to which he was to send wires.

"It's a place called Sheafward Manor, in the New Forest, alright? Now lemme go!"

Houdini left Venter with some small reward for his unwanted services in the form of a proper drubbing. He was quick about it, though. He needed to check the Sunday service from Waterloo to get him down to the late Major Saxhallow's rural estate.

And Sabine.

<hr />

64 This would be 'the king of blackmail' described in "The Adventure of Charles Augustus Milverton". Milverton's downfall is commonly held to have taken place in 1889.

An account about Mr Martin Beck:

Given his previous experience, Martin Beck elected to take breakfast in his room. The message from Watson arrived with his tray. Beck hastened to dress to attend the proposed meeting at Baker Street. He was just fastening his cravat when there was a deferential knock at his door.

The page Bobby, on day duties this week, hovered in the corridor. "There's a visitor for you, Mr Beck, sir," he announced with a sly grin. "A *lady*."

"A lady? Who?"

"She didn't say." Bobby winked. "Shall I show 'er up, sir?" It was customary when a gentleman received a lady in his hotel room that the bellboy on duty received a generous tip for the sake of discretion.

"I'll come down," Beck answered disappointingly. He descended with Bobby to the reception lounge, where he immediately recognised the trim fashionable shape of the Marquise de Confontaine.

"M. Beck!" she cried when she spotted him. "I had to come."

"Marquise…"

"Sigrette. Remember?"

"Sigrette. It's great to see you, but I don't understand…"

The lady moved in to kiss his cheeks in the French manner. "I have word from Houdini," she whispered as she was close to his ear.

Beck took it in his stride. He had not survived this long as Houdini's manager without learning to roll with the punches. "Shall we head into the coffee lounge?" he suggested. "There is a family room."

"That would not be wise. Come with me. I have a coach outside where we can speak privately."

Beck hesitated. "Did Harry give you any special message to pass on to me?" he enquired. *A pre-arranged codeword, perhaps?*

"Yes. I will explain all when we are safe." Sigrette glanced around the lobby. She gripped his arm. "Please, M. Beck… Martin…"

"See, the thing is," Houdini's agent explained, "Harry and I have a little system for sending each other messages. A precaution, you might say. Phrases and quotes to prove that… to prove…"

Beck realised that his arm hurt where Sigrette held it. It felt like a pinprick, or the tine of a brooch jabbed into his bicep.

The room began to swim.

"I will help you out to the fresh air," the Marquise told him.

"What ha' thoo…" Beck managed to struggle out with an impossibly thick tongue.

Then he remembered nothing.

—⁊⍳⇜—

From the account of John Watson MD

When we heard the bell sound we assumed that it was Beck come to confer. Morgaine and I were surprised when Galpin shuffled into the sitting room.

"What brings *you* here on a Sunday?" I asked Doyle's secretary. "I'm afraid this isn't a very convenient time."

The fussy man was wan and stiff. "I have been given a note to convey to Mrs Kent," he answered. He held out a folded sheet of plain white paper.

Morgaine received the message from him. Her eyes widened. "This is Yve's handwriting!"

"Yes," Galpin answered tightly.

I realised that something was very wrong. "What's this all about?" I demanded of our unexpected guest.

"I am afraid, Dr Watson, very afraid, that something beastly is happening. I'm terribly sorry. This letter…"

"Read it, John," Morgaine insisted, pressing the note to me.

> Dearest Morgaine –
>
> I am writing this against my will. I am being held by men I do not know who burst into the house and dragged me away. I do not know where I am. I am very frightened.
>
> I am directed to write that you must accompany the man who delivers this note. He has instructions where to deliver you. I am assured that if you comply then neither of us will be harmed.
>
> Yours in desperation
> -Yve

I glared at Galpin. "What is the meaning of this, sir?"

"I don't know," the secretary spluttered. "Why is this happening to me?

They… they are holding my mother, Dr Watson. They say that if I do not follow their instructions then they will… hurt her."

My mind was racing. The threats to hostages had the same ruthless stench as that encounter on the steps of our lodgings a week before. Our adversary had discovered a way to circumvent all the careful precautions to protect Morgaine while she sheltered with us. Holmes' pugilist associates, the young ragamuffins on our street corners, my own readied service revolver were all useless against this coercion.

"They allowed me ten minutes to return with Mrs Kent," Galpin warned.

The lady rose. "I must go, John," she determined. "They have left me no choice."

"Where was Yve?" I asked her.

"Yve was married a little over two years ago, to Mr Francis Morrison, a stock-broker in Ealing. She is carrying their first child. I should have *thought* that my enemies might strike through her. I am a fool!"

Galpin shifted uneasily. "I am further commissioned to instruct you, Dr Watson, that if anybody attempts to leave this house other than Mrs Kent in the next twelve hours, more throats will be cut amongst the innocent poor. No alarm must be sounded, no warnings sent. Your premises are quarantined."

I rang for Mrs Hudson and apprised her of what had happened.

"What shall you do, doctor?" she asked me.

"I must go. Right now," Morgaine insisted, frightened but determined.

"Of course," I agreed. She was a lady of the finest quality, brave, noble, and self-sacrificing. "But you must not go alone."

Galpin objected. "My instructions were…"

"Damn your instructions! I will escort Mrs Kent. I daresay the criminals behind this will be glad of another hostage they can use as a lever in their machinations."

Morgaine stared at me. "You would come? Into this nightmare?"

"I must insist."

Mrs Hudson nodded fervently. "Dr Watson will see you alright, ma'am. And I'll have Mr Holmes after the pair of you as quick as I can, see if I don't."

"But…" Galpin tried to object.

"Time's up," I told him. I laid the hostage note on Holmes' desk. Who knew what the great detective could discern from those few plain lines?

Morgaine and I followed Galpin out of Baker Street to a waiting carriage. There was no-one inside the box except for the three of us. The scarf-swathed coachman made no objection to my presence, but shook the reins and headed away as swiftly as he might without causing remark.

We were taken away to meet our foe.

A report about Mr Harry Houdini:

Houdini had no way of knowing if any of the loafers around Waterloo Station worked for members of the Far Edge Club. He took precautions anyway, disguising himself with a white beard and walking cane from his collection of props at his secret lock-up. He doddered aboard the Southampton train just before the guard blew his whistle and waved his flag. He chose the endmost compartment, so if he had to leap out at some intermediate railway station he might more easily drop and roll without notice.

The train eased away from the platform, gathering steam as it passed along the elevated tracks running south parallel to a loop of the Thames. Out of the window Houdini could see the Palace of Westminster across the river—the Houses of Parliament, with the stately tower that housed Big Ben and its clock. The route skirted Archbishop's Park, passed Lambeth Bridge, then rattled on beside Albert Embankment. Over the water was the new National Gallery of British Art,[65] built on the foundations of demolished Millbank Prison. Then the train speeded past Vauxhall Bridge, where an unidentified murdered woman had been hauled from the Thames.

As the train rattled over the multiple points changes at Clapham Junction and steamed on towards Wimbledon, Houdini relaxed fractionally and opened his newspaper. Inside were the notes and maps he had assembled about his destination.

He would reach Southampton in just under two hours. From the southern coastal resort it was less than thirty miles across one of the last large woodland tracts in England to the private estate within the unenclosed pastureland, heathland and Crown forests.[66]

---

65 This building is nowadays known as Tate Britain.

66 Although called the New Forest, the landscape is actually ancient, designated by William the Conqueror as a royal hunting forest about 1079 and referred to as the *Nova Foresta*

Sheafward Manor was near the westward edge of the New Forest, accessible by a single road that branched from the route to the village of Godshill. Houdini would need a horse, then, or else a hire carriage. Could he trust a driver? He might arrive at Lady Saxhallow's estate about two and a half hours before dusk, offering him an opportunity to scout the area before making any move.

Caution was important. He knew from past experience that the dilettantes of the *Club de Bord Lontain* enjoyed going armed and liked to have brutal efficient lackeys at their call.

Houdini reviewed the options. Sabine Saxhallow was involved with the Far Edgers. She had confessed as much to him as they whirled around the dance floor at Devonshire House. She had been set on him by a man other than her husband, to whom she had been "loaned". De Maupassant? Was she victim or conspirator? Pawn or queen?

And who was the other masked woman? Mlle. de Confontaine? If so, who had the dead woman in the river been? Why did these dangerous women wear plaster masks of a long-dead mystery-girl?

Houdini was jerked from his reverie by the opening of his compartment door. An elderly vicar struggled in with a huge carpet-bag. "Pardon me, but may I join you?" he asked. "The children in the compartment where I was before are making a terrible racket."

The escape artist regarded the intruder with well-disguised suspicion. "Take a seat," he agreed, disguising his American accent. Then, impulsively, he added, "Try not to get the spirit gum holding your whiskers in place onto the seat fabric."

The vicar plumped down across from him, snorting. "Very good, Mr Houdini. I am not disappointed."

Houdini's hand jerked to his pocket for his revolver.

The vicar held up a reassuring hand. "Come now. If you have the wit to recognise a sloppily-applied disguise you can discern my true identity."

Houdini's hand on the butt of his weapon relaxed. "Mr Sherlock Holmes!" he replied. "Of course it is!"

---

in the Domesday Book tax survey of 1086, the only forest that is described in detail. Covering 219 square miles, and drained by three rivers, the area is an ecological treasure-house, home to many rare species including the indigenous wild New Forest Pony. The New Forest is now designated as a Site of Special Scientific Interest, an EU Special Area of Conservation, a Special Protection Area for Birds, and a Ramsar Site (Convention on Wetlands of International Importance, especially as Waterfowl Habitat). Ancient rights of the forest dwellers "from time immemorial" still remain and are used by locals, of common pasture, estovers (fallen wood gathering), turbary (peat cutting for fuel), marl (clay digging), pannage (grazing pigs on acorns), and fern (gathering bracken as animal litter), arbitrated by Verderers, Crown-appointed forest wardens.

The men shook hands. "I apologise for my tardiness in not paying my compliments before," the detective declared. "I have been up and down the length of the train appealing for subscriptions to the War Orphans Fund and have not identified any agent of your enemies."

"Thanks for that. So what takes you to Southampton, Mr Holmes?"

"I suspect we have mutual business at the country seat of the late Major Sir Horace Saxhallow."

"You know about the Far Edge Club? About their lethal game?"

"I suspect that you are the quarry whom they hunt. I imagine they have threatened to eliminate anyone with whom you share the problem."

"Pretty much. Now I'm going to address 'the problem' directly."

Holmes pressed his hands together, index fingers pressed to his lips, as if in prayer. "An ugly problem it is too—though fascinating from a professional point of view. I was hoping that we might exchange information and arrive at a mutual solution."

"If you mean we should team up and give the bad guys a licking then I'm for it," Houdini replied.

Holmes nodded. "Let us then reconstruct the circumstances as best we might. You have encountered this Club before?"

"The Club yes. These particular guys, no. I ran into the Marquis de Confontaine and his buddies recently over in Paris. The Marquis didn't walk away. His sister's here in England now, possibly making trouble."

"You have also crossed paths with Lady Saxhallow," Holmes noted. "I have access to the notes taken by those following you. You encountered her at a Guildhall banquet and again at the Devonshire ball."

"Yeah. Interesting lady. She likes plaster masks."

"I thought as much. Sabine Saxhallow may be the key to this affair. We must discuss her in more detail later."

"There was a third girl in a mask, who turned up dead."

"That would be Fancine Maison, formerly Dolly Coppard, a demi-monde at the establishment of Mme Deschilde in Piccadilly. She vanished one week ago today. The house was well compensated for her loss and was reluctant to speak of it."

"A prostitute? How does she fit in?"

"Miss Coppard bore a remarkable resemblance to Lady Saxhallow."

Houdini frowned. "Someone thought he was murdering Sabine?"

"I said she was key to all this. First I need to mention Amile Kent, whom you may not yet know was the original *l'Inconnu* of the Seine. As best I can reconstruct given the time that has passed, she was seduced as a means of trying to gain an 'in' to the affairs of her sister-in-law's uncle. Previous attempts by the then-Marquis de Maupassant to suborn Amile's brother and to seduce the brother's wife having failed, I believe the younger Maupassant was turned loose on inexperienced Amile."

"They killed her?" Houdini growled.

"It may be more complicated than that. That uncle, you see, was the notorious Professor Moriarty, the most dangerous man I have ever encountered, who was at that time the undisputed co-ordinator of the criminal underworld, with resources that stretched beyond Europe to every continent on the globe. The Maupassants and the Far Edge Club who sought his secrets were spectacularly out of their league."

Houdini had read Dr Watson's account of the clash between Holmes and his arch-enemy. "Moriarty was not a guy to tangle with," he agreed.

"It seems as though Moriarty took a dim view of this interference in his affairs. A man called Naudé was dispatched to Paris—and Nestor de Maupassant died."

"And this girl Amile?"

"There were at least three deaths," Holmes recounted. "Naudé was paid for two of them. I think his other victim was Giles Kent, the brother, who had foolishly given away a secret that had set the Maupassants on in the first place. I believe he was silenced, though his death was officially classed as an accidental fall from a horse. Moriarty was always thorough. Thereafter Amile became a dangerous toy for the younger Maupassant to keep. She was either murdered by him or driven to suicide. By pure chance her face attracted the attention of the mortuary pathologist and caught the interest of the mask-maker who was commissioned to prepare a cast of her corpse's features."

"Gabriel de Maupassant… if it was him I encountered in my hotel room when I was told about the Far Edge Club's wager then he likes to travel around with girls wearing the mask of his most famous victim. I guess he gets a thrill out of it."

"Amile Kent shall receive justice," Sherlock Holmes promised.

"You bet she will," agreed Harry Houdini. "But what about Moriarty's secret?"

"You ask good questions," Holmes approved. "Before his death, Moriarty concealed a manuscript which *may* have had mathematical formula or even practical applications for causing major tectonic upheaval. Methods for destroying whole cities. He left clues to the document's location engraved upon his own death-mask and ordered it conveyed to me on the tenth anniversary of his death should he fall in our struggle. Due to the recalcitrance of the niece who was charged to send it, Kent's widow, the clue did not reach me until a week ago."

"There's a city-breaking formula out there?"

"Perhaps. Watson and I recovered the manuscript but were compelled to surrender it when a masked woman threatened the lives of children, and indeed nearly killed one to enable her escape."

"When you say a masked woman…"

"She wore *l'Inconnu*'s visage, yes. That in itself is an interesting choice."

"Like she wanted you to look into the case," Houdini considered. "Another game?"

The train steamed through Basingstoke. A guard checked travellers' tickets.

"So there are two things going on with the Far Edge Club," Houdini considered. "They've come here to chase down this Moriarty thing they've been wanting for donkey's years. Must be a big thrill to them, seeing a whole city on the brink of destruction. And while they were in the country they decided it would be fun to settle the score with a guy who'd bloodied their noses before."

"The immediate start of current events appears to have been Mrs Morgaine Kent's decision to post me Moriarty's death-mask," Holmes agreed. "It was a decision she was assisted to by the counsel of Lady Sabine Saxhallow."

"They wanted you to flush out the document for them!" Houdini exclaimed.

"That is likely. Their stratagem worked."

The escape artist frowned. "Hold it! Here, in my paper… it says that Colonel Moran has broken loose from jail."

"It seems as though Moran wishes to play some part in the present drama also," Holmes owned.

Houdini's mind was racing. "So we have the members of the Far Edge Club competing to get at me. But they're working together to get a hold of Moriarty's calculations. And Moran's a wild card. But what about Major Saxhallow?"

"He was with the Far Edge Club. He died during a kidnapping attempt of Mrs Kent that Watson and I ultimately thwarted. Of interest was that he had no idea we did not still possess the manuscript. The Far Edge Club does not know where it is."

"Only the gal in the mask who took it from you," Houdini breathed. "You said Sabine was the key."

Holmes brought out a thin yellow international telegram paper. "I have only received this information today, all the way from South Africa," he revealed. "I believe that I can now fill in the missing pieces of past events and show where Lady Saxhallow connects them."

Houdini braced himself. "Tell me."

—⁄⁄⁀—

From the account of John Watson MD

Armed men met us on a lonely country road. We were searched, hooded, and bundled back into another carriage. We travelled for another hour.

At last we came to a halt. I heard the coach's wheels grinding on gravel. From the birdsong and air quality we were still in some rural setting.

We were bustled up a flight on nineteen steps. Changes in acoustics told me that we were now inside. The floor was stone, possibly marble, and then we were treading on carpet.

I heard a door open and we were bustled forwards. A young woman's voice gasped, "Morgaine!"

"Yve? Is that you? Are you alright?"

"Yes. No. What's *happening*, Morgaine?"

I was manhandled onto a chair. My wrists were wrapped with cord and bound behind the back of the seat; a professional job. My ankles were looped to the chair's front legs.

There was a pause while Morgaine was similarly restrained. Then my hood was pulled away, allowing me to see my situation.

Morgaine and I were secured in a pleasant, tastefully-furnished sitting room. Beyond the bay window was a vista of well-maintained gardens leading down to an ornamental lake. A pair of peacocks preened on the terrace. A young woman with a pregnancy-swollen belly was trussed on a chaise lounge, laid more comfortably in deference of her condition.

There were three huge brutes in the room. Morgaine glared at them. "I know you," she accused one. "You attend…"

"Me," declared an attractive blonde woman who swept through the doorway. She wore expensive town clothing with matching jewellery, but was in no way a comparable lady to Morgaine Kent.

"Sabine!" Morgaine cried, shocked and puzzled. "What are you doing here?"

"Madam, explain for what reason you have resorted to coerceion and kidnapping to bring us to this place."

"She's the one in charge!" Yve blurted tearfully. "They all do what she says. These are her brutes!"

"These are retainers that I brought back from the Transvaal," our captor replied. "They were with my late husband in the *Vryheidsoorlog*- the Freedom War."

"These men worked for Major Saxhallow?" Morgaine puzzled; from that comment I identified the stranger as Lady Saxhallow.

Our captor snorted. "These men worked for my *real* husband, not that cowardly pimp whom you so kindly rid me of two days ago."

"Madam," I interjected, "kindly have the goodness to explain for what reason you have resorted to coerceion and kidnapping to bring us to this place."

Lady Saxhallow looked at me curiously. "Dr Watson. I'm almost impressed at your stupidity in accompanying Morgaine here. It's quite touching."

"Dr Watson has proved a loyal friend," Mrs Kent answered. "I question your friendship now though, Sabine."

"Well, I at least bear you no ill-will, Morgaine. You are one of the few people in the world of whom I can say that. But since Dr Watson is accustomed to getting answers to mysteries from his celebrated friend I suppose I should indulge his remoseless curiosity and address his question."

Lady Saxhallow poured herself a sherry and took the remaining chair in the day-room. "I was born near Bethulie in the Boer Free State. My name was Sybella du Plessis."

"The name in the visitor's register at Newgate Prison!" I remarked.

"Yes. Colonel Moran was not as helpful as I hoped he might be. That was why I had to resort to Morgaine after all. But that was much later. In 1897 I was Sybella du Plessis, when I met the love of my life. We married and were happy for a short time."

"You have never mentioned him?" Morgaine accused.

"That would have been most unwise. When the war of resistance to British imperialism began two years later, my husband was at the forefront of the movement. He was not Boer by birth, but he had become one in spirit by our union. Anton had skills and experience of immense value to our cause."

"Anton?" I noticed. "Not Anton Naudé?"

Lady Saxhallow's head jerked up. "How…?" she gasped, then spat, "Sherlock Holmes!"

"Anton Naudé was Moriarty's assassin," I accused. "Naudé was most likely responsible for Giles Kent's death!"

"He was," Sabine admitted to the horrified Morgaine. "It was from that Paris mission that Anton came to know about Moriarty's unexpurgated version of *Dynamics Of An Asteroid*. In our years together he told me all about his time with 'the Professor'; told me not for any gain but just because we were close. I knew about Moriarty's concealment of the manuscript, but of course not its location. Anton discovered the plan about the death mask."

"So you sought me out when I was part of Mrs Garrett-Fawcett's Ladies Commission," Morgaine realised. "Was that Naudé's plan?"

"Anton was killed!" Lady Saxhallow snapped. It was the first real anger I had seen her display. "Christmas Day, 1900. Anton was ambushed in a cowardly British attack. He was shot down by a dozen rifles and left to rot where he fell!" She took control of herself again and added stiffly, "Then the British destroyed Bethulie. Every barn and field was burned. Every animal was slaughtered. The town was turned into one of their refugee concentration camps. Our people had the choice of starving or placing themselves at the questionable mercy of the British Empire."

"You know I do not support those deeds," Morgaine answered her.

"Many more do, though. Some are *proud* of it, how they brought the fearsome Boer to heel like whipped dogs. I would not go, though, would not crawl and beg to the very men who slaughtered my husband. Not then. Not though I starved."

"You went to Viljoensdrift, though."

"In February of 1901 I was part of a group of survivors living rough in the veldt. We were found by British troops and force-marched to the camp. I could not identify myself as Sybella Naudé, widow of the notorious freedom-fighter, so I became Sabine Cronjé. Nobody questioned it.

"Viljoensdrift was... You and your Ladies Commission, and Emily Hobhouse before that, were only permitted into the camps that were considered safe. The furthest camps from British central administration were the least regulated, the most dangerous to visit and most terrible to inhabit. Viljoensdrift was the worst. The guards who administered it were pigs. The officers who commanded them were worse. There is no atrocity you can imagine that could be wreaked on starving helpless captives that was not perpetrated there."

"I am sorry for it," Mrs Kent said. "It must have felt as if no-one cared, as if there was no justice; but not everyone forgot and nobody will be allowed to forget again."

A flash of fury from Lady Saxhallow again. "It is already being brushed away, Morgaine. Horace Saxhallow oversaw the cruelties at Viljoensdrift.

He organised them. He sold his camp to the sadists of the Far Edge Club so that they could have unfettered sport with the prisoners interned there. And for that, for all he did and all he permitted, he was merely required to retire in wealth and comfort back to his English homes. Where is justice there?"

"Then why did you marry him?" I demanded.

"What other means did I have, to survive Viljoensdrift or to destroy him? Only by matching and bettering the excesses of de Maupassant and his cronies, by impressing them with my innovative cruelties, could I avoid being subject to theirs. I gained access to their Far Edge circle by being as wicked as they. I used every skill that Anton had taught me and every wile of my own. I captured Horace as surely as he had imprisoned me. At first it was me who wore the fetters. By the end it was him."

"You married him to accomplish his destruction," I understood. "So Mrs Kent's kidnapping…?"

"I spurred de Maupassant to that bungled effort at the National Gallery," Lady Saxhallow revealed. "Given its poor planning and flawed execution it was bound to fail. It served its purpose, though, prompting Morgaine Moriarty to flee her home and seek refuge with a friend she had come to trust—me."

"I thought you *were* my friend," Morgaine admitted, sadly.

"Horace thought my actions served the Far Edge Club, congratulated me on my initiative. He gladly arranged to extract Morgaine from Berkley Square to question her about the whereabouts of Moriarty's mask."

"It had already been sent to Mr Holmes," Mrs Kent objected. "You knew that. You urged it of me."

"Horace did not know. The secret of that dispatch was shared only by you and I."

"Then you were the ruthless fiend who cut that girl's throat in the road at Baker Street," I accused.

"I have done far worse in my Viljoensdrift days," our captor assured me. "That same night I also killed the whore whom I had retained to impersonate me with Gabriel de Maupassant, to give me an alibi with the Far Edge Club. Men scarcely look at their women's faces anyway, do they? Certainly not when they are masked."

"Why kill her, then?"

"To silence her, and because I despised her; despised what both of us do for men. I left her mask on to draw your friend Holmes closer to Gabriel's trail."

Morgaine shivered. "You arranged for my kidnapping by Major

Saxhallow to bring Mr Holmes and Dr Watson against him, to cause his downfall. You murdered some poor girl just to set them against de Maupassant in the same way."

"The blank bullets in the Major's gun!" I remembered.

"You may thank me for your life, Dr Watson. At least for preserving it then. I offer no such assurances today. And I have claimed you from Baker Street, Morgaine, so that Holmes will move against my enemies anew," Lady Saxhallow explained. "But not for that reason alone. That is why I shall allow Dr Watson to live on for a short while longer."

"Do not cross her," Yve warned us. "She has a temper and she knows how to cause hurt."

"I have Professor Moriarty's manuscript and his death-mask," Lady Saxhallow revealed. "I have his formula. But it makes no sense. It is still encoded."

"And you need Holmes to break that code," I understood. "He will not."

"Not even when I begin to send him slices of Dr Watson and Mrs Kent? We shall see."

One point remained. "What about the business with Houdini, then?" I demanded. "How does that serve your mad revenge?"

Lady Saxhallow smiled. "Can you think of a more dangerous foe against whom to pit the Far Edge Club?" she challenged me. "What enemy is more likely to push them off that edge?"

A report about Mr Harry Houdini and Mr Sherlock Holmes:

"There are guards round the perimeter," Houdini observed.

"The remnants of Soapy Ventner's miscreants who did not fall to the law after the unpleasant Milverton's demise," Holmes recognised, "and a few men who move more like ghillies or hunters. You are expected."

"So de Maupassant or Sabine are setting a trap for me. Why would they expect me here?"

"You mentioned interviewing some of the underlings who were set to watch your hotel. Surely one or more of them must have sent word that this location was betrayed?"

Houdini ranged his binoculars over the Sheafward Manor estate. "I count seven men on patrol, plus one on the roof of the coach-house and two on the balconies over the portico."

"There is also the baying of hunting dogs. Your adversaries expect to enjoy a chase before completing their wager."

"Well the first rule of stage magic is never do what they expect."

Holmes borrowed the field glasses. "Sheafward Manor follows the same layout as many such country residences. The main residential block has a formal frontage with a ground floor raised slightly above ground level to allow window lights to domestic rooms below. An upper floor is devoted to guest bedrooms with an attic tier for servants' use. Domestic buildings at the rear linked to house, stables, and a meadery to form a courtyard. Formal gardens to the western side of the range. Orchards and apiaries to the south."

"There's got to be more goons inside that we can't see. Probably other traps too."

Holmes played the binoculars over the windows. "It would be useless to summon the constabulary yet. There is no crime in holding a country gathering, no matter how many seedy retainers of low character one brings along. Unless one of those retainers is a known and wanted felon, the police would be helpless to interfere."

"By the time we got evidence to bring in the bulls we'd be in too deep to go fetch 'em," Houdini concluded. "I don't fancy our chances in the firefight, two of us versus everyone who's waiting for us. We've got to be smart."

"You have an idea, Mr Houdini?"

"I might have, Mr Holmes. What say we wait and watch until night? There's no rush, so we might as well gather as much information as possible. About one or two in the morning we set a diversion and sneak inside. We try to find the boss-men, whoever's in charge there. Probably this de Maupassant character. We work out how Sabine's tied into this too, because if what you said on the train is right she might not be on the same side as the Far Edge Club at all."

"Sybilla du Plessis has every reason to hate them—and us. That is why the possibility of her having possession of Moriarty's equations is of much concern. Imagine the revenge a bereaved and vengeful widow might take on the capital city of the Empire that killed her husband if she had a process capable of triggering cataclysm."

"So we go in the magician's way, secretly, and we pick their pockets before they know what's happening. We've got plenty of time to set up something clever, so…" Houdini paused, then reported, "There's a carriage coming."

Holmes and Houdini hunkered down in the greenery by the treeline from which they were observing the house. A four-wheeled enclosed carriage rumbled down the drive to the manor and halted beneath the portico.

Houdini had the field glasses. "Three more grunts by the look of it—and a lady. That's the Marquise de Confontaine. Makes sense, I suppose. She's one of Maupassant's entourage of likely suspects. And someone else is climbing down out of the… Beck?"

The escape artist turned to Holmes in dismay. "They've gotten Martin Beck! That's how they intend to lure me down here. They have my buddy."

Holmes and Houdini watched as the impresario was bundled up the steps into the hall.

"This shifts the timetable somewhat," Holmes observed. "We cannot discount the possibility of our opponents attempting to extract your location from Mr Beck using force."

"Beck doesn't know where I am," Houdini pointed out, "but they won't believe him, will they? They'll just keep on torturing him. So we have to go in now."

It was almost dusk. The sun was red and low over the trees to the west, casting long shadows on the eastern side of the estate where the wash-house and potting sheds lay. Houdini's eyes ranged over the scene. "You up for a climb, Holmes? Because I'm guessing that second storey window there by that drainpipe might be a way in—as long as everyone's looking the other way."

"The window may be trapped, of course," the detective cautioned. "The diversion will need to be lengthy and significant."

"Don't worry about that," Houdini promised. "These guys snatched Beck. I'm going to set fire to their coach house and stables."

➳❀❧

A report about Mr Martin Beck:

Gabriel de Maupassant sat on a chair that might as well have been a throne. He regarded the masked woman who glided in with the guarded Beck and asked in French, "Where is Sabine?"

"She never made the rendezvous," Sigrette replied. "I told you there was something odd going on. That woman the newspapers spoke of, with the cut throat and the plaster mask… was that Sabine's doing?"

"No orders of mine. Perhaps her useless husband? But where is she now?"

"I do not know."

"I do not know, what?"

"I do not know, master."

De Maupassant nodded, satisfied for now that at least the Marquise remembered proper submission. He turned his attention to Beck where the manager had been thrown to the floor. "Has the situation been explained to you, little man?"

"You're another of those spoiled rich sadists from the *Club be Bord Lontain*, in England to have another go at Harry Houdini," Beck summarised. "There are five of you over here having some kind of competition to see who can kill him first. Four now that Lady Saxhallow's husband has turned up dead. Houdini was warned about your game as part of the sport, and told that you'd kill anyone he told about it. That's why he's been so secretive and suspicious this past week. You've grabbed me in the hopes of luring him into whatever trap you're setting here, and what you really need is kicking in the pants so hard you won't sit down for a week and being made to do an honest day's work."

"I briefed him on his role as bait as we travelled down here, master," Sigrette confirmed. "He was…" Beck was the first man who had listened with any degree of sympathy to her story of abuse and servitude since her youngest days with her wicked brother. "He does not know where Houdini is or what Houdini is doing."

"Well, that's still to be tested properly," de Maupassant pointed out. "They've set up my work-table in Saxhallow's gun room." He gestured for his men to haul the bound Beck to his feet and bring him along. "Was there any further word on Morgaine Kent or the Moriarty formula when you left London?"

Sigrette followed through the house after captive and captor. "There are rumours that Mrs Kent may have been rescued by Sherlock Holmes. That is what happened to Saxhallow. He evidently got his hands on the woman but was killed before he could discover the location of death mask or manuscript."

"Sherlock Holmes." De Maupassant's eyes glinted. "There would be a fine hunt, don't you think?"

"It may be that Holmes has also found Sabine. That could be why she is not here."

"If not then she is being disobedient. I'd have thought by now she would have learned the penalty for displeasing her betters. As you have, Sigrette."

"Yes, master."

The billiards table in the Gun Room had been converted into a makeshift interrogation slab. Beck was shackled down across it spread-eagled before he could resist. Fear washed the last of the drug that the marquise had used to capture him out of his system. "For a man who supposedly likes close-death experiences you seem an awful coward," he told de Maupassant.

"I save my encounters for those who are worthy of me," the French aristocrat replied. "You are nothing more than a seedy petty variety-show tout, a nobody scarcely crawled from the gutters. Your only part in this is to scream and to tell me where your friend is."

"I wouldn't squeal even if I knew. Go to hell and take all your Club with you!"

De Maupassant glided over to the side-table where a case of silver surgical instruments awaited his selection. "You are the entrée, little man. We shall devour you while we await the main course. You can shorten your agony by helping to serve him up, or we shall just have to make you last. I have managed to maintain subjects in unspeakable pain for many hours. Be certain that your torment will be no less than theirs."

If Sigrette was distressed at Beck's fate or if she anticipated it, l'Inconnu's mask covered all.

De Maupassant chose a small simple scalpel to begin with. It could cut away clothing and make a few small incisions to get some blood flowing. That always helped his subjects understand their position. "Nothing to say, M. Beck?" he mocked his prisoner.

Beck replied, "Can you smell smoke?"

De Maupassant turned sharply. "Investigate," he ordered Sigrette. "Houdini may be here, Lancier," he told his most trusted retainer. "Activate those precautions we set."

His minions scurried away. De Maupassant leaned over Beck. "Tell me, do you think your friend will surrender when he arrives and finds I have a blade at your jugular, or will he sacrifice you and choose life?"

Beck glowered but said nothing.

The Marqisa hastened back into the gun room. "The stables are ablaze. When men tried to run in there to douse the conflagration they set off some kind of trap that dropped the estate's beehives on them. The swarms were furious. The flames have got a grip of the coach-house too. I do not think they can be stopped."

"A diversion, then. Houdini wants us looking that way. He is a conjurer and so thinks he is clever. Have men check the upper floors. He will be sneaking in that way."

"And the fire?"

"Abandon it. Let Saxhallow's place burn. We will not need it soon."

Sigrette swept away to pass instruction on to Lancier. The hallway outside was filled with smoke-stained men with scarves and cloths wrapped about their faces. She directed them to leave off the bucket-chain and attend to the Houdini hunt.

"There!" someone cried. "On the next floor. This way!"

The halloo went up. Thugs armed with blades and cudgels, some better equipped hunters with guns, all charged up the main staircase.

"Some of you go by the servants' stairs," Sigrette called. "Fan out. Take every route."

"In here! This bedroom…"

"The dumb waiter! The dumb waiter is going down. He's in the moving cupboard!"

"The basement. The kitchen block. That's where he is! Down! Down!"

"Some of you remain upstairs," Sigrette called. "It may be a ruse. Don't all stampede to the cellars."

"That door moved! He's in the wine store. This way!"

"Where is he? It's dark in here. Fetch a lantern!"

"Check between all the racks. Spread out and search it all."

"Where's that light? What idiot has shut the door?"

"It's locked. Bolted from the outside! What…?"

"We're shut in! Find another way out."

"It's a wine cellar, idiot. There are bars on the windows. Break down that door."

"It's reinforced. What's that smell?"

"Gas. We're being gassed. What is it?"

"It's bleach. It smells like bleach. My eyes sting. Agh!"

"It's coming through that broken ventilator. It *is* bleach—bleach with acetone!"[67]

"I can't breathe. I can't see… Get that door open!"

"Who… who led us in here? Who…?"

"Get out of my way. I'll kill you all!"

---

[67] On a ratio of 50:1 this is the formula for chloroform. Ice is usually added to ensure the chemicals do not immediately form poisonous clouds. Holmes and Houdini may not have bothered to raid the ice house on this occasion.

In the main hall upstairs, Lancier was fuming. "Idiots! Everyone was covering his face while we fought the blaze. He came in with us as part of the bucket chain, then led us on the hunt for himself!" The mercenary fired his gun into the air. "Shaddup! Nobody moves. Nobody speaks. Just everybody take your scarves off so I can see who you are. Now!"

One swathed figure dodged away into the breakfast room and from there through the connected chambers of the eastern range.

Sigrette pointed. "Him! Stop him! Catch him *now!*"

The chase proper began. The fugitive crashed through a picture window and escaped onto the terrace.

De Maupassant watched with amusement. "I'm quite impressed. Your friend did rather well, M. Beck—to a point. Now he's going to get chased through the forest and brought down like the animal he is. What have you to say about that?"

"I'd say you've underestimated Harry Houdini," Beck replied.

The Frenchman turned to retort and caught a roundhouse punch from Houdini right in the face.

De Maupassant tumbled back, steadied himself, and assumed a boxing stance. "How did you manage that?" he demanded.

Houdini assayed a feint left and a straight right. "Punching you in the face? Balance on the balls of the feet and put your whole weight behind it. Very enjoyable. The two-places-at-once thing? Professional secret."

The Frenchman responded with a pair of taps that Houdini fended away with his left but still managed to land a reasonably solid stomach blow. "Did you think I would be easy prey, American? I have trained with the finest boxing tutors in Europe. It will be my pleasure to instruct you."

Houdini feinted to the right and caught de Maupassant a buffet on the left ear. "Well I learned on East 79th Street, New York City, and the guys there would eat your instructors for breakfast, buster."[68]

Beck called from his position on the billiards table. "Houdini, would you please just beat the fellah to a pulp and get us out of here? This place is filling with smoke. Is a burning house really the best place to exchange *bon mots* with the bad guy?"

"He's the one running out of time," the escape artist called back to Beck. "Once the fire's seen there'll be all kinds of people coming. Fire brigade, police, eventually the press. I don't think the Far Edge Club likes publicity much. All I have to do is keep hitting him, and that's no hardship at all."

---

68 Houdini was thirteen in 1887 when he and his father moved to a rough part of New York, four years before he began his at-first-unsuccessful stage career (not counting his trapeze debut at nine as Ehrich, Prince of the Air).

There was an explosion outside the house. A couple of window-panes cracked.

"That'll be the meadery," Houdini explained, landing another right hook on the distracted de Maupassant. "It was kind of rigged to go up when your searchers chased in there. Alcohol is a great accelerant."

Holmes was doing a splendid job leading the hunters away from the house into a series of prepared traps. The criminals were up against not one but two of the most dangerous men in England, whose abilities and knowledge were complementary and who were not renowned for their conventional behaviour. The detective had chivvied the Far Edge minions into the cellar and out to the meadery leaving the way open for Houdini to remove the traps and open the locks that guarded his friend.

De Maupassant fell back and reached his instrument case. He selected a carving knife to change the balance of power in the confrontation.

"Oh, we're cheating," Houdini scorned.

"I am merely demonstrating my superior resource, you buffoon," sneered the Far Edger.

"Ah, right. Well here's my superior resource, then," the showman responded. He pulled his gun and aimed it at de Maupassant.

"A shot will bring my people in here at once," the Frenchman sneered.

"First five of them will be in trouble," Houdini replied as he fired into de Maupassant's leg. The arrogant nobleman fell to the ground screaming.

Sigrette burst in to see what was happening. Houdini hesitated to shoot at a woman.

Lancier burst through the other door, rifle aimed. "Hold it there, Houdini! Weapon down and hands up! Right now!"

Holmes appeared behind the henchman and applied a baritsu nerve-jab to disarm him. Another blow dropped the brute to the floor.

The Marquise de Confontaine levelled her own Derringer at Houdini. "I could win the contest right now," she told him.

"You might, madam," Holmes told her, "but then you would never be free of de Maupassant and his friends."

"Sigrette," called Beck, "Don't!"

The masked woman fired three shots into Houdini's chest.

―ゝ│ヽー

From the account of John Watson MD

Sabine Saxhallow, or whatever she chose to call herself, confined us for the night in an underground room at whatever estate she had hidden us away in. "I apologise for the unpleasant confinement, but I have only a few loyal men to act as guards," she told us. "Better to hold you all in a windowless cellar where one sturdy door requires only one armed sentry than try to be civilised and offer you better accommodation."

"Civilised?" spat Morgaine, "After you tortured Dr Watson to try and wring from me information I do not have about my uncle's code?"

"I believe you now," our captor replied. "You have a fondness for the gallant doctor which would have caused you to betray whatever you knew. You know nothing. As for him, I have no fondness for British soldiers."

I was more concerned for Yve Morrison, who was approaching her third trimester and should not be subjected to shocks and hardship. "Some comfort for a mother-to-be would not betray your vengeance," I told Lady Saxhallow.

"I've seen plenty of miscarriages caused by your Empire," Sabine snarled. "Another lost baby is of no matter to me."

This was indeed the monster who had coldly slit an urchin's throat merely to facilitate an easy getaway.

"At least assure us that you have allowed Mr Galpin's family to go in peace," Morgaine asked her.

Our captor snorted. "Oh, Galpin's family are perfectly safe."

"And Galpin himself?"

"You will see him again when the time is right."

Sabine turned to go, but Morgaine had one more question for her. "You have asked me many things. There is only one thing I want to know from you. Why did you wear that mask of Amile's face?"

Lady Saxhallow's own visage might as well have been plaster for all the expression it showed. "That was not my fetish, but Gabriel's. Your foolish sister was the first girl he ever killed. When her face became famous he was surprised and delighted. He adopted the mask as his own personal trophy, for every whore and victim he had afterwards to wear. I think he enjoys hurting Amile still. But fear not, Morgaine. Your sister and all who have played her part shall soon be revenged."

The door closed, leaving us in the gloom of a sealed space with but a single candle.

Morgaine hastened over to me to check my hurts. "I will be fine," I assured her. "I've had much worse. Sabine was working to spur you to speak, not to harm or break me. There's nothing that a few bandages and a bit of time won't mend."

"You have suffered these wounds because you came with me. If you had not been there, Sabine would have inflicted these injuries on me—or on poor Yve. John… I…"

"Now, Morgaine. You've been a rock until now. Hold fast, dear lady, and we'll see our way through."

"You don't understand, Dr Watson. I did not know the answers to Sabine's questions so I could not tell her what she wanted to know. But if I had known… I would still have remained silent!" The lady looked away, ashamed.

"But of course you would," I answered. "We cannot yield to coercion, can we? It is not done."

"You… you understand?"

"Absolutely."

"But you cannot forgive."

"There is nothing to forgive, Morgaine. Your resistance does you credit. I am flattered that your confidence in my character is such that you would honour my wishes not to be used as some lever by our enemy."

Yve watched us with confused, frightened eyes. "But what is to become of us?" she worried. "What about my baby?"

"We must all hold on," I told her. "Tomorrow night is the gala opening of Houdini's show. When the curtain falls at the end then the Far Edge Club's challenge is evidently defeated. By then Holmes will have found our trail and will be ready to bring the wrongdoers to book. All we need do is remain calm and be prepared."

We made Yve as comfortable as possible on a pile of sacking. The exhausted mother-to-be quickly curled up and passed into a dreamless sleep.

I leaned against the far wall and stretched my legs over the cobbles. "My shoulder is somewhat more padded than the stones," I noted. "Would you wish to make use of it, Morgaine?"

The lady nodded mutely and came for shelter in the circle of my arm. "You are a good companion in adversity, John Watson," she whispered.

"You are a good companion always," I answered her.

We did not notice when the candle guttered out.

A report about events at the Lyceum Theatre
Monday, 12th May, Houdini's Gala Opening

The man who wrote as 'Langdale Pike' looked as elegant as ever in formal evening dress with black tie.[69] He glided down the ornate main staircase of the refurbished Lyceum, pausing to nod or exchange some salacious word with the famous and the beautiful. He wove through the rich crowd milling in the foyer and located his target.

"Quite the show, Mr Galpin," he greeted Doyle's nervous-looking secretary. "Delicious, isn't it?"

"Nobody knows where Houdini is," Galpin replied. "He is still missing. Yesterday's dress rehearsal was cancelled. Some people are saying he's dead, that he drowned in the Thames."

"Oh, there are much better stories than that," London's foremost gossip columnist promised. "Did you hear the one about his being shot leaving his hotel room? That the management covered it up to maintain their reputation? Or else he was stabbed by a lady at some secret love-nest in the New Forest. Or perhaps he was kidnapped by a foreign power who want to know about his secret work for the War Department."

"Are any of those true?" Galpin frowned.

Langdale Pike shrugged. "Do they have to be? I thought stories were your employer's stock in trade. Was Doyle very unhappy that you failed to sign Houdini for a series of adventure yarns?"

The secretary started. "What? How can you know about...?"

"Oh, my dear chap, it's common knowledge. Doyle himself was going on about it at his club. Apparently he felt you pushed a little too far."

"If I had got the contract, all of this publicity would have made a magazine series into best-sellers," Galpin replied sullenly.

"I could have told you Beck would never let that happen, old boy. Houdini's all about being in control. He wouldn't surrender his literary destiny to you or Sir Arthur."

Galpin frowned. "Doyle's no knight," he objected.

Pike tapped the side of his nose. "The post of Deputy-Lieutenant of Surrey is becoming vacant before Christmas," he purred. "The incumbent

---

69 The "strange" and "languid" celebrated gossipmonger makes the briefest of appearances to assist Holmes in identifying a suspect in "The Adventure of the Three Gables". Secondary sources have fleshed out his background significantly but never authoritatively. It is generally accepted that Langdale Pike is a pseudonym; Langdale Pike is actually a prominent geological feature in the Cumbrian Lake District.

usually picks up a knighthood to go with it. You didn't hear it from me, though. The Crown likes to keep these things a surprise."[70]

The secretary shook his head. "So you know where Houdini is?"

"No idea, old thing. But I'd love to know. And look at this mob here. They're panting to know as well. *Will* the celebrated Houdini make a surprise sudden appearance at the last minute? All entrances are watched. Will he once again baffle and astound? We will be on the edge of our seats."

Galpin shifted slightly away from the effete columnist. There was something unsettling about the elegant, sophisticated Pike. "They're saying that Martin Beck has vanished too. Disappeared off with a woman yesterday and didn't come back."

"Bully for him if that's what he likes," Langdale Pike approved. "Would have expected him to be here to shepherd this crowd, though. Half of London society is here, and a few choice specimens from over the Channel."

Galpin looked around. "Who do you mean?"

Pike extended a delicate index finger. "There, being helped to his box, that's Gabriel de Maupassant. Old émigré money, lives it large in *fin de siècle* Paris. The nymph supporting him is the delicious Marquise de Confontaine, who is a very lively lass by all accounts. I wonder who arranged those bruises over Gabriel's face? I must find out."

The gossip columnist looked about. "The turbaned fellow is Prince Dakir, son of the Rajah of somewhere-unpronounceable-or-other. Rich as Croesus. Gives sybarites a bad name. And there's the Graf von Sigren, Bavarian big game hunter. Wouldn't have thought this was his cup of tea at all. Not enough blood around. And there's the Spanish gambler Alançon. Hmm. Takes a lot to get him to these chilly climes."

"You seem to have catalogued the whole theatre," Galpin observed.

"Oh no. The uppermost galleries are closed tonight. No-one is allowed in the gods.[71] And there's a Personage or Personages in box five with the curtains drawn. Très mysterious, my dear."

"You really think Houdini will appear?"

"I very much doubt a fellow like that could resist an audience like this. Don't you?"

"I expect... I think tonight will be very interesting," Galpin told Pike. "Wait—look there!"

---

70 On November 11th, 1902, six months after our present narrative, Conan Doyle was made a Knight Batchelor (the lowest rank of British knighthood) by King Edward VII and appointed Deputy-Lieutenant for Surrey (second in command to the Lord Lieutenant of the shire, both ancient senior military posts appointed directly by the Crown).

71 The very topmost tier of seats with the very worst view, usually the cheapest seats in the theatre, were unlikely to be utilised at a gala performance where the hoi-poloi were excluded.

Martin Beck appeared on the balcony above the foyer. "Honourable guests, ladies and gentlemen, would you be so good as to take your seats?"

"One missing player found then," Langdale Pike noted. "No sign of the great man yet, of course."

"Take your places, please," Beck called to the gala crowd. "The show is about to begin."

From the account of John Watson MD

Morgaine and I were placed in box five, handcuffed to our chairs to prevent any sudden decision to escape if threat to the gravid Yve Morrison proved insufficient. The presence of two of Sabine Saxhallow's three loyal Boer retainers sat behind us was an added precaution.

Sabine seemed very excited, peering through the box's closed curtains at the circle and the other boxes, identifying people she knew. "Von Sigren... Dakir... Alançon. Yes, they have all come to be in at the kill. Even de Maupassant has crawled out of whatever hole he fled to after the events at Sheafward Manor. So he has reason to believe that Houdini is still alive too?"

"If you intend to gloat, madam, then you will need to offer better context for it," I told our captor.

Sabine turned to me. "Ah, but of course, Dr Watson. I do apologise. I want you to fully understand the nature of the little drama that is about to play out here."

"You have all the Far Edge Club gathered together in one place, where they can make their final attempts on Mr Houdini's life should he appear," Morgaine understood.

"As many as I could lure to London with the game, yes, or for a chance at your uncle's amazing manuscript. Enough for now, anyhow. And also so many of 'the great and the good' of your British Empire too. Nobles, guildsmen, politicians, ambassadors, captains of industry, the rich, the idle, the *parasites* who backed the destruction of my homeland. All here at last!"

"What do you intend, madam?" I demanded.

"Well first I intend to enjoy the show," Sabine assured me. "I hope that

Mssrs Houdini and Holmes do not disappoint. And then I intend to bring the house down."

I realised that she meant it literally. "You want to blow up the Lyceum?"

"It will have been searched, of course. Each member of the Far Edge Club has his own security precautions and all will have been looking around for Houdini as well. All of them have overlooked one thing. Can you tell me what, without help from your clever friend, Dr Watson?"

I was baffled. Morgaine was not. "The Lyceum has been closed for refurbishment after a fire. Builders have restored it to its former glory."

"Men working for me," Lady Saxhallow boasted. "Men who were able to conceal explosives in the very walls, to sabotage every support beam, to turn this whole edifice into a death trap to slaughter over two thousand enemies!"

"Mass murder!" I gasped. "Whatever happens with the Far Edge Club's Houdini-hunt, you intend for *everyone* to die!"

"Not you and precious Morgaine, doctor. Not yet. I need you alive and sliceable tomorrow to convince Sherlock Holmes to do my bidding. You are here as my witnesses, not as my victims." She glared again at the filling auditorium, an unholy joy in her countenance. "This destruction tonight is only down-payment. One day I shall use Moriarty's method and reduce this whole city to rubble and ruin."

"Your torments in Viljoensdrift have driven you mad," Morgaine recognised, not without sympathy.

"The British Empire has taken from me my husband, my honour, and my future," Sabine Saxhallow declared. "I shall take from it its leaders and its capital."

"I shall not allow it," I told her.

"Nor I," agreed Morgaine. Our eyes met in perfect agreement. We would die to stop her if we must.

"Then you will sacrifice Yve and her unborn child," Sabine pointed out. "Now at last you begin to understand the mathematics of the concentration camp."

Whatever retort we might have made was interrupted by the dimming of the house lights and the rustling as the stage curtain rose.

A report about events at the Lyceum Theatre

The audience fell silent. A low drum roll vibrated from the audience pit. A spotlight lit the centre of the stage. The only furnishings, behind the circle of light, were a hatbox on a pedestal and the ornate glass-walled water-filled tank where Houdini was expected to escape his chains before drowning.

A trapdoor glided back, allowing a coffin-sized box to rise up from beneath the boards. Martin Beck's voice boomed around the theatre. "Lords... ladies... gentlemen... From the centre-stages of America, from the great theatres of Continental Europe... The master of his art, the wonder of the age..."

Five shots burst into the wooden frontage of the rising box. The bullets came from the gods' gallery, where an assassin lay with a sniper rifle.

A quick spotlight wheeled around to illuminate the killer as he abandoned his weapon and tripod to race for the exit stair. The audience, unsure if that was part of the show, watched in alarm as he made his escape.

A second spotlight found Harry Houdini, racing to intercept the would-be murderer, vaulting over dusty empty bench-seats and jumping on the assassin.

"May I present: Harry Houdini!" bellowed Beck as the escape artist took the gunman down.

The audience went wild.

Uniformed officers and Inspector Merivale of the Yard hastened up to the highest balcony to accept custody of the apprehended killer. The assassin's weapon would later be proved to have also killed the policeman at St Pancreas, another offence that would have sent its owner to the gallows had he not already been swinging there.

Houdini tossed a rope over the edge of the gallery and rappelled down to the stage. He took a bow.

"Thanks for the welcome," he told his crowd. "Sorry about the heckler. I guess you've been wondering what's been going on, where I've been these last few days. It's quite a story. And there's only one guy could tell it properly."

He moved over to the box whose front was marred by bullet-holes. He unclipped the clasps and threw the lid open.

Mr Sherlock Holmes appeared on the stage, announced by Martin Beck.

Holmes was not inexperienced on the stage or averse to a touch of drama. He took a bow.

"There has been a plot laid against England," he told the distinguished members of the audience. "A plot laid by those who fancy that their wealth and privilege shield them from the consequences of their actions. The attempt you just witnessed to do away with Mr Houdini is not their first attempt nor intended as their last. Tonight, before your eyes, we shall expose these criminals and lay their machinations bare. Then we shall see if their connections and corruption can truly shield them from the power of British justice."

In his box, Gabriel de Maupassant stirred to leave. "Come now," he ordered Sigrette. "This is going sour. Houdini somehow survived your shots. He and the detective have laid some scheme against us. We must leave—now."

The Marquise rose obediently, but her troubled eyes were drawn back to the stage and the confident, striding showman who commanded it. She had chosen murder over salvation, yet here Houdini was, alive and whole.

In the rear access corridor outside the theatre box, de Maupassant's two remaining enforcers were struggling with constables. Inspector Lestrade aimed a snub-nosed pistol at the fleeing Frenchman. "Stay just where you are, sir. I am an officer of the law, and I am h'apprehending you on a charge of..."

The phlegmatic Scotland Yard officer was distracted by Sigrette hurling herself into his arms and crying "Save me!" Before Lestrade could react she had twisted the gun from him and kneed him in the groin. As the inspector doubled over, before the constables pinning de Maupassant's guards could react, the Marquise and her master raced away down the lavish carpeted access hall.

"This way, Sigrette!" de Maupassant called to her. "Put on your mask and come with me."

"Gabriel—master—we have to get away from here."

"Not yet. If there are police here then the regular exits will be watched. And one player in our game is not yet accounted for." He sped across the almost-empty saloon bar behind the auditorium into the access corridor on the other side of the house. "You noticed the drawn curtains in box five?"

He drew a revolver and went to find Sabine Saxhallow.

Box five was empty.

Holmes and Houdini still commanded the stage. "There is a society of rich sadists and wastrels known as the Far Edge Club," the great detective told his distinguished listeners. "They hold themselves above the law by virtue of their rank and privilege. They thrill at murder, at hunting and torturing to death whatsoever victims they choose for their perverse sport. They operated in many distant corners of the world but tonight they have chosen London for their entertainment."

There was a susurrus of disapproval from the patriotic audience.

"I've taken them on before," Houdini declared. "Crossed 'em in Paris last year. That's why they're trying to kill me, as you saw tonight. They tried before in the Thames under London Bridge. I guess you all read in the papers how that worked out."

"They have committed to a wager amongst themselves as to which of them can murder Houdini," Holmes revealed. "The bet expires at the end of tonight's show, so their quarry's disappearance made them desperate, but also hungry for the kill. They are amongst us here tonight."

The crowd looked around, each assessing the others as potential murderers.

"That's fine," Houdini announced. "We wanted to bring them all together, where we could drag them from the shadows in front of witnesses no-one can deny. Ladies and gentlemen, I need some audience participation."

"A number of traps and assassins have been deployed here tonight," Holmes noted. "Several felons are already in the hands of Scotland Yard. A number of ingenious methods of administering poison, releasing venomous creatures, or delivering death by mechanical trap have already been deactivated." The detective turned to the large glass water-tank behind him. "Here is another one. This has been cunningly attached to the theatre's electrical generator, so that the frame is electrified when a pressure plate at the tank's bottom detects the weight of a man upon it. Ingenious but obvious."

"Nobody beats me on my stage," promised Houdini. "So I want some volunteers from the crowd. Come on down here, Prince Dakir. I've got a trick to show you that you won't enjoy as much as those you like to play. And you, Senor Alançon. I'll bet you won't like the gamble you're about to take. Oh, and you, Graf von Starken. No, don't leave. This hunt is over."

As the showman spoke, spotlights picked out each of the discomfited members of the Far Edge Club. The audience's attention on them was rapt and unwelcoming.

"I see our other special guests are already trying to exit the premises," Houdini noted. "Don't worry. They won't get far."

"Break off those chains!"

"Bring those men down here," Holmes commanded the officers who appeared to bundle the surprised gamesters from their seats. "Houdini, would you retrieve the others? Especially…"

"On it," the escape artist assured him. "Orchestra, keep 'em amused. Give 'em *Camptown Races.*"[72] He tossed the stalls a wave and hastened offstage, leaving Holmes to co-ordinate bringing the captured and protesting Far Edgers together.

Sabine Saxhallow had already led her captives and minions down to the deepest level of the theatre's cellars. There was the grating that led into the lost watercourse. She had identified the secret way during the weeks that masons in her pay had been working on the Lyceum's refurbishment. She had always intended it as an emergency exit.

Now she understood it was also the means by which Houdini and Holmes had entered the closely-watched establishment. The grating was padlocked shut, as professionally and thoroughly as the handcuff king could accomplish.

"Break off those chains," Lady Saxhallow commanded her Boers. "Quickly. The clockwork timing mechanisms that will trigger the theatre's destruction may not be that precise."

"Trust Holmes to find a way to thwart a sinister plot," Watson told her.

"What is that cloth that also ties the bars shut?" Morgaine Kent puzzled. "A ribbon? *Yve's* ribbon? She was wearing it when we left her!"

Sabine recognised the flimsy scrap too. "How could that be here, unless…?"

"Unless Holmes and Houdini have already located your country hideaway and liberated Mrs Morrison?" concluded Watson. "The ribbon is a sign to us that we need no longer fear for your hostage, madam."

Sabine aimed a Mauser auto-loading ten round pistol at them. "Then fear for yourselves," she warned.

Morgaine did not flinch. "If Mr Holmes has retrieved Yve, has he also recovered the manuscript you took from him?" she wondered.

A mad fury played over the Boer woman's face. "*Ag jou hol man!* No! This has gone too far! I've given too much, endured too much, to be thwarted now!"

Shots echoed in the enclosed space of the undercellar. Sabine's men spun to the floor, bleeding out their lives in short seconds. Sabine screeched.

De Maupassant and the masked Sigrette had trailed their former partner. They had caught and slaughtered the Boers by surprise. "What

---

72 Stephen Foster's popular minstrel song was first published in 1850.

you've endured, Sabine?" the French nobleman sneered. "It will be nothing compared to what you will suffer next, you common tramp."

Sabine's gun was aimed at Watson. The Marquise and de Maupassant had weapons aimed at her.

"This entire building will explode in a very short while," Sabine warned. "Only I can save you. Ask Mrs Kent."

"She is lying," Morgaine answered coldly. "Nothing can save you, de Maupassant. You killed my sister Amile. You took her face as your vile badge of triumph. I will see you dead."

It was distraction enough. As de Maupassant and the Marquise stared upon the vengeful countenance of their accuser, Sabine spun her Mauser round and shot Sigrette three times in the chest. The expensive black evening gown the French aristocrat wore offered none of the protection of Houdini's silk-layered bulletproof waistcoat.[73] These shots were not deflected with minor injury. La Marqisa Marie Sigressa Alotta Francoise-Claire Saint Sirene de Confontaine et Asnières-de-la-Châtaigneraye fell back lifeless, her blood draining through the grate to the storm drain below.

Sabine emptied off the full ten rounds of her clip at the other people still living in the cellar. Watson dived to shield Morgaine with his body, pressing her to the ground as bullets spanged about them. De Maupassant spared not even a glance for his fallen mistress but ducked away, scrambling back up the stairs to make some other escape.

In her blind fury it took Sybilla Cronjé a moment after her gun clicked on an empty chamber to realise that her killing rage was thwarted. Watson made a split-second decision not to tackle the madwoman. Rather he lifted Mrs Kent to her feet and scrambled with her towards the exit. When Morgaine tripped over Sigrette's corpse Watson hauled her bodily up the staircase where de Maupassant had just fled.

The old soldier's instincts had been right. Sabine reloaded her weapon with practiced speed and fired again after them.

---

73 Several kinds of multi-layer silk vests were used as moderately effective body-armament at the end of the 19th century. Tombstone physician Dr G.E. Goodfellow published an article in the *Southern California Practitioner* documenting how a silk pocket handkerchief had protected faro dealer Luke Short from a fatal gunshot and offering the results of practical experimentation with layered silks. This prompted Fr. Kazimierz Żegleń to construct a working "bulletproof" vest.

By 1900, some American gangsters were wearing $800 silk vests for protection. Archduke Franz Ferdinand of Austria, heir to the throne of Austria-Hungary, was wearing such a protection at the time his assassination triggered World War I, but he died of a shot to the neck. A silk vest constructed by 1901 by Polish inventor Jan Szczepanik, whom Mark Twain dubbed "the Austrian Edison", saved the life of King Alfonso XIII of Spain.

Watson dragged Morgaine by the wrist, dodging with her behind dusty old props and stacked scenery to avoid the pursuing killer's gunfire.

"There are only so many places to run or hide," Sabine warned him coldly. She reached for another clip.

It wasn't in her pocket. It was in Houdini's hand.

"Lady Saxhallow," the escape artist greeted her. "Time for another dance?"

She fired point blank at the showman's head. No bulletproof vest could save him this time.

"Sorry, honey. I can count to ten," Houdini warned her as the gun clicked empty.

As she lashed at him he clapped a cuff on her wrist, spun her round, and closed the other circle to pinion her arms behind her.

"Game over," declared Harry Houdini.

Gabriel de Maupassant was still loose. He tried to make it back to front of house but was thwarted by a limping Lestrade and his searching bobbies. He ducked back under the stage, seeking some back exit by which he could depart.

Dr Watson blocked his way. "You're not going anywhere, Frenchie, except the dock of the Old Bailey."

De Maupassant raised his pistol to finish the army doctor in his path.

"*Murderer!*"

The cry came from *l'Inconnu*, appearing death-masked behind him, one hand pointed like Nemesis. The mask was Sigrette de Confontaine's, but Sigrette was killed, another victim of the Far Edge Club's deadly games. There was blood across *l'Inconnu*'s perfect porcelain face, as there had been when Amilie Kent had died.

A moment's superstitious dread gripped de Maupassant's guilty heart. Even as he realised that he faced Morgaine Moriarty Kent, Dr Watson was upon him like an agent of the Furies.

It was Morgaine herself who told Watson, "Enough, John. We are not killers. Leave him now for the courts. We will see him dead but we will not be murderers."

Watson climbed off the fallen Frenchman. Morgaine came to him. He held her. She cast the mask aside, letting it drop and shatter on the floor.

"This building is going to blow up!" Watson recalled. "We must warn Holmes, evacuate. Hoi, Lestrade! Down here. We have your man for you! Where is Holmes?"

Sherlock Holmes still commanded the stage. He strode in front of the captured Far Edgers and the constables who restrained them. "The other purpose that brought these men to our shores was a manuscript, a document prepared by the late Professor James Moriarty. It allegedly contained mathematical formulae and instructions for utilising them to fashion a weapon of mass devastation. These people wanted it for their amusement. A woman who had been wronged by them used it as a lure to assemble them all for my attention. Ah, I see she is joining us now."

Houdini bundled Sabine out to join the others. "The Victoria Station murderess, all trussed up for the law," he assured Inspector Merivale.

Sabine spat. "Fools. You will never hang me. You will see."

Watson and Morgaine hastened onto the stage with warning. Lestrade bustled the battered de Maupassant after them.

"She means it when she says she won't stand trial for her crimes," Watson warned his friend.

"Because of the explosives buried inside these theatre walls?" Holmes suggested.

Lady Saxhallow stared at him. "Yes," she answered. For the first time her rigid self-confidence was cracked.

Watson's mouth gaped for a moment, and then he snorted and laughed. "Hah! I should have known you'd be ahead of me, Holmes. You always are!"

Morgaine took the doctor's arm. "*You* have done very well tonight, John Watson. I shall not forget it."

"Hold on!" objected Inspector Lestrade. "There's still a bomb in the theatre?"

There were the first stirrings of real panic in the audience.

"It's fine. I discovered the explosives the night before last when I was on the run," Houdini told them. "An empty theatre at night is a great place to think things through. I came to pick up some supplies I'd need while I was hiding out and chasing down the Far Edge Club, but while I was here I got to pondering."

"Rely upon a conjurer to wonder what preparation the opposition might be making," Holmes observed. "Is this the moment to open the hatbox, Houdini?"

"Sure, why not?" agreed the escape artist. Beck lifted a clockwork device from the container that had been stood on stage all along. He passed it to the showman to demonstrate to the murderess. "Lady Saxhallow, is *this* the timing mechanism you set to blow everyone here sky high?"

There were some shrieks from the audience and a smattering of applause. This gala opening was unlike any other.

"I believe that wraps up the investigation," Holmes suggested. "All that remains is to arrest these men for their various crimes and await justice to be done."

"You imbeciles!" de Maupassant scorned. "You have no idea with whom you trifle! You will regret the day you ever crossed the *Club de Bord Lontain!*"

"I have diplomatic immunity," Prince Dakir warned. "You *cannot* arrest me!"

"And I am…" began Graf von Starken, before a near red hole appeared in the middle of his forehead.

The second shot burst Alançon's head open. The third took Dakir between the eyes.

De Maupassant had one moment to look up to the grand chandelier over the auditorium, where Colonel Sebastian Moran hefted a unique air rifle with such deadly precision. Moriarty's finest agent squeezed off another shot that took the nobleman in the face.

Fifteen seconds had passed. Four men were dead. James Moriarty had reached from the grave and avenged their trespass on his affairs.

Sabine saw the air-gun orient on her. She stared back at her executioner, defiant to the last.

The last bullet caught her in the throat, spilled her back into the glass of the escape tank. The plate broke, spilling water out across the stage. Sabine fell onto the base of the container. The trap was activated, electrifying the apparatus, searing the Boer woman with lethal currents.

Moran oriented his gun at Holmes, gave a fey grin, and set his empty weapon aside. He remained where he was to await recapture. His work was done.

And then the show was over.

─╱╲╲─

From the account of John Watson MD

It took as much police time to clear the audience and fend off excited pressmen as to clear away the results of Moran's bloody vendetta. Beck supplied evacuated theatregoers with complimentary tickets for another night. "We'll easily make the cost back in publicity for this," he assured us. "*Everyone* is going to want to know what happened here."

"Publicity that will make it hard for the Far Edge Club to operate again," I ventured.

"What of the explosives built into the fabric of the Lyceum?" Galpin worried. "The whole place will have to be stripped out and rebuilt again!"[74]

"I imagine lawsuit against the de Maupassant estate might compensate for that," Holmes suggested. "In the meantime, Mr Galpin, there remains the question of your involvement. By what means was Lady Saxhallow placed in contact with the builders she suborned? How did she know of Doyle's literary gathering to first have Mrs Kent encounter Dr Watson? And why were you so eager to press Mr Beck into a literary deal concerning Houdini, a contract that might prove suddenly very lucrative if something untoward happened to the showman?"

The secretary paled. "I... you... there is no proof..."

"You told us that Lady Saxhallow was threatening your family," I recalled.

"Holmes and I found no evidence of any family," Houdini mentioned, "but the last of Sabine's henchmen, the one who was guarding Mrs Morrison when we got him, I bet he'll sing like a canary now she's dead."

"M-mr Holmes," Galpin stammered, "I assure you..."

"Oh, do go and turn yourself in to Lestrade, there's a good fellow," The detective told him impatiently. "Do not compel me to direct my attention upon you."

Holmes' gimlet gaze seemed to melt the secretary like butter. He shied away, then scuttled off.

Houdini chuckled. "Well this has turned out better than I expected. I can take a few bruised ribs and a ruined silk bullet-vest, even if it did allow de Maupassant and Sigrette to make their getaway from blazing Sheafward while Holmes was fixing me up. We still got to put on quite an act. I admit I didn't anticipate the last minute body count, but..."

"Colonel Moran is nothing if not loyal to Moriarty," Holmes confessed.

"There are still injustices to be addressed," Morgaine insisted. "I accept Mr Doyle's argument that the Afrikaners were usually treated no worse than our own poor settlers, but that does not excuse neglect, mismanagement, or cruelty. Having made a commitment to do an honourable thing we should have done it, properly, thoroughly. We are British; it is our duty. Having made an error we must investigate, correct it where we can, punish where we should—and learn." She looked to my

---

74 In 1904, the Lyceum was almost completely rebuilt by Bertie Crewe in richly ornamented Rococo style, retaining only Beazley's façade and grand portico.

friend. "A consultation with the world's foremost investigator might prove invaluable."

Holmes glanced at me and smiled. "As with everything touched by a Moriarty, it will be given my full attention."

I had not seen Lestrade join our little group at the side of the stage. "Speaking of the Professor," he interrupted, somewhat reticently, "I am instructed… ordered, like, to collect that manuscript you discovered. It is judged too dangerous to be allowed in private hands, even yours. It is a matter of national security."

"Why - you want to get your hands on the weapon yourselves!" Beck objected.

"It is not yet decoded," I warned. "I doubt that a cypher prepared by James Moriarty to challenge Sherlock Holmes would be comprehensible to any other intellect."

"I still need the papers," Lestrade apologised.

Holmes fetched a satchel from concealment under a canvas. He lifted out the rusty box in which we had retrieved *Dynamics Of An Asteroid* and showed the manuscript to Morgaine. "This is your uncle's hand? Verify if for the Inspector."

"It is his. What will become of it, Mr Lestrade? Surely no-one will be mad enough to try and apply those calculations, formulae so terrible that even Uncle James sealed them away and never used them."

"I don't know," the pale policeman admitted. "I just has orders."

Holmes handed the document over. "Take it and be done with it," he declared.

Lestrade scuttled away, carrying the box as if it was another bomb.

"Was that really a smart idea?" Houdini asked Holmes. "Or did you palm the real thing?"

"That was the genuine article," my friend confirmed. "No copy exists. That, and that alone, is Moriarty's final trap."

Morgaine looked at him in puzzlement "What do you mean, Mr Holmes?"

"I mean that if the Napoleon of Crime had the means of such destruction but never used it then he was either a wiser or more moral man than I took him for. But the *rumour* of such an invention… ah, that would set whispers across the criminal underworld, rumours that could only enlarge Moriarty's prestige."

"You said a trap," I pointed out.

"A last revenge on me, Watson. On the tenth anniversary of his death I would receive the puzzle-mask. I would retrieve the manuscript. I would find the code concealing Moriarty's greatest secret. I would bend my intellect to breaking that cypher."

"And then what?" asked Beck breathlessly.

"And I would continue to do so. Trust Moriarty to craft a document that looks as though it is the most cunning of encryptions but is actually gibberish. Imagine him chuckling at the idea of me going mad unable to solve his riddle, of me devoting my declining years on that futile quest. That was his intended revenge, from a man who knew how my mind works and how my obsessions command me."

That seemed horribly likely to me once Holmes had spoken it. "You gave the trap away, so that others might be caught in it rather than you."

"It is no bad thing for the enemies of our nation to fear that we have acquired a weapon of such terrible potency. The manuscript's confiscation removes the chance of any more plots aimed at or using Mrs Kent or Mrs Morrison. Let secret boffins drive themselves mad trying to decode the impossible while their secret superiors rage."

Morgaine had a question. "If my uncle understood you so well, if he shaped this manuscript as a stab at you from the grave, then why did it not work?"

Holmes looked to me. "Watson?"

"Moriarty knew the Holmes who was eleven years ago," I answered. "Since then Holmes has wandered Europe under the name of Sigerson; has thwarted Dr Grimesby Roylott, Holy Peter, James Windibank, Don Juan Morillo, Baron Maupertuis, Charles Augustus Milverton, and countless other villains and monsters;[75] has prevented the loss of vital military plans,[76] saved the reputation of a promising young lawyer, solved the sudden death of Cardinal Tosca, recovered the famous Black Pearl of the Borgias, and accomplished many other feats. In short, he has learned. He is no longer the man whom Professor Moriarty fought."

"If I am less obsessed and more sensible, Watson, you can ascribe the credit solely to yourself," my friend declared. He watched Lestrade hasten from the theatre. Only the slightest twinge of doubt crossed his features; so Moriarty had some small revenge.

---

75 Holmes encountered these villains respectively in "The Adventure of the Speckled Band", "The Disappearance of Lady Francis Carfax", "A Case of Identity", "The Adventure of Wisteria Lodge", "The Adventure of the Reigate Squire" (passing reference) and "The Adventure of Charles Augustus Milverton".

76 See "The Adventure of the Bruce-Partington Plans", "The Adventure of the Norwood Builder", "The Adventure of Black Peter" (this case is only mentioned), and "The Adventure of the Six Napoleons".

Beck clapped his hands. "Well, we've got a heck of a lot to do to get this place back in shape for a show tomorrow," he announced to the world. "Heaven only knows what mess the box office will be in without me checking on it, and there's repairs to be done all over where you fellows ripped death-traps apart. And the blood-stains! Maybe we'll just leave those for now and charge people extra?"

Houdini extended his hand to Holmes. "It's been a thrill working with you. I'm glad we're on the same side."

"Same here," Holmes assured the escape artist. "You would present some singular challenges if ever you turned to crime."

The showman looked over to the shattered glass tank where Lady Saxhallow had died. "Shame about Sabine. She must have been quite a woman once, before misfortune destroyed her. But before she died she saw her real enemies fall."

"The female of the species is deadlier than the male," Holmes remarked; and I knew at once that he was thinking about another adversary from long ago who to him would always be The Woman.

Mrs Kent was still gripping my arm. "Where shall I escort you, Morgaine?" I asked her.

"Wheresoever you please, John," she promised me.

In July of that year, Holmes did me the honour for the third time of being my best man as I escorted her down the aisle to become Mrs Morgaine Watson.

THE END

AFTERWORD: REALLY FICTIONAL
In which I.A. Watson considers our protagonists

Sherlock Holmes is a creation of literature that we sometimes like to pretend was real. Harry Houdini was a real person whom we sometimes like to write about as if he were fiction.

The Sherlock Holmes that the authors of Airship 27's Consulting Detective series (eight volumes out now, two more ready in the wings, doubtless more thereafter) strive to depict is the character as his creator Sir Arthur Conan Doyle imagined him. We are expressly warned not to include elements of fantasy or science fiction or any other anachronistic or anomalous material that would not have appeared in the Canon, nor to contradict that august body of work. We are encouraged to find ways of covering new ground that Doyle never did but that he might have done had time, contemporary tastes, and Victorian literary conventions allowed.

The Harry Houdini who stars in Airship 27's The Amazing Harry Houdini (volume one now available) is a stylised, fictionalised version of the real artiste, carefully repurposed without encumbering and intrusive personal detail – or beloved accompanying wife – to stand alongside entirely-fictional pulp protagonists such as The Shadow or Doc Savage. This is somewhat authorised by Houdini himself, who permitted to be published various short stories wherein that same imaginary version of himself faced adventure and horror; he even survived the pen of H.P. Lovecraft.

In real life, Houdini and Doyle were friends and correspondents, although that bond cooled somewhat over Doyle's spiritualist beliefs. The fictional Houdini and Doyle's most famous literary avatar Holmes doubtless have even more in common than their progenitors, including a fierce dedication to uncovering the truth whatever the cost.

My brief was to bring together these fictional men and their respective associates in a single novel-length account, within the rules of engagement for both Airship 27 series, and offering a showcase by which the characters were compared and contrasted.

I felt at once that Holmes and Houdini could not share the stage often; both blaze with star quality and demand the focus. Each is set up with a companion to do necessary narrative heavy lifting. The logical route was therefore to divide the tale into four sections, mimicking Airship 27's favoured four-short-stories-per-volume format in which these characters are usually presented. I decided on a Holmes section, a Houdini section, a Watson and Beck section, and finally a team-up free for all. In this way each combination of characters could be featured. My only regret was that the plot did not allow for Holmes and Beck or Houdini and Watson to have their day.

Given the scope of a full book rather than the short story format of the Consulting Detective series, I felt I had liberty to push rather more in what was presented. In particular I ventured into the usually-sacrosanct preserve of Doyle continuity to suggest an identity and circumstance for the (presumably) last Mrs Watson, to offer a final curtain call for Colonel Sebastian Moran, and to allow one last groan and rattle from the spectre of Professor James Moriarty.

I was also able to exploit the purview available to a writer of historical stories – as opposed to Doyle, who wrote his Holmes material as contemporary fiction – to weave in elements of real world events to a degree that would have been insensitive and controversial had Doyle attempted it. As our story depicts, Doyle was a strong defender of British actions in the Boer campaign; had he attempted to feature the events in his fiction there would have been severe backlash. At over a century's distance we can review those things with a more detached mind.

The Canon often uses far-off events to spur Holmes cases; Mary Morstan came with an Indian connection, and The Valley of Fear referenced Mormon America, for example. Drawing consequences from the world's first concentration camps seemed possible in a modern work.

Houdini's literary adventures have mostly been "an American abroad", featuring that vigorous New World protagonist against Old World adversaries, values, and sins. For that reason, the effete, elitist aristos of the Far Edge Club seemed like good opponents, epitomising the clash of entitled, wealthy, conscienceless hedonists with the rough, self-made, life-toughened, naturally-decent Houdini and Beck. That these villains also feel like intruders in Holmes and Watson's staid, ordered, moral Victorian society is a bonus.

Arthur Conan Doyle invited himself as an extended cameo; although he is, of course, the literary avatar of Doyle as much as Houdini is of the real Erik Weisz – no resemblance is intended to any real persons living or dead, as they say.

Here then, were the elements from which it seemed appropriate to build a book. And here is the book. I hope the blend was to your satisfaction.

Ian Watson
Gradually becoming fictional himself
June 2016

ABOUT OUR CREATORS

AUTHOR -

I.A. WATSON's criminal career had been tragically curtailed by his literary duties. He has been kept honest by producing short stories for *Sherlock Holmes: Consulting Detective* volumes 1-8, most of which have been nominated for Best Pulp Short Story in their time, and one of which has won the award. With Airship 27 he has published four *Robin Hood* novels, *King of Sherwood, Arrow of Justice, Freedom's Outlaw*, and *Forbidden Legend*, and contributed to the anthologies *Sinbad: the New Voyages* 1 and 3, *Zeppelin Tales, The Amazing Adventures of Harry Houdini,* and the mammoth, award-winning *Legends of New Pulp Fiction.*

To avoid recidivism, and since Airship 27 insists on publishing material from authors other than him, he has also authored seven novels, four novellas, and the non-fiction essay collection *Where Stories Dwell* for other publishers, and contributed to thirteen of their anthologies. New novels *Labours of Hercules* and *Premium Delivery to the Centre of the Earth*, will debut later in 2016 from Chillwater Press.

A full list of his publications and hidden clues to his many criminal plots may be found at http://www.chillwater.org.uk/writing/iawatsonhome.htm - but you'll never catch him alive!

INTERIOR ILLUSTRATOR

ROB DAVIS is one of the vanguard artists of the New Pulp movement. His work for the SHERLOCK HOLMES CONSULTING DETECTIVE series won him the PULP FACTORY AWARD for Best Interior Illustrations in 2010, again in 2015, and he has been shortlisted every year since the awards' inception. His extensive and influential work has recently been profiled in the deluxe art-book PULP! THE ART OF ROB DAVIS.

From a beginning illustrating role-playing games in the 1980s, Rob moved to pencilling black and white comics for small publishers. Most notable of these was Eternity Comics (later Malibu Comics), collaborating with writer R.A. Jones on SCIMIDAR. For Marvel and DC, Rob drew likeness-intensive comics such as QUANTUM LEAP and STAR TREK, and especially Malibu's DEEP SPACE NINE series and Marvel's PIRATES OF DARK WATER. He has developed small press and self-published comics like Caliber's ROBYN OF SHERWOOD and is publisher and designer for his small-press production REDBUD STUDIO COMICS. His output includes video games, advertising illustrations, and T-shirt designs.

Rob is Art Director, Designer and Illustrator for New Pulp production outfit AIRSHIP 27, partnered with writer/editor Ron Fortier. His illustrations have appeared in dozens of their books, making him probably the most prolific contemporary artist in the genre. One of the most active figures of the New Pulp movement and a regular feature at conventions and shows, his work and the encouragement and support he offers fellow creators help to define the character of the genre.

Rob works and lives in central Missouri with his wife and two children. He currently has plans to update his online gallery at his website: robmdavis.com for future perusal.

www.ingramcontent.com/pod-product-compliance
Lightning Source LLC
Chambersburg PA
CBHW052033260626
47163CB00006B/221